Medusa Untold

By

Porsha Deun

Books by Porsha Deun

<u>The Love Lost Series</u>
Love Lost
Love Lost Forever
Love Lost Revenge

<u>The Addict Series</u>
Addict—A Fatal Attraction Story
Addict 2.0—Andre's Story
Addict 3.0—DeAngelo's Story
Addict 4.0—DeMario's Story

<u>The Hot Holiday Series</u>
Santa's Pleasure
Cupid's Lust
Jacks Thrills

<u>Standalones</u>
Intoxic
In Over Her Head

<u>Children's Book</u>
Princesses Can Do Anything!

<u>Devotionals</u>
Childlike Faith

<u>Fantasy</u>
Medusa Untold

ISBN (paperback): 978-1-970943-00-9

ISBN (hardcover): 978-1-970943-02-3

ISBN (eBook): 978-1-970943-01-6

Trigger Warnings:

There is an **attempt** of an SA.

There are battles and fight scenes that lead to death.

Medusa Untold

Glossary

Bwana (Swahili)—lord

Mugeni (Swahili)—foreigner, alien

Ụbọchị izu ike (Igbo)—day of rest

Moeder Heelal (Africaans)—Mother Universe

Ejo nla (Yuroba)—giant snake

Iṣẹ́gun àwọn oríṣà (Yuroba)– the highest praise to the goddess

Neem stewig vas (Africaans) – take firm hold

Íyá Àgbà (Yoroba) – grandmother

Prologue
Three years ago.

Sisay sits between my legs on the steps below me. We always sit at the back of the temple, facing Joro's vast mountain range when I work on her hair at the end of each week. After working clay from the riverbed into her hair and scalp, I pick up a pitcher and dip it into a bowl of clean water before rinsing out her hair. Grayish-red water flows down the steps from her hair until it eventually runs clear.

"Do you ever feel that something is missing?" my teen daughter asks me as I use a wrap to dry her soft curls.

"What do you mean?"

"If the Elders are the gods of the gods, wouldn't Moeder Heelal be as well?"

Feeling that this wrap has soaked up all the water it is going to, I pick up the second we brought with us and continue drying her hair. "The Elders are the creators of the gods, their parents, so to speak."

"Like how you're considered my parent?"

I think fondly of the day I took Sisay in. There was no thought behind it, but something I knew I needed to do. "Yes, only I didn't give birth to you." I continue drying her hair. "Remember, the Elders are not like the gods we worship."

"Because Kemet and Songhai don't survive on our worship the way the gods do. They and Moeder Heelal just exist."

"Precisely."

Sisay is quiet again, but I know it won't last for long. She's always been a curious child. Hair day is when she likes to pick my brain about the gods the most. We've spent countless hours on these back steps of the temple since she was of nine years, talking about the gods, Moeder Heelal, and the history of the four lands that make up the Ashi realm, our universe.

"I don't understand why Moeder Heelal felt the need to create the Elders if we are all a part of her, anyway. Have you ever wondered that?"

"I can't say I have." I hold my breath, hoping she doesn't ask why Moeder Heelal created our world to function the way it does because I wouldn't have an answer for her. Picking up a small jar of oil, I pour some into my hands and rub it through her hair.

Sisay stays quiet as I massage her scalp. My fingers rub the herb-infused oil into her head in small circles, working from the front to the nape, and back up to the top. When I finish, she stands and stretches.

"Are there other realms out there…like ours?"

"You already know the answer to this, Sisay."

She sighs. "It makes little sense that we are all that exists out there."

"It doesn't have to make sense to us now. We have faith that the Elders and our gods will never steer their children wrong."

Satisfied or dissatisfied with my answer, Sisay changes the subject.

"Can I go help Zendaya in her garden?"

Finally, a question I can answer.

"Yes, but help me take all of this back to our quarters. And be back in time for dinner." We pour out the rest of the water and pick up the pitcher, bowls, oil, and wraps before heading inside the temple.

"Oh, I'll be back early. I overheard Cairo say we're having goat curry tonight, and she likes to hoard extra of it."

"You both love your goat curry," I chuckle.

"Will you be in your favorite sanctuary for the rest of the day?" Sisay asks.

"I was, but now I want to go to the palace library."

"I've always wanted to see it."

"You will one day." Being my adoptive daughter only gets Sisay privileges in the temple, which is unprecedented, as those of the priesthood don't have children, or at least, not of their loins. Though she's considered my daughter, she is not of the priesthood. Only members of the priesthood, those of royal blood, or the highborn, are allowed access to the palace and temple libraries. I've read every tablet and scroll in the temple library more times than I can count. Sisay's questions have me curious if there was something mortals of old days missed or failed to pass down. *Is there more to Moeder Heelal than just us?*

Chapter 1
Medusa

Nothing brings me peace as much as worshiping the gods, other than healing people and raising my daughter. Unlike my brothers and sisters in the priesthood, I prefer to worship alone. When I'm alone in my favorite of the smaller sanctuaries of the temple I reside in, I can worship the gods of Joro, Jata and Nthanda, without the watchful eyes of others or the jealous eyes of Kunle, the High Priest. However, it is ubochi izu ike, *day of rest*, which means the people of Joro are resting today while the priesthood sends up praise for another blessed week past and prayers for a blessed week ahead.

Kunle, with his thin and tight tawny skin, stands in the middle of the circle the priests and priestesses form, singing the call back to the song of praise the High Priest leads. As we sing, our voices rise higher and higher, filling the large sanctuary until the sound passes the outer columns and floats up to the heavens. In response, from Jata and Nthanda, their glory falls down on us, gently wrapping around our bodies like thick ropes of gold and red. The people have said the temple glows like the sun on ubochi izu ike. I've never seen it from the outside.

When we praise together like this, the gods share their glory among us equally. It is when we praise separately that it is noticeable who the gods favor more.

I put that out of my mind and focus on my praise. Though Joro and its gods are not the land and gods I was born into, I love this land and it's gods all the same. I inhale deeply, preparing to raise my voice higher, but a loud bong from the cymbal just outside the temple distracts everyone and interrupts our song of praise.

In the ten years that I've lived in Joro, never have I heard the gong ring. The other priests and priestesses asking if it was the gong informs me they've never heard it either. It is only to be used when the attention of the priesthood is needed for emergency situations while we are together in praise and prayer. Other than that, it is forbidden even to touch it.

Two soldiers bearing the rose and dove crest of the princess walk into the temple.

"You'd better have a good reason for this interruption," Kunle quips.

"The princess requests the immediate presence of priestess Medusa on behalf of the king," one responds.

Excitement and dread always fill me whenever the crown requests me. Excitement, because having the favor of the crown and the gods means everything to me. Dread because Kunle knows keenly that the crown, the princess, her prince husband, and her father-in-law, all prefer me to him. Everyone knows Kunle fears being ousted as high priest when the new king and queen of Joro take the throne.

"Princess Nia requests on behalf of the king? Since when and for what reason?" Kunle asks.

The soldiers look at each other, and the silent one shrugs his shoulders. "The king's time is nigh."

Rising to my feet, I say, "Allow me a minute to gather my things." They nod their heads, and I take off to my chambers, walking as briskly as I can. In my room, I gather my satchel and stuff it with small jars of herbs and ointments. It is an honor to be requested by the crown, but it comes with complications. Mainly, Kunle and his jealousy. I know I'm going to have to deal with his wrath later.

When I return to the sanctuary, I inform the soldiers that I'm ready to go.

"Cairo," Kunle calls, "take over leading the prayers and praise. Do not stop until you have completed all the rituals. I don't know how long it will be until I return."

Cairo fails at hiding her glee at being the one Kunle chose to take his place in performing this week's rituals. Her dark brown freckles seem to dance on her cheeks and shine brighter as she smirks.

Everyone looks around at each other. "The request was only for the priestess, Your Grace," one guard states.

"King Ahmose appointed me to the position of high priest shortly after he took the throne. While I approve," he says with a strained tone, "the mugini—"

"Priestess Medusa," the talkative soldier corrects.

Kunle takes immediate offense, and it shows. "Remember your place," he snaps.

Silence falls heavy in the temple until he continues.

"While I approve of her performing the rites to pass the king's spirit, I am the High Priest. My presence is required on such an occasion as this."

I almost feel sad for Kunle. He wouldn't have to worry about being removed from his position if he were good at fulfilling his duties.

The soldiers nod and lead the way, with me following behind Kunle. The sound of the remaining priesthood chants grows faint as we leave the temple. This is the one day in the week I never leave the temple. Seeing the vast courtyard between the temple and the palace so empty is strange to me. Typically, the courtyard is full of vendors from Joro and the other three lands in the realm. It's loud, bustling, and filled with the scent of salted meats, spices, and fresh-baked breads. There are no loud calls for the purchase of fabrics and jewels. The courtyard feels as foreign to me as I must do to Kunle and others who chose to only see me as a mugeni, a foreigner.

I turn back to see the light of the gods' glory filling the temple. It is a magnificent sight to behold. The golden light streams up to the heavens where Jata and Nthanda live. I wish I could look at it longer, but I have a duty to the crown.

Refocusing on my tasks ahead, I turn to catch up with the soldiers and Kunle, only to nearly run into Kunle's chest. I stumble to keep from tripping over him and knocking us both onto the courtyard's sun-bleached pavers. "Is something amiss, Your Grace?"

"Amiss indeed. What private dealings do you have with the crown?"

Not this question again. "As I've told you before, Your Grace, I have no private dealings with the crown, or anyone else."

He stares at me in disbelief, but no matter how many times he asks me this, my answer has not changed.

"From now on, you are to notify me whenever the crown requests your presence and for what reason. Then I can determine if I need to accompany you."

"And if you aren't available?"

"Excuse you?"

"When the crown requests me and you are otherwise occupied, preventing me from notifying you. Should I make the crown wait for your approval?"

Kunle's follies with some priests and priestesses, as well as temple interns, are well known both inside and outside the temple. Just last week, Priestess Cairo came to me for an elixir to cleanse her womb, though she put it as if another Joroan woman asked her to ask me for it. Cairo and Accra always do it that way when the seed of Kunle or another priest takes hold.

"Then inform an intern and have them tell me as soon as I'm available. We wouldn't want to keep the crown waiting."

"Your Grace," the soldier says.

Kunle steps closer to me. "You will not replace me. If I as so much hear about you campaigning your way to my title, I will have you executed for treason."

We stare at each other; him waiting for me to back down and me waiting for him to back off. I would never say I hate someone, but my feelings for Kunle are close to it.

"Do you understand me?"

"Whatever the gods will, Your Grace. The crown awaits."

From the way he looks at me, I can tell he wishes to be rid of me. My response didn't satisfy him, but it wasn't blasphemous. He's going to have to find another way to take me down, not that I would ever give him the opportunity.

When he turns and resumes following the soldiers, I'm relieved. Though I'm honored for the crown's trust in my abilities, I just want to get this over with so I don't have to be in the same room as Kunle any longer than I have to.

Catching up, I notice there are a few people in the courtyard. Highborns. Today is the only day they can mull about the courtyard and not be forced to interact with the commoners who live across the Tehenu River. They don their fine garments and bow their heads to Kunle and me as we pass. I can't help but wonder what is going through their heads at seeing us escorted to the palace by the princess' guards. *Do they have any idea how close they are to having a new king and queen?*

The four of us walk up the many steps that lead to the palace's outer vestibule. We pass thick and tall pillars made of limestone. There is a stillness in the air, as if the winds know death is near and they dare not approach. It's unsettling. I've done the death rite many times over as priestess, but never for a high-ranking royal. I realize in this moment that neither has Kunle. The former queen's execution for treason left her soul lost, and the king's only brother died when they were kids.

Kunle has no problems letting his jealousy show, but now I know he is raging on the inside. I'm never going to hear the end of it. It will be worse than when Prince Gainde constantly came to me for prayer in the weeks leading up to his nuptials to Princess Nia. Kunle swore I must have been seducing or colluding with the man since he was coming to me and not him for prayer. I whisper a prayer to Jata and Nthanda, asking that Kunle will be too preoccupied with the king's passing and soon coronation of the new king and queen to repay me for being more favored by the crown than he is.

Just as the highborns in the courtyard, servants and guards stop in their tracks and bow their heads as we pass. We make the journey through tall and long corridors until we reach the doors of the king's chambers. The guards open the double doors to let us in, and I'm immediately humbled.

The sounds of King Ahmose's strained breathing and Princess Nia's soft sobs are the first to greet us. It is a heady song of death and grief. She is only of nine and ten years old, and her entire life is about to change in more ways than one. The princess sits on the bed next to her father, holding his hand, while the royal physician stands close by. Her husband, Prince Gainde, stands off to the side, along with his father, Captain Baraka, leader of Joro's soldiers.

"Priestess Medusa," Baraka greets in a soft tone.

"Prince Gainde. Captain Baraka." I bow my head to them, each in turn.

"Kunle," Baraka says dryly.

"Prince. Captain."

"It is good to see you, priestess," Gainde says. "Albeit, I wish it were under better circumstances."

I give him a small smile, not sure of what to say in this situation.

"How much time does he have?" Kunle asks.

"Any hour, according to the physician," Baraka says.

"I'd better get started then. Excuse me." I give the prince and his father another bow of my head before walking over to the other side of the bed. "Princess." She doesn't look up. I call her name two more times before she does. "I'm going to anoint his body and pray for his soul's safe journey to Muhabura."

She nods her head. Her tear-stained face breaks my heart. I've not seen anyone look so in despair since the plague of fevers that took my daughter's birth parents and the rest of her family. Nia has her husband, but my Sisay, she had no one else.

I set my ointments, burners, herbs, and crystals up on the bed table near me. Closing my eyes, I pray.

Gracious Jata and Nthanda. Our great King Ahmose will soon make his way to the place of your birth to be with the elder gods, your parents, Kemet and Songhai. Guide and strengthen me as I prepare the way for him. Bless him so that his journey is successful.

I crumble dried sage leaves, red and white rose and sunflower petals, and lemon peels into a burner bowl before laying small strips of parchment on top and giving it a stir. "By the power of Joro's great gods, Jata and Nthanda." Warmth fills my hands, and I do a single clap over the bowl, igniting its contents. I blow on the fire after a few moments because I want this to smoke. "Thank the gods."

It isn't long before the room fills with a floral and citrus scent. It mimics the smell of the fields of Muhabura, as passed down from the Elder gods, Kemet and Songhai, and then from mortal generation to generation.

Taking the oil into my hands, I rub them together and start anointing the King's feet. As the princess continues to weep next to her father's dying body, I can feel the eyes of the men in the room watching us. It's unsettling the way men feel they have to watch, or take witness of what women do, outside of chores and childbirth, of course. Especially highborn men. Except for Prince Gainde, these very men, along with royal males from the other three lands, stood behind a lattice wall and watched as the prince and princess consummated their marriage a mere three full moons ago. Every marriage among the highborns starts that way.

I take a deep breath to start a chant, but Kunle interrupts. "I'll do the chant."

"No," Baraka corrected. "We requested the priestess for this. You are welcome to stay, but she will perform all the rites. She has the favor of the gods. No one has seen their glory fall on you in sometime."

Baraka's last sentence was the quiet part no one else dared to say out loud, especially to Kunle's face. It is true that outside of the group prayer and praise on ubọchị izu ike, no one has seen the golden glow of the gods' glory fall on Kunle in years. Even he has to be aware of this, and I'm sure it adds to his paranoia. Whether it was the harvest festivals, the wedding of the prince and princess, the crown has continuously requested that I perform the rites only for the duties to be split between Kunle and me. This is the first time they've adamantly closed him out.

I refocus my attention on the task at hand.

Bless the king's journey ahead. Reunite him with the Elders, who created us all. Give his spirit the strength of Kemet and the fierceness of Songhai to get through the trials he will face along his journey.

Bless the king's journey ahead. He has been a great king on land. May his spirit be great in Muhabura. Take in your child and count him as one of your blessed, great Elders, Kemet and Songhai.

I repeat this as I anoint his feet and legs with oil, then again while anointing his free hand and arm. When it's time for me to do his other hand, Princess Nia moves to the end of the bed and kisses her father's feet. After anointing his body with oil, I go back to the side table with my supplies and add cedarwood to the burning bowl before enclosing it with a matching top, making it a sphere. I hold the sphere over his body, moving it back and forth.

"Return to the elder gods, great King Ahmose. Kemet and Songhai await you with blessings. Your spirit knows the way." I say. When I repeat it, the men in the room join in with me. We say this seven times together.

The room falls silent again, aside from Princess Nia's sobs and the gurgling breath of King Ahmose. I continue moving the incense sphere back and forth as I say my own prayers. Joro is going to need them. I pray for a smooth transition of power and for Joro, as King Ahmose has reigned so long that many here do not remember being under the rule of another king. My prayers also include that the kings of other lands don't take advantage of this time and try to start a war. The last war between the lands, which was decades before I was born, left my home of Ginawa and the land of Himba without royal families. The war also caused Ginawa to be without a priesthood. Himba held trials to select a new king and queen from amongst its highborn society, while Ginawa made the high priestess queen and she selected a husband and king from amongst the people, and dismantled the need for a priesthood. The people of Ginawa were each to develop their own relationship with its gods, Kush and Ife. It's been that way in my homeland ever since.

I also pray for Kunle. Although there is no love between the two of us, if Kunle is removed from his current station, he will need to find a new purpose. I don't see him settling to be just another priest of Joro. It's always been his intent to die as the High Priest of Joro. Whatever happens, I pray, too, for my safety if I am to be the next High Priest.

Chapter 2
Prince Gainde

Standing next to my father, I watch Medusa as she performs the rites over King Ahmose, my father-in-law. The gods have cursed me with a burning desire for this woman. My heart quickens as her leg comes through the slit in her dress as she maneuvers onto the bed to anoint the king's body. There is no one like her in all the land, which is fair, since she's not Joroan. Her dark skin is richer than the soil that provides food. Her ample hips could bring any man to rise and bear many children. The small softness of her stomach looks like it wants to be squeezed, and her long, thick locs are in need of a powerful hand to twist around.

"Have you heard anything I said?"

Blinking my eyes, I turn my head towards my father, but I keep my eyes on Medusa. In a hushed tone, I respond. "My mind was somewhere else. There's a lot of change coming."

"Change that I've been preparing you for since you were of two and ten years."

"I'm aware, Babba."

"You need to think about the transition of the priesthood."

This catches my attention, and I turn my full body towards him. "What do you mean?"

"Joro needs a high priest who can bring about change. That can bring the blessings of the gods."

"Joro is the most blessed and richest land in the Ashi Realm."

"Haven't I told you that there is always more to want and strive for?"

"Babba, what are you proposing?" I'm losing my patience with this conversation, but now is not the time to show it.

"Medusa needs to be placed in the high priest position. The sooner after your coronation, the better."

"Medusa?"

"Yes. She is the most favored of the priesthood. More favored than any priest or priestess I've seen. There's not a prayer of hers that goes unanswered."

I am aware of this. That is why I went to Medusa for prayer so much during the weeks leading up to my nuptials with the princess. My mind goes back to one of those times.

I kneel before the inner temple statue of Jata. There is no way out of this marriage for me, short of murder. I'm not willing to do that anymore than I'm willing to be killed. The sound of soft footsteps comes to me, and then her perfume. Peonies only grow in Ginawa, so perfumes made from them are highly valuable when vendors come here with them. What is unique about Medusa's scent is that she makes her own and pairs it with earthy tones like teakwood instead of citrus like the perfumers do. I stand to greet her.

"Priestess. Young lady." Her ward is with her.

"Lord Gainde," they both say with a bow of their heads.

Medusa Untold

Medusa looks ravishing in her black dress, always with a high slit in the front, and layered gold necklaces and bangles. Does she truly have no idea what she does to me; the torture I feel whenever I'm in her presence?

"I came looking for you, priestess. Do you have a moment?"

She nods and sends her ward off to their living quarters.

"Does something trouble my future king?" Medusa asks me.

Oh, how I long to hear her call me her king while bonding with her!

I released a frustrated sigh. "King Ahmose has set a date for the wedding. I am to marry the princess in two fortnights."

"Do you not want to marry?"

"Yes, but…" I look around to see if anyone was listening. If word got back to King Ahmose that I don't want to marry Princess Nia, it would be considered treason for me and my family.

"You do not wish to marry the princess," Medusa answers quietly.

"I want the throne. My father's raised me for it ever since I was a child. Nia doesn't… she's not…"

"Do you love someone else?"

"I don't know if it is love or not. In our world of advantageous marriages, can that sort of love ever exist?"

Medusa stays quiet.

"But there is someone else I would like to be my wife."

"The law allows a man to have more than one wife," Medusa reminds me.

"Yes, but King Ahmose never took a second wife, not even after his first wife soiled their marriage bed. I want to be a righteous king like him." The last line is one I've never verbalized before, but it's the most completely honest thing I've said to anyone in my life.

"That does not mean you can't have a second or even a third wife," Medusa says with a bit of hope in her voice. "You can be your own man, your own king. The number of wives you *have does not determine the king you will be. If you wish to take a second wife, you can do so."*

"So, there's a chance?" I intentionally leave out who I want my wife to be.

"Someday you will be king. Probably sooner than you think, given King Ahmose's age and health. You'll write and rewrite laws as you see fit. With the gods on your side, there's nothing you wouldn't be able to do."

For the first time since my father arranged this marriage with the king when Nia was two years old and I ten and two years, I feel my life as king would not be so bleak. I could pray my way to the wife I desired and deserved. "Priestess, you have the ear of the gods more than even the high priest. Pray for me. Beseech the gods on my behalf that I will make my life so as king with the wife and prosperity I desire."

"As you wish." Medusa directs me to kneel in front of the seated statues of Jata and Nthanda. Standing behind me, she places her hands on my shoulders and prays for my peace, strength, and happiness not only with life, but with the woman set to be my wife and the woman I desired to be my wife.

The priestess doesn't know the wife I'm praying for is her.

"No. I have other plans for the priestess," I say, bringing my mind back to the present moment. "None of which includes the priesthood."

"Don't let your loins damn us all. Joro needs the favor she has with the gods."

"The problem is…"

Medusa says something that catches my attention. "He is gone."

"Are you sure?" Kunle asks.

The room is dead silent. Everyone watches King Ahmose's body closely.

"Babba," Nia says as she shakes his shoulders. She does it two more times, and nothing.

King Ahmose is dead.

Nia wails. For the second time since the date of our wedding announcement, I feel sorry for her. The only parent, the only family she's ever known, is now gone. It wasn't long before she found out that what she had been told about her mother dying in childbirth was a lie.

"Fetch the royal physician," Kunle orders.

The lone guard inside the door gives the word to the guards outside the chamber door. It isn't long before the physician is in the room and checking the king's vitals with his gold-inscribed onyx bead bracelet.

With a shake of his head, he confirmed what we already knew. Only now, it is official.

"Long live King Gainde and Queen Nia," Kunle says. With the exception of Nia, everyone looks at him with disgust. Nia most likely didn't hear him over her crying. I'm sure Kunle wanted to be the first to say it as an attempt to gain favor. He doesn't realize that it is my father who wants him out, not me. I couldn't care less about who the high priest is, as long as it is not Medusa. Given my father's disgust for women in leadership roles, I'm surprised he is being so adamant about her taking the title. But of course, it's because he sees something in it for himself.

"Have the royal embalmers come prepare his body for its final viewing and rest," Baraka orders. Because he didn't say a name, no one moved. Other than Medusa, no one else in the room recognized themselves as someone my father could order around, but she had to finish the ritual of guiding Ahmose's spirit into the next world. "Kunle!" he snaps.

"Oh, you want me to do that?"

"Do you have any other purpose at this point? The priestess is more than capable of finishing here."

Kunle looks at me as if I'm supposed to correct my father. Little does he know, I'm not paying attention to the conversation. My eyes and mind are on the prize I know is mine, but have yet to claim. Realizing I'm not changing my father's order, Kunle tilts his head in a half attempt at a bow. "As you wish."

"While you are at it, send in Nassir. Also, prepare for the coronation of our new king and queen to take place one week after King Ahmose's burial. Since you are still the high priest, you will work directly with me in planning the festivities."

"Of course," Kunle says in a tone that did little to hide his disdain for being ordered around.

Kunle leaves quietly. My eyes continue to roam the curves of Medusa's voluptuous body. The thought of bonding with her and making her my wife… even my second wife… it's the only thing keeping me planted in this room. I have to figure out how and when to approach her.

The king's secretary and the father of my best friend, Nassir, enters and bows to everyone. "It's true," he whispers.

"It is," my father states. "I will need you to stay on duty for some time after the coronation to ensure your son is ready for his new posting as King Gainde's secretary."

"Of course. Would you like me to send the royal messengers out to inform the people now?"

"Yes, Joro needs to begin mourning their great king."

Nassir bows his head and leaves to dispatch the messengers.

"Are you always going to be this distracted whenever she's in the room?"

"Until I make her my wife, probably so. Maybe still after then," I say.

"She is the future and first high priestess of Joro."

"As I've said, that is not her destiny. Find yourself another high priest or keep the one we already have. Leave her out of it. I've made sure the gods are in alignment with my will."

My father's eyes widen at me. "What is this you speak of?"

"Babba," I whisper, and look at the ladies to make sure they aren't listening. When I'm satisfied that they aren't, I continue. "I've done everything you've asked of me. Because the princess was not of her father's loins, he couldn't marry her to a royal son from another land, so you offered me. I didn't ask to marry her or to be king, but I did, and I am. You wanted this. I will do what is necessary of me as Nia's husband and as king of Joro, but I will have Medusa. She is the only thing I want."

This is the first time I've ever stood up to my father, and it feels damn good. He stares at me, and I hold my ground. He must know I'm not budging or changing my mind about my intentions with Medusa.

"If you are going to be a husband to the wife you currently have, comfort her in her time of sorrow."

I hate the fact that he is right. Nia has been crying nonstop since we entered this room hours ago. She has received nothing from me because my eyes and mind have been consumed with nothing but Medusa. Sighing, I make my way over to Nia, but my father stops me by placing a hand on my arm.

"Be careful what you wish for, son," Baraka warns. "Pretty doesn't always make a good wife. Think of the story of your mother-in-law for reference."

"I couldn't care less about what Nia does or with whom, but that one," I say with a nod of my head towards the priestess, "she will be mine."

"You need to care about what Nia does. She is the only one who can give you a rightful heir to the throne. We don't want a repeat of the previous queen."

"I've been king for less than two blinks, and you are already thinking of my heir."

"I'm thinking of our legacy. You are the start of a new dynasty for Joro. I will not see it cut short. You will have an heir, a male heir, with the queen, so help me, Jata."

I haven't visited Nia's chambers since our wedding, nor do I intend to anytime soon. Still, she has continued to send one of her maids down to my chambers to make her requests known every other night. My father is right again. Any child, even a girl child, with Nia would be preferred to sit on the throne than a child I had with any other wife.

I nod my head and go to my wife. Picking her up, I carry her to her chambers. As her bedroom doors close behind us, Nia whispers to me.

"Please, I don't want to be alone."

"I'm here."

I'm here, and at this moment, I hate my life.

Chapter 3
Jata

I stare at the back of my wife's head with disgust. I never thought I could dislike her more, although she is who I asked the Elders for after fighting valiantly in the Great War, Nthanda. Considered to be the most beautiful of the goddesses, is selfish, vain, lazy, and miserable to be around. The daughter of Joro's original gods, Kinshasa and Malabo, marrying her secured my place as a ruling god after the war. What I saw as a fiery spirit turned out to be an unattractive disposition. *Oh, how I would love to be rid of her!*

"Jata, the king is dead," Nthanda says. "That should please you."

"Why would such a thing please me? He was an excellent king. The best our mortals have had. I've not inhabited his body in hours, or years, in their time. From what I can tell with Gainde, it would be better for all the land if Ahmose lived forever."

"That new one has never prayed to me."

I don't respond. Nthanda refuses to get to know the mortals we serve outside of the royal female she inhabits. Also, her comment shows she doesn't care about how I feel about the king's death. As usual, she's talking for the sake of hearing herself talk.

"There's nothing in her head. Nothing!" Nthanda continues, this time about the new, but not yet crowned, Queen Nia. "In all the time of possessing queens and future queens of Joro, never have I seen a more empty mind. I don't know if she is dimwitted or just intentionally closed off." She takes another swig of marca, the wine of the gods. "The problem is, they raised her to be a doting wife instead of a powerful queen, despite her many pleas to be allowed to rule alone. Mortals kill me with that."

"Nothing but another god can kill you, Nthanda," I retort, as I lie on a chaise made of clouds listening to prayers from the mortals that appear before me as gold feathers. The feathers appear in front of my wife, too, but she ignores them. I no longer have the patience for her dramatics. Many times, I've thought of killing her, but the Elders would kill me and give my beloved terrestrial land to a younger god and goddess couple. A couple so young that they wouldn't have fought in the war against the demigods nearly a millennium ago. I fought too hard to earn my place as Joro's god after the prophesying demigod, Asmara, betrayed Kinshasa and Malabo. I can lose my wife, but Joro, I cannot.

"Too bad the former queen didn't have a son before she died," Nthanda continues, as if her husband had said nothing. "That way, he would be the one set to rule and marry a mortal woman with more of a brain and better looks. I avoid anything reflective when indwelling Nia because she is so plain."

I'm exhausted by Nthanda's selective memory. "If the queen hadn't been involved in an ongoing affair with one of the king's gentlemen while indwelled by you, which produced said plain-looking child, you wouldn't feel the need to avoid her reflection. Since you often seem to forget, the king caught his wife in the said affair, an affair you only engaged in to make me jealous. If you hadn't set your eyes on using her in such a way, the queen might've birthed another child. Instead, they buried her head and bones in different parts of Joro."

"If you had only paid me some attention—"

"And I still don't, so what good did that affair do?" I look into her eyes for the first time during this conversation, pupil-less gold eyes to pupil-less gold eyes. We're both well past the point of sparing the other's feelings. "I wonder, wife, would you be able to handle it emotionally and mentally if I were to use the body of the one to be crowned king to bed a mortal, just as you used the former queen?" I rise from my seat and start walking to my private quarters while Nthanda screams at my stardust back.

In my chambers, I use my quartz looking sphere to see into Joro. I love looking in on the mortals I have the power of life and death over. Before the war, the serving gods interacted with their mortals directly. I, however, was created during the war to fight the demigods. Being with mortals, interacting with them, is an experience I've never known. This is another point of contention between me and Nthanda. She could once interact with them, but she is indifferent towards them. I have to be satisfied with indwelling in the existing male ruler, or the next king, as had been the case recently. Answering prayers will have to do, though some of the mortals' prayers are nothing short of ridiculous.

There is one person whose prayers I always listen to intently and answer abundantly. One person who brings me the greatest joy with her praise. To me, her praise is perfect, especially when she dances for me. Granted, the praises aren't only for me. She always includes Nthanda, the Elders, Kemet and Songhai, and Moeder Heelal, but I love to let myself think they are just for me. I look forward to answering Priestess Medusa's prayers because of the praise she will give later. The thought of her makes the stardust of my body shine brighter.

I release a contented sigh. There she is in the palace, praying over the dead king's soul while his daughter lies crying next to him. Even among the goddesses, no one is as beautiful as Medusa is to me. I watch her as she purifies his body with scented smoke and prays for his passage to Muhabura, the birthplace of the gods and home to the souls of worthy mortals.

Though others are praying to Nthanda and me for the same as word spreads throughout the palace, it is Medusa's whispered prayer I actively listen to. Her soft, husky tone excites me in ways I hadn't felt for an eternity. In fact, I don't think I've ever wanted Nthanda the way I want Medusa.

Like the young new king I indwell, I want to make her mine. However, it isn't as easy for me as it could be for him. All he has to do is bond with her to make her his wife.

The only way she can become my wife is through my turning her into a demigod, which is forbidden unless another god is attacking the said human. The latter's forbidden as well. Though the Great War was why Kemet and Songhai created me, I hated what came because of it. Gods had no rules before the war, as I understand it. The restrictions result from a failed coup to overthrow the mother and father of the gods by a few demigods. The demigod Asmara leveraged her gift of prophecy to gain an audience with the Elders, Kemet and Songhai, as mortals and demigods are not permitted in Muhabura. If I had been there, she wouldn't have been able to lead other demigods into my birthplace to start the war; Joro's original gods, Kinshasa and Malabo, wouldn't have become her martyrs. Then again, I wouldn't be a ruling god of Joro if she hadn't done what she had done.

Asmara's betrayal changed everything for the gods, especially the ones who served over lands. The Elders created a separation between the gods and mortals. Through tablets made of onyx, the Elders instructed the four lands to form priesthoods to perform rituals and sacrifices to the gods. From the day the war ended, gods sent their word to the mortals they served through the ruling royals by indwelling them.

Still, no one can convince me that Medusa is not the perfect partner for me. Not only is she beautiful beyond measure, but she has an alluring combination of strength and submissiveness. She knows how to stand her ground and submit her all into what she believes in. She believes in me; of that, I'm sure. I've proven myself to Medusa repeatedly and will continue to do so, hoping that one day, somehow, I will become more than just her god to her.

Once again, I consider making a personal appeal to Kemet and Songhai. If only they could see her as I do. I know they feel her worship of them. But what if they decide they want her servitude for themselves? For that reason alone, I can't go to my creators with this, because to me, Medusa is worth starting a war over.

I've watched her ever since she traveled from Ginawa, her homeland, and declared her priesthood in Joro. Unlike the others who lived in the temple dedicated to me and my wife, and pray only when it was convenient or fashionable, Medusa prays faithfully every day and rarely ever for herself, just like now.

I listen intently as Medusa prays for the strength of Nia and Gainde and the smooth transition of power.

Great Jata and gracious Nthanda, your blessings have been abundant. For all of Joro, I give thanks. It is also on behalf of all of Joro that I come to you now. Keep the princess and prince, now queen and king, in your grace. Comfort them, especially Queen Nia, in their time of grief. Allow no one to take advantage of or make a mockery of this sensitive time in our land. Bless our new king and queen to rise in this new phase of their life and for Joro. I do not pretend to know your will, but I know greatness from and of your people is your desire. Don't let death impede that. All honor, thanks, and praise. Asé.

The finished prayer manifests in front of me as a white feather, as all prayers do. I move my hands in circles around the feather, and shimmery gold dust flows from my hands and infuses with the feather until it turns solid gold. With a blow of my breath, I blow the feather out and into the sky, where the sun dissolves it so the dust falls onto Joro. Prayers from others I dismiss with a wave of my hand, and they turn into black dust as if they never existed.

"Pathetic," Nthanda's voice snaps from the opening of my chambers. She is jealous of my obsession with Medusa. I don't blame her, but I also don't care. "You always answer her prayers, but what could she ever give you in return?"

"You mean besides the worship and submission a god deserves as opposed to the constant snarky attitude you give me?" I say over my shoulder. There's no need for me to turn around to know my words had the desired effect on Nthanda. I mean to hurt her. I can feel the anger rolling off of her in waves.

"Ignore her prayer even once and she will turn on you," Nthanda says through gritted teeth.

"If you would answer more of their prayers, maybe you would feel the love that you don't and won't get from me. Maybe, just maybe, that will make you satisfied enough to leave me alone," I say with my back still to her. The conversation is over, as far as I'm concerned. I want to go back to watching and listening to Medusa as she prays in silence while the embalmers prepare to take away the dead king's body.

I'm not foolish. Nthanda is still watching me. Her seething rage sends ripples through the clouds at my feet. She was supposed to be my prize, and instead I desire a mortal. I can see how that would make any god enraged beyond belief. At the same time, her disdain for the mortals we serve and lack of partnership in serving have made me turn my eyes and heart cold towards her.

"Just so you know," I say, acknowledging her presence, "I've thought of the same with you."

"What's that?" she asks, using a cool tone that doesn't match the rage she feels.

This time, I turn around to look at her. A smile slowly plays across my face. One that would give Nthanda hope and make her smile, thinking I was going to say something thoughtful or kind to her. "Killing you." I wait until the smile on her face fades away. "I decided in the end it wouldn't be worth the trouble it would give me."

We have a stare-off for a few moments before I've had enough and turn back to watching the woman I want as my wife, but Nthanda asks me something she's never asked before.

"What happened to us, Jata?"

I sigh, and she manifests a chair next to me before sitting down. "I realized you didn't appreciate any of this, not only as much as I do, but not nearly as much as you should. We gods have it easy compared to the mortals we're charged with. All we have to do is answer a few prayers, and we get all the glory and praise, but you don't want to do that even though our power comes from their praise."

"That's not true."

"When was the last time you answered a prayer? Huh, Nthanda? Female mortals pray to you regularly to help them with their barren or painful wombs, their marriages, equal status, or whatever, and you haven't answered one in centuries. The praise you get comes from my work, when the people pray to both of us. Your existence from the time I became your husband until now is because of me. Unfortunately, I can't stop them from including you in prayers to me so you could just wither away, and I'd be permanently free from you.

"On top of all of that, you have the nerve to take credit for my work at every gathering of the gods. Other goddesses comment on your aura and how our people must love you to make you glow the way you do. You say something about the circle of blessings between you and our people, but you don't deserve any credit, any praise, any blessings, any aura, or any power. You are nothing more than a loud and needy weight I'm forced to carry around. I saw past your beauty to who you really are, and from that moment, we were doomed. Wife or not, you don't deserve to be in my presence, or that of any god, for that matter."

Tears roll from Nthanda's gold eyes and down her starry bronze cheeks. I can tell she wants to say something to me, come back with some snarky remark, but every word I said was true. Nthanda transports from my chambers. It isn't until I hear her screaming and crying that I'm able to determine she's in her chambers. Her emotions cause a storm of heavy rain, thunder, and lightning on Joro. I pretend as if I don't hear her as I listen to a prayer from the new young king that may solve my problem.

This isn't the first time I've heard such a prayer from Gainde. It is, however, the first time I've seen it as an opportunity. Granting Gainde's prayer is the next best thing to making Medusa my godly wife. Already, I'm making plans to inhabit Gainde more often just for the pleasure of being in Medusa's presence. With Medusa as Gainde's wife, I'd know the pleasures of her body and get her praise in person. Through the king, we can have kids I would bless immensely. I'll have an escape from my wife. Hope for me is not all lost either.

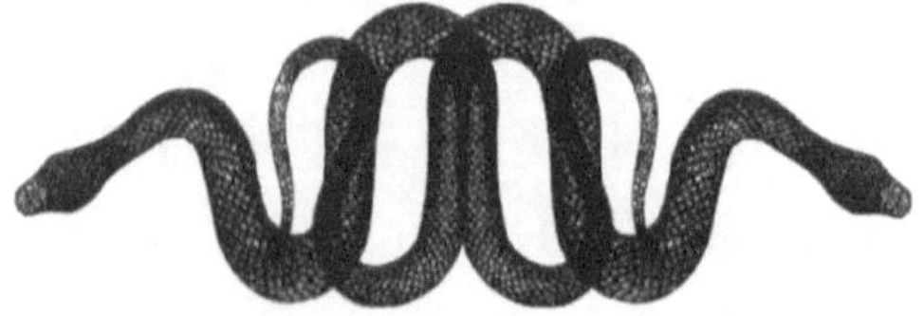

Chapter 4
Medusa

I am grateful for the storm, no matter how unexpected it is. The smell after the rain always reminds me of my beloved homeland, Ginawa. Though not as strong here in Joro, the mix of fresh rain, earth, and the diverse plants that thrived off them gives the air an alluring scent. Though my quarters in the temple were more than accommodating, there are some things about a simple hut made of strong vines and leaves longer than an adult male formed between the trees of the forest that I will always miss.

Once the rain slows down to a drizzle, I leave the palace and head to the Commons, where the everyday people of Joro live. Where the best people live, if you ask me. I need to get to my daughter, Sisay, who is visiting with my only genuine friend in Joro, Zendaya. The rain feels cool on my skin as I walk through the now empty courtyard to the bridge over the Tehenu River. Each of the four lands in the realm has a river that flows from Muhabura through the heavens of the serving gods and down onto the land as a waterfall. My homeland has the Akan, Himba has the Nzambi, and San the Hausa. It's been a blistering hot few days in Joro, so the rain is much relief. I stop on the edge of the river to fill my leather water sack and take a drink before walking across the slippery cobblestone bridge.

The Commons is busier than the courtyard where the highborns reside. The people are not only more about community, but they also do not let a little rain keep them from going about their day.

Just before I get to the road Zendaya's house is on, Zendaya's brother Nyani spots me. I try not to make eye contact, but he still excuses himself from the men he's talking with and makes his way to me, cutting me off, so I have no choice but to talk to him. Though his sister is a dear friend, Nyani is not. I find his personality to be repulsive.

"Have you heard? The king is dead."

"I was there," I answer.

"You were? Death is a sensitive thing. They should've had the high priest or one of the other priests there to spare you of such a burden."

The comment is not worth responding to. Joroan men are proud, and some think little of women outside of bonding and raising kids. I could've let him know that I'm highly favored to be the next high priest, but some battles aren't worth it. That energy will be better used in the transition of power to come.

"I want to thank you for what you did for my sister and her boy last week," Nyani continues. "His soul would probably be with the Elders if it were not for your knowledge of herbs. It hasn't been easy for Zendaya since her husband died a year ago."

"It was my honor. Zendaya has always been kind to my girl, Sisay, and she was the first welcoming person I met when I came to Joro. Helping her in any way is the least I could do."

He nods. "Still, thank you."

I nod in return. Giving him more than necessary is something I'm not willing to do.

"I would like to do something for you in return," Nyani says as his eyes turn from thankful to heated with lust.

It is a look I know all too well. Knowing what is coming, I try to cut it off early. "The gods supply me with everything I could ever need," I state. I try to step around him, but he puts himself in my path again. I consider whether it's wrong for me to ask the gods to open the ground so it swallows him.

"But you haven't heard my proposal. How could you know it's not something you need or want without knowing what I am going to offer you?"

I sigh, and it takes everything in me not to roll my eyes. It always exhausts me how men can be so sure of themselves that they miss all the obvious signs of disinterest. "Go on then."

"I know you've dedicated your life to the gods, but you did it so early in life. By doing so, you have denied yourself the privilege of passion and a lucky man the honor of you bearing him a child or few. The other women of the temple never had the looks or charm to live such a life. That is why they are there."

I stare at him for a few moments, waiting for him to make his proposal. After a bit, I no longer have the patience to point out that there was no question in his statement, nor his audacity in assuming I want his so-called passion and large-headed kids and, that none of it is the compliment he thinks it is.

As if he has to clue me in on what he meant, Nyani leans in and says, "your husband. I'm offering to be your husband."

"No," I say firmly, which, based on how he pulled away, takes Nyani by surprise.

"As beautiful as you are, don't you want to fulfill your duty as a woman?"

My body stiffens as my anger rises and pours out of my eyes and tone. "My duty is to the gods. The very gods who blessed me with the knowledge that saved your sister's child. Show some respect."

With that, I storm off. Nyani is hot on my heels, begging me to listen to him and to give him a chance. I ignore him. When we get to his sister's house, Nyani stops talking and walks into the small sandstone home with a clay tile roof that is typical of the homes in the Commons.

"Brother, you were just here," Zendaya says. She doesn't care much for her brother, either. "Medusa, so good to see you, my friend." She stands to hug me, then holds me out at arm's length. "Wait, something must be wrong. You never leave the temple on the day of worship."

"Something is indeed wrong, sister," Nyani states. "That is why I returned so soon."

Again, I roll my eyes.

"Whatever it is, Nyani, it is not your news to tell if Medusa is here on this day." Zendaya nods for me to tell her, while her brother huffs his frustration at not being respected by yet another woman. He doesn't care for the independence his sister has established for herself after the passing of her husband.

I smile in thanks. "First, where is Sisay? You both need to know."

"She is in the garden out back with Wambua."

Zendaya leads us to the back garden where Sisay and her son are playing. Sisay, who is of two and ten years old, is showing the boy, of five years, how to do the latest dance the kids are doing. Sisay has always wanted to be a big sister, but her mother was not willing to go through childbirth again. Then she died of the fever plague that ravaged Joro a few years ago. Wambua is her closest thing to a sibling.

When Sisay looks up and notices me, worry sets in her oval, copper-toned face and green eyes. She stops dancing immediately. "What has happened?"

"King Ahmose has begun his journey to Muhabura to meet Kemet and Songhai."

"He looked so strong at the wedding months ago," Zendaya says.

"That was a farce," Medusa explains. "The royal physicians gave him a powerful tonic to suppress his cough for a few hours. When it wore off, not only were his lungs worse, but the tonic was like a slow poison to the rest of his body. He insisted on taking it so he could look the proud father and strong king everyone had known him to be for the wedding."

"Poor Princess Nia," Sisay says.

"Poor Queen Nia," I correct. "She was distraught as he took his last breaths and when he was gone… our new king had to carry her out."

"We should say a prayer for her," Sisay suggests.

"We will," I respond.

"All of Joro will," Zendaya says.

"Do you have enough provisions to get you through the mourning time?" I ask Zendaya.

"Yes, I should."

"All of my households should make it through just fine," Nyani says, as if someone is talking to him.

"Of which my household is not a part of," Zendaya reminds him.

"You women," he huffs before storming off.

I watch Zendaya's child as he chases a butterfly. "It is good to see your boy doing so well."

"Praise the gods and thanks to you." She pauses for a moment. "With the new king and queen, there could be a new High Priest soon."

"I'm not thinking about that," I respond.

"You may not be. The princess, I mean, the queen, most definitely is not at this time, but other people in the palace are. His Grace, without a doubt, is thinking about it."

"He is always in fear of being replaced," Sisay says. Kunle has never treated either of us well, so she has very little respect for him.

"All I'm focused on right now is doing what I can to make sure Joro gets through this mourning period. After that, the coronation of the new king and queen. Whatever happens from that point on, I will cross that bridge when I get there."

"Will the king's journey to the Elders differ from anyone else's, since he was Jata's inhabitant?" Sisay asks.

"Yes, in several ways. I can tell you about them as we make our way back to the temple."

Sisay nods. We say goodbye and depart for our home at the temple.

The stone streets of The Commons were filling up with people coming together to mourn King Ahmose. We could still hear people sobbing as we crossed the bridge over the Tehenu River.

"The king's journey?" Sisay asks.

I smile for the first time since leaving the temple this morning. I've always loved how eager Sisay is to learn. Placing an arm around her shoulders, "First, tell me what you remember of the journey of any other person."

"When a person dies, their soul goes to Muhabura, where the Elders, Kemet and Songhai, live. The Elder gods show the person their life and weigh their deeds and their heart. If the good outweighs the bad, the soul becomes a new star, and the Songhai & Kemet release the star to the Mother Universe. If the bad outweighs the good, the Elder gods send the soul back to live another life for it to learn how to be better."

"Good job. Kings, queens, warrior leaders, and high priests are also accountable for the quality of life and souls of their subjects. If the good outweighs the bad, their soul becomes one with Kemet and Songhai. If the bad is greater, their soul gets destroyed. Now, do you remember the origin story and the various kinds of gods in Moeder Heelal?"

"At the top is the Mother Universe herself, Moeder Heelal, who is both an entity and everything under the stars. She created Muhabura and the Elder gods, Kemet and Songhai.

Kemet and Songhai created all the gods under them and the lands. Serving gods have dominion over the lands, like our Jata and Nthanda, and Ginawa's Kush and Ife. There are the messenger gods, like Eshu, who send messages between the Elders and the serving gods, as well as delivering new tablets with a word directly from Muhabura to each land's High Priest. There are warrior gods, which Jata started out as during the great war of the gods."

I feel a bit of pride listening to Sisay as she rattles off the deity system of Moeder Heelal. Most teens her age in Joro don't know the god-system as well, whereas in Ginawa, I had to know all of this and more by the time I was of ten and three years. "You are going to make a great priestess one day."

"That is because I have the greatest priestess as my teacher and mother."

Sisay's last word stops me in my tracks. In the four years that Sisay has been with me after the death of her birth parents, she's never referred to me as her mother. Parent, yes. Mother, never before.

"Zendaya referred to you as my mother earlier today. It felt… right."

"Other than serving the gods and the crown, raising you has been my greatest joy."

Sisay gives me a wide and bright smile that somehow makes her cinnamon skin even warmer. "So, Mother, what is being served at the temple for dinner today?"

"Your favorite, I believe."

"Egusi?"

I nod my head. If given the chance, she will stuff herself full of egusi until she can't move.

Sisay picks up her pace and pulls me along. "Hurry! We must get there before Accra! She likes to restrict how much everyone else eats so she can take all the leftovers to her room for her and Cairo to eat all night."

"There is always enough to go around, Sisay."

"But I'm starving!"

I laugh because I know she is exaggerating. She's been at Zendaya's all day, so I know she's eaten. Zendaya lets her munch on the vegetables and fruits of her garden all day. Still, I entertain her and run with her back to the temple.

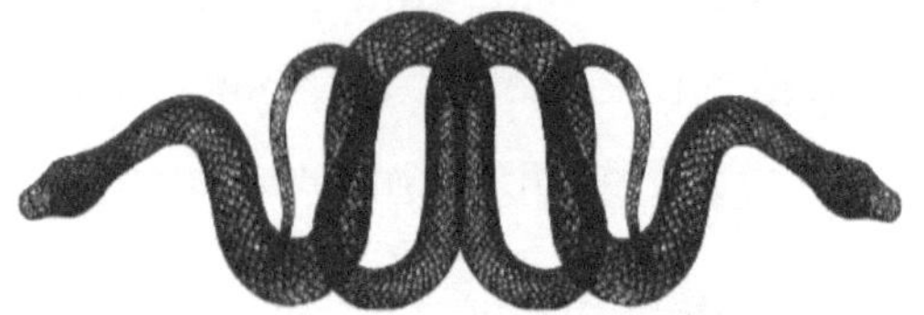

Chapter 5
Medusa

It is now up to the people of Joro to help King Ahmose reach the Elders. The royal groomers are now in possession of his burial cloth, which was made shortly after his coronation, from the royal library. They will prepare his body and dress him in his finest garments and jewels for his funeral service.

All the people of Joro are expected to contribute to the construction of the dead king's final bed, which has been taking place in the center of the courtyard throughout the six days of mourning. Every day I watch as men and women alike bring in timber from the nearby woods, hay from the fields, flowers and vines from their gardens. Some even hide coins in the hay so King Ahmose could pay for whatever he needs in order to get to the Elder gods, where he'll receive a reward for his life and service and become one with Kemet and Songhai.

While the people prepare and mourn, Kunle is on the verge of quarreling with the palace. According to him, it's my fault. His problem is King Gainde's father, Baraka, who wants me to preside over both the funeral and coronation ceremonies.

"She ranks below me!" Kunle states while pointing at me as I stand right next to him in the throne room of the palace. "As the High Priest, I am the only one who can receive new tablets directly from the Elders."

I've been standing here listening to them go back and forth about me for at least a quarter of an hour.

Baraka has something for every reason Kunle comes up with about why I'm not qualified. "And yet, she is more favored by the gods than you, which in my eyes makes Medusa the true High Priest. You merely have the title. Tell me, Kunle, how does that work for you, hmmm? Knowing the one you trained outshines you in every way and no one else in the priesthood shines nearly as bright as Medusa? That the people seek her counsel and intercession before thinking of coming to you?"

"A *mugeni* cannot serve as High Priest of Joro!"

"What law of man or decree from the gods, even the Elders, makes that so?"

Kunle has no response.

Baraka turns his attention to me. "How long have you been in Joro now?"

"Ten years, my Bwana."

"Ten years. She is no longer a *mugeni,* a stranger to us. The people know and adore Medusa. Jata and Nthanda know her, and it shows in her favor. As much as you do not want to admit it, you are old, Kunle, and your ways are old. This land needs refreshing. That is starting with the new king and queen. It will get that with a new head of the priesthood, as well."

"Will the same refreshing take place with the leader of Joro's warriors, too?" Kunle retorts.

"You will watch your tongue before I have it cut out!" Baraka yells.

"May I return to the temple?" I ask. My presence is unnecessary if all they are going to do is provoke each other.

"Yes!" Kunle snaps.

"No!" Baraka yells.

"What is the meaning of this?" Gainde asks as he casually walks into the throne room.

"My King," Kunle and I say as we bow.

Baraka rises from the king's throne. "I was handling some matters on your behalf. I figured you would still be with the queen."

"She is sleeping for the first time in days, so I am here."

"Please give the queen condolences from all of Joro," I say. "I know it is not the same, but we all grieve with her."

I can see Kunle staring at me from the corner of my eye and can feel his disdain for me. Knowing him, he just took my words as me trying to gain favor with the new king before he had a chance to. He doesn't understand that I'm not in on the campaign to replace him.

"Priestess Medusa," Gainde says with a wide smile. "How is it I didn't notice you when I entered?"

I'm not sure how to respond, but Baraka saves the awkward moment by clearing his throat.

"I will let the queen know. Now, what matters have you two yelling at each other? I could hear you halfway down the corridor."

Kunle waves a sheet of woven paper with a broken purple wax seal in the air. Purple was a color only the royals could use or wear. "I received this not long ago. It says the funeral ceremony is to be performed by Medusa. I am the High Priest. It is my right and duty to perform the funeral rites."

A look passes between the father and son that says a lot. I can easily gather that the king is not happy with Baraka about this. Why, I am unsure. It is because of the requests for my intercession by the then prince, now king, that sent Kunle's paranoia about me replacing him beyond Joro's four moons.

"Kunle is right," Gainde says.

"Medusa is more favored," Baraka says. He seems irritated that he needs to explain himself to his son, king or not. "If we want to ensure our fallen King Ahmose's soul survives the passage to Muhabura, she needs to do the rites."

King Gainde is silent as he mulls over his father's words. He looks back and forth between Kunle and me, though his eyes linger on me. I can only imagine he is thinking of a peaceful way to go about this, one that will respect Kunle's current position and the crown's apparent desire to have me as the next High Priest. "I propose a compromise. Both Kunle and Medusa perform the rites for the funeral—"

"And the coronation," Baraka interrupts.

Gainde sighs. I don't think I ever realized that the relationship between Baraka and Gainde was as contentious as it appears to be now. Maybe some of it is grief over King Ahmose, but they are definitely at odds with each other. "And the coronation. You two will split the duties equally."

"My King, as part of your counsel, I must say I do not think this is wise," Kunle says.

"Are you confusing me with the old king already, Kunle?" Gainde asks. "I've yet to form my counsel, as I've been occupied with the queen's mourning."

"No, my King. Apologies."

"Split the duties equally. I do not care how, just do it," Gainde orders.

"Yes, my King," Kunle and I say in unison.

"Priestess Medusa, I am glad you are here. I was going to come see you. I could use your prayer if you have time for your king."

"Yes, of course," I respond.

"Leave us," King Gainde orders to everyone else in the room.

His father leans down and whispers something in his ear. The king keeps a stoic face, but his hands noticeably grip the armrests of his throne. Kunle gives me a "hmph" before crossing in front of me to leave. *Oh, the gods, this man!*

"Would my king like me to pray for his and the queen's strength during this time of grieving?" I ask.

"No. I mean, yes, but that is not the prayer I am seeking." Gainde remains silent and stares at me until the silence forces me to speak.

"What troubles you, my king?"

"You have the ear of the gods. That is why I come to you to intercede on my behalf. How will I know the right time to approach the woman I desire to be my wife with a proposal?"

Though he's expressed his desire for another wife to me before, I find it odd that this is what he is thinking about at such a time. "Let the gods lead you, but I might suggest waiting until after your coronation. Both you and Joro are going through substantial changes right now. Adding another wife now may seem insensitive not only to this land, but to your wife, the Queen."

The way he stares at me leaves me unsure if my answer was satisfactory or not. "My king?"

"How much do I need to consider the Queen in such affairs?"

"She's the queen by birthright. Any additional wives you take will have to understand that Queen Nia will be their queen until her last breath, even if you favor them more than her. They will never be queen of Joro or this palace. They must respect the Queen at all times. It will be easier for you if your additional wives were someone who already has great respect for the queen and whom the queen likes."

"Birthright… hmmm."

The king is questioning my choice of words. "He was the only father she ever knew. He called and treated her like his own. Same as I do with my daughter. Only my daughter was old enough to remember her parents when I took her in."

"Tell me, if you were to move out of the temple, would your daughter come with you?"

"Why would I move out of the temple?"

"Allow me to rephrase. If your king were to require you to move into the palace, would your daughter come with you?"

"Wherever I go, my daughter comes with me. But I am confused about why you would ask me to do such a thing. The priesthood resides only in the temple, and I am available whenever my king or queen needs me. I serve you both just as much as I serve the gods."

He gives me a slanted smile. "That is good to know, priestess."

"That prayer?"

"Yes. Please, pray for the queen and everyone mourning."

I kneel before the steps of the throne, and after a few moments, King Gainde rises and joins me.

Great gods Jata and Nthanda, our creators, Kemet and Songhai, and the almighty Moeder Heelal, the mother to the stars and everything under them,

"In this moment of sorrow, all of Joro turns to you for solace and comfort. We are heartbroken and seek your loving embrace. Help us find peace in the knowledge that our great king will soon join you in Muhabura. May his soul find eternal rest in you,

and may his memories continue to glow in our hearts, especially the heart of his daughter, Queen Nia.

"Grant her the strength to bear this loss, and courage to move forward in their honor. Let her cherish the memory of her father in the quiet of her heart and remember his joy in the echo of her laughter.

"May all the people of Joro honor King Ahmose's legacy by living their lives with kindness, love, wisdom, and compassion. In Your infinite wisdom, power, and love, we find solace and peace. Asé."

The king quickly stands and holds out his hand for me to take.

"Thank you, my king," I say once I'm on my feet.

His hand lingers on mine. "Thank you, Medusa."

I wait for him to release my hand, because I don't want to seem rude. An uneasy feeling settles in my stomach. He's never called me by my name before. It's always been "priestess" or "Priestess Medusa". He's been holding my hand for far too long. When he rubs his thumb across my knuckles, I come up with an excuse to leave.

"I need to get back to the temple. With Kunle on a tangent about his diminished role in the upcoming ceremonies, my daughter is not safe from his wrath."

He lets go of my hand. "If you do not feel safe in the temple, you are always welcome here, and your daughter, of course."

"Thank you, my king. That won't be necessary. I can stand up to Kunle. Sisay, however, is just a child."

"Very well then. The invitation will remain open."

"Thank you, King Gainde." I bow and quickly exit the throne room. As I walk through the corridors of the palace until I am on the stone of the courtyard, I tell myself not to overthink my interaction with the king. *He is the king, after all, and I am just a priestess devoted to the gods. What could he want with me?*

Chapter 6
Jata

Being a god has its perks. One of them is being able to look in on mortals in multiple ways. Using a looking sphere is the most common way to do so, but sometimes I want to get closer to them… closer to Medusa. This is when our incognito power is the most useful these days, for me at least. I used it a lot more during the Great War, but now that all the demigods are gone and there's been peace, my only use for it is to be near my most cherished mortal. The problem is we can use the incognito power for only so long.

I lean against the wall in her chambers as she listens to her daughter animatedly tell her of the latest happenings in the temple and in the Commons. Medusa sits casually on her bed with her legs crossed wide, soaking up everything being told to her and gently reminding Sisay that it's not good to gossip. She gives the girl her undivided attention, the same as she does to us gods when she is praying, meditating, or praising.

What I would give to have her attention only on me in that way.

The child asks her what the crowning ceremonies in Ginawa are like. A natural question, as the coronation of Joro's new king and queen is coming up.

"The ceremonies are simpler, I think. There is no priesthood to perform rites as the king and queen share the priesthood duties. If there is an apparent or declared heir, the glory of Kush and Ife will fall upon them and their spouse. All the people, along with the new king and queen, pledge to serve the gods. Kush and Ife indwell the rulers, accept the people's pledge and pledge to serve the people in return. They provide a feast for celebration and bless everyone with coin in their purse."

"And if there is no heir?" the girl asks.

"Then Kush and Ife will select rulers from amongst the people. That has happened less than a handful of times in Ginawa's history."

For the first time since I've been with them, Sisay stops talking. I watch Medusa as she watches the girl. Medusa's skin glows in any setting, but especially in the candlelight illuminating her room. Her long locs, which she usually wears down her back, are up high in a messy bun on the top of her head. Sitting next to her, I look at her beauty even more closely. I wonder if she's ever noticed the speckle of green just on the edge of her irises. Her full lips look as soft as the clouds that make up my home. I imagine that the hollows of her clavicles and her breasts hold the sweetest scent. The way the thickness in her hips spreads when she sits sends a charge through me. The leg closest to me comes through the split in her dress. She always wears dresses with a high slit, which is perfect. Her long, thick legs deserve to be seen and admired.

I want to feel her flesh. Gainde needs to bond with Medusa soon, for all of our sake.

"Let's go," Medusa says as she jolts onto her feet.

"Where?" Sisay asks.

"Ginawa. It's been a while since we've gone. I'm sure my mother would love to see how tall you've gotten."

"Do you think she will cook egusi?"

"For you, yes!"

Watching them as they leave the room, I wait a few moments before opening a portal and transport to the heavens of Ginawa. I won't be able to see her in Ginawa from Joro. I walk through the portal and into Ginawa's heavens, the home of their gods, Kush and Ife.

"You know, brother," Kush says, "you don't have to only visit whenever your favorite mortal returns home." He doesn't even look up as he watches his looking sphere.

"I know, and I'm sorry. It's just that I worry…"

"About what Nthanda would do to her if you weren't around?" Kush finishes. This time, he looks at me.

I nod as I sit beside him.

"I already know the answer to this, but," Ife asks, "are things still strained between you two?"

"Strained is a pleasant way of putting it," I answer.

"What is it with this one?" Kush asks. "Why is this mortal so special to you when she's not even from your world?"

"She's different."

Kush chuckles. "Aaah. I see. You aren't accustomed to being praised or credited for something as simple and ordinary as the wind blowing, even in your own marriage. That is what our mortals are taught from birth, and now that you have a taste of it as her god, you want more."

I nod while watching Medusa enjoy her family and old friends. When word gets out that Medusa has returned home, everyone moves their dinners outside, and it becomes a gay feast.

"So much more. I want her to be my wife," I respond.

"It would be much less complicated to get your mortals on board with the ways our mortals do things," Ife comments. "She was here recently. Nthanda, that is."

I look away from Medusa and ask my question with my stare.

"First, she wanted us to swear to kill Medusa on her next return here, which would be now."

Instantly, I'm ready to defend Medusa. My power rushes over my body in golden waves. The warmth of my rage at Nthanda's request heats my very core and radiates throughout my body.

"We denied her request," Kush says, putting a hand on my arm to calm me.

Ife seems to have taken offence at my assumption. "Are we not as family to one another? Do you not know us, the gods we are? We would never harm a mortal, especially one of our own."

"She also asked you to kill me?" I ask.

Ife nods. "And we denied her again."

I take a seat. "Apologies to both of you. I've thought about killing Nthanda, but I've never acted on it or dared to ask someone else to do it for me."

"Even as the youngest of the four of us, you understand consequences," Kush explains. "Nthanda is the eldest of us, and she does not."

"What else did she say?"

"Oh, she swore to take us down with you for not helping her," Kush says nonchalantly.

Now I chuckle. "That's it?"

Ife speaks. "I told her that there is no problem in letting you have your fantasy. It will pass along as the brief lives of mortals do. If she weren't a priestess, I'd say indwell the king and bond with her. Nthanda's done it."

I silently stare at the looking sphere. I don't want to tell them that, priestess or not, I plan to do just that.

Kush sits up straight. "Brother?"

"Aaht," Ife says. "I am going to excuse myself now so that when the moment you, Jata, do something stupid, and you will, I can remain innocent in the eyes of the Elders." Before either I or Kush can say another word, Ife vanishes.

Kush decides it is wise to drill home his wife's point. "Jata, you know a mortal cannot be your wife. And this mortal has taken the oath of the priesthood in your land. Don't take that away from her."

"Medusa."

"What?"

"Her name is Medusa," I inform him. "None of Joro's priesthood is chaste. They've even corrupted the interns with lust."

"Except Medusa." Kush stares at the side of my head like he's trying to get his seed of sense to take root in me. "Okay. Still, you know Medusa can't be your wife. Not to mention you are a god, an immortal, meant to answer prayers, give out blessings and punishments from the heavens. You can't abandon that to be a husband to her?"

I don't want to hear it. "There has to be a way."

"And that right there is your problem."

"What? Being in love with a mortal?"

"Oh, please. You aren't in love with her. This is lust. Lust and greed. Those are the same reasons you chose Nthanda as your wife, without getting to know her."

"Greed has nothing to do with it." I intentionally leave the lust part out of it.

"Greed has everything to do with it. You said it yourself; you want more of her type of praise, so much that you want it from her, but as your wife. That is all about you. Did you ever stop to think that if you opened the hearts and minds of your people to worship the way she…Medusa…does, not only would your people prosper more with you doing less work, but you would be all the more satisfied? Instead, you work yourself over answering more prayers than any other serving god for the love of mortals you have trained not to appreciate you. Things became so much easier for Ife and me when the former queen got rid of the priesthood."

"My mortals appreciate me. They love me as they should."

"They appreciate your constant blessings. When's the last time you've gone a day, a mortal day, without answering a single prayer? Have you ever had a day where you received nothing but praise and not a single prayer asking you for something? When was the last time you caused a famine to remind them to be grateful for when there is plenty?"

"They had a sickness that killed many mortals not long ago."

"Was that yours or Nthanda's doing?"

I don't respond. How I've hated Nthanda for sending the fever plague. I knew she did it hoping it would take Medusa out and to get a boost in praise for when it passed. Through her own knowledge of medicinal herbs, Medusa didn't even get sick.

"That's what I thought," Kush says. We are silent for a few moments before Kush speaks again. "I don't want to know what you plan on doing or what you will do when you come up with a plan. You are as aware as I am of the punishment you may very well bring upon yourself. Be prepared, and you need to be absolutely certain she is worth it."

I sigh. "How are your kids the Elders so graciously gifted you with?" I ask to change the subject.

"Living in Muhabura with our creators, Kemet and Songhai, serving them dutifully.

"I do envy you there, brother. You built a nice family for yourself."

"You could have done the same."

"I don't trust Nthanda with our mortals because of how she acts when she feels she isn't getting enough attention. She would get rid of any child of ours for the same reason."

"I tried to warn you about her. I can't prove it, but I still think she was in on it with Asmara."

"For what gain?"

"Control. To be the first god to rule solo, just to prove a point to the Elders who insist we serve in pairs."

"Have you looked into this so you'll have proof?" I ask.

"It's not that important to me."

I wave him off. Kush is the only person in all the godhood with that theory.

Now it is Kush's turn to change the subject. "Have you ever wondered what it would be like to be so fragile?"

The two gods look on at the mortals eating, telling stories, and laughing together. "No, I get enough of a taste when I indwell Gainde."

"Understandable."

"I will say this about them. Mortals have no idea how frail they are in the grand scheme of things."

"You are right about that."

Me and Kush entertain ourselves by watching Medusa and the other mortals of Ginawa until she and her daughter travel back to Joro.

Chapter 7
Medusa

I stand behind Sisay, combing out her soft curls. After pulling the top half back, I secure it with a leather cord decorated with turquoise beads at the end.

"I don't want to go into the woods today, or any day," she says to me.

Turning her around by her shoulders, I look into her innocent green eyes. "We have to. All of those who are of able body must go into the woods to lay the king to rest in the tomb of kings."

"But the *ejo nla...*"

"Is nothing more than a fairy tale."

"A cruel fairy tale. I remember my parents telling me that if I did not go to bed without a fuss, the giant snake would snatch me away in the middle of the night. What do you suppose happened to the cattle that sometimes go missing without a trace and never return?"

"Stolen, or the stories are false. No one has ever seen the thing, and you would think someone would've spotted a snake large enough to take a dozen cows at once."

"Nyani said he looked it right in the eyes once."

"Nyani? Zendaya's brother, Nyani? Looked into the eyes of the snake claimed to eat cattle and people who wander into the woods alone at night?" It surprises me that Sisay used him to make her point, which only invalidated hers. That man is full of lies to make himself seem more important and braver than he is.

"I suppose you have a point. But it lives *in* the mountains. They bury the royal family *in* the mountains. We are walking into the snake's home."

"Only a few guards, Queen Nia, King Gainde, Kunle, and I, are going into the tomb. The rest of Joro will stay in the woods just outside of the mountain."

"The woods are the *ejo nla's* garden! Better yet, it's hunting grounds. Are you saying that you have no fear of it whatsoever?"

"It's just a story, Sisay. The only thing that scares me is how much you are growing up. Look at you. Soon you will go from a beautiful child to a beautiful young woman."

"I know you changed the subject to distract me from my fear. Thank you… and thank you. I will say this one thing. You didn't grow up hearing the stories of the ejo nla like I did."

"You are welcome, and I understand. I will do anything to protect you, you know that, right?" She nods her head. "If there is any sign of danger, I will get you out of there. I won't let anything happen to you."

"Yes, Mother."

"Alright. Go find a place near the king's bed in the courtyard where I will be able to see you. I must go to the palace to be a part of the royal procession, then you will walk with me to the tomb."

The two of us leave our chambers and take the side exit closest to them to get to the courtyard. For the last six days, the courtyard hasn't been the usual hustle and bustle place it usually is during the week. The markets have not reopened after the announcement of the king's death.

"Can I stay in the village with the other teenagers afterwards?" Sisay asks as we approach the bed.

"I do not see a problem with that. I will probably spend some time with Zendaya before returning home. See you later."

I continue across the courtyard to the palace. Inside the vestibule, a royal guard greets me, then escorts me to the great hall where the dead king's body lies on a smaller bed and his daughter, son-in-law, and warrior leader wait. I bow first to King Ahmose, then to Queen Nia and King Gainde, and last to Baraka.

"You have been in my constant prayers, my queen," I say.

"I have felt them. Thank you."

Baraka says out loud what I've been hoping to avoid. "Priestess Medusa would make an excellent High Priest. Don't you think, Queen Nia?"

"I haven't given it any thought, but I am surprised to hear this coming from you, Baraka, considering how you feel about a woman's purpose. You, along with my father, insisted that Joro needed a male to rule beside me when I asked that my engagement to your son be called off."

This is news to me, and by his face, it is news to Gainde as well. He looks at his wife, then at his father. "What's she talking about?"

"For the love of the gods, I am standing just here. You can ask me about what I said." The queen shakes her head. "You men and your constant need to be involved and in charge, yet you can't talk directly to a woman when it matters most."

This was a side of the queen I've never seen before. She always seemed quiet, soft-spoken, and amenable. I know emotions are high for her today, and understandably so, but she surprisingly has a snarky side. I wonder how much of what she just alluded to is true—that she didn't want to marry the then-

Prince Gainde, or maybe not have married at all. We may have more in common than I thought before.

"You weren't my choice for a bride either," Gainde says.

"Gainde!" Baraka snaps.

"I am aware," Nia responds. "Servants have overheard you say just that to your friend and secretary, Assir. Your words eventually made their way to me."

"What are *you* doing here already?" a voice from the entryway of the great hall says.

Everyone turns to see Kunle staring me down, while the guards set to carry the king's body take their places on what will be the top of King Ahmose's ceremonial funeral bed.

"I came directly here," I answer.

"Early and without me to impress the new king and queen, no doubt."

"She," Baraka interjects, "was on time and, unlike you, did not make the said new king and queen wait for his grand arrival as if he ranks above them. Know your place and take it. We've been ready to go."

Kunle wasn't late. I imagine Baraka felt the need to change the focus from the marriage he forced upon his son to Kunle's jealousy. Everyone lines up behind the king's body, with Kunle and me first, Gainde and Nia a couple paces behind us, and Baraka last. As our procession starts, Kunle puts the end of his staff in front of my feet to keep me from moving, effectively putting me a few paces behind him.

"Of all days…" the queen says.

If Kunle hears her, he pretends not to. The guards carry King Ahmose's body through the palace and out to the courtyard, where the people of Joro and the royal families of Himba, Ginawa, and San are celebrating the life of the dead king.

The people have adorned themselves in clothing of vibrant colors with painted designs on their faces and bodies in reds, oranges, yellows, and greens. They dance and sing in the courtyard while drums and horns play. We, the procession, join in on the song and dance as we make our way through the crowd.

Journey on.
Journey on.

*May   your
soul journey
on.
Let the gods
welcome
you, and let
your reward
be great.
We
celebrate
you, child of
the Moeder
Heelal.
Joyous was
your life.
Now   that
mourning is
over,
Joyous   is
your death.*

The people repeat the song over and over until the guards place King Ahmose's body on his burial bed. Me and Kunle stand before the crowd. Others of the priesthood surround the bed and toss brightly colored flowers over the burial cloth that lies over the king's body.

Kunle raises his arms to quiet the crowd and lowers them as he begins speaking. "The sun has set on our beloved King Ahmose the Great. He saw us successfully through battles and brought much prosperity to the land. Most Joroans have never lived under the rule of another king. Many of us here would say he is the best king Joro has ever known. He surely had the longest reign of any king within the Assi galaxy."

Now it is my turn. "On behalf of Joro, I'd like to welcome and thank our guests from lands near and far. Thank you for your thoughts of condolence and prayers of comfort for us, especially for our new queen. Also, on behalf of the crown, thank you for your gifts, declarations of support to our monarchy as it transitions and continued peace, and the memories of our king that you've shared. With and even against some of you and your forefathers, King Ahmose ushered in unprecedented peace throughout the Moeder Heelal."

Bright gold light falls on Queen Nia and King Gainde, nearly blinding everyone in attendance. The light is the telltale sign that Jata and Nthanda are joining us through our royals, along with the joyous sound of harps and horns that always announce their arrival and departure. When the music stops, everyone knows to bow until they speak. Silence passes for a few moments before Jata's baritone laced over Gainde's tenor addresses the gathering.

"My precious Joro."

Everyone rises and takes in the golden glow that dances around the king and queen, as well as the gods' gold eyes, the only physical attribute of the gods royals take on when indwelled by a god.

"We grieve the loss of King Ahmose with you," Jata continues, "and have all confidence that he will become one with Kemet and Songhai."

"Our commitment to you, and your new king and queen, will not change," Nthanda says in her bell-like soprano voice that makes the perfect melody over Queen Nia's alto tone. She continues speaking, but I have a hard time focusing on it as I've caught Jata staring at me.

He doesn't look away as I wonder why he's looking at me so intently. I'm not the only one who notices either. Kunle slowly turns from Jata to me and back.

"What have you done?" Kunle whispers to me.

I turn from Jata's gaze to look at Kunle. "Nothing. I don't know what that is about."

I nearly pale when I turn my head back to see Nthanda looking at me, then turning to her husband. Jata finally removes his eyes from me and looks at Nthanda from the corner of his eye. He steps forward, stretching his arms over the crowd.

"Feel comforted, Joro, for we are with you." A strong sense of peace falls over me, and I imagine everyone else. The chorus of harps and horns starts, and the blinding gold light returns. When it is over, our king and queen are back to themselves.

After a few moments, Kunle raises his arms to the heavens, and drummers start a rolling beat. "Gods of Joro, guide your faithful servant, King Ahmose the Great, to the heavenly mountain from which you were born. Give him all the advice he needs in order to pass the tests of Muhabura so that he may present himself before the Elders, Kemet and Songhai, to receive his eternal reward and become one with them."

I finish the prayer. "Though his body remains here on Joro, we commit his soul to you, to the Elders, and to Moeder Heelal. Asé."

Kunle claps to start a single beat, and others join in. The people clap and dance as Queen Nia walks up to her father's body and gives him a last kiss on his forehead. When she stands again, she wipes away tears from her eyes before joining in on the song.

There were no words to this song, only the energy of grief and joy that rises and falls throughout the crowd. Some shout or hum their own tune; others let their hands and feet make their song for them. It is boisterous, chaotic, and beautiful.

The fallen king's guards position themselves on either side of the bed and lift it up to their shoulders. They lead the way through the courtyard to the riverbank of the Tehenu just outside the gates of the Proper. The path between the river and the stone wall that encloses the Proper is just wide enough for the guards to walk across with the body. As we pass the end of the stone wall, we follow the river into the woods that eventually give way to the mountains. The drummers and most of the people follow the procession into the woods, and the collection of songs continues until we reach where the Tehenu River falls from the heavens onto the land. Just behind the falls is the royal burial cave.

I notice Kunle's lips moving like he is saying a silent prayer or fussing about something he doesn't want anyone else to hear. Like most Joroans, he doesn't go into the woods unless he has to, and even then, it isn't for long. Kunle believes in the stories of the ejo nla, too. Knowing him, he wishes the guards are quick about placing King Ahmose's burial bed in its ultimate resting place.

The music of the procession grows louder and louder, as if it's battling for dominance over the roar of the waterfall. It's also believed that the louder groups are while in the woods, the less of a chance of the *ejo nla* would show up. According to legend, the creature likes little noise. Since no one has ever witnessed the giant snake, there was no actual way of knowing this to be true. But maybe, just maybe, they were right, and the ejo nla was real.

Only a few of us are allowed into the royal burial cave, which is just as well because the sight of skeletons under thin cloths is not for the lighthearted. A few of the guards struggle to keep the contents of their stomachs. They place King Ahmose's burial bed next to the bed of his father, who is next to his father, and so forth. Me, the guards, Kunle, Queen Nia, and King Gainde all walk backwards out of the cave with our heads bowed, to show respect to all who lie there.

The celebration continues as everyone dances and sings on the way back to the courtyard. Those who are older or have grown tired go to their homes. Even the new king and queen return to the palace, allowing Queen Nia to continue mourning her father in peace. I walk arm-in-arm with Zendaya to her place.

"Is it just me," she asks, "or do you have the favor of our god in more than one way?"

I look around us to see if anyone heard her. "There are too many ears around for this conversation now."

Zendaya nods, and I am grateful, but I'm also worried. I'm sure others in the crowd noticed Jata staring at me. I wish I had answers, if anything, for myself, as to what that was about.

Questioning the gods is not in my nature, so I'm not sure how I'd go about finding out. It couldn't possibly be what Zendaya is suggesting. Jata *is* a god, and I'm… I'm human. It makes no sense to think a god would look at me the way these men do. *Will I really be the next high priest, the first female high priest of Joro?*

It could be my nerves, but I feel like the gaze of everyone we pass lingers on me longer than usual. I can only imagine the rumors that will spread after Jata's stare. People really will think I'm favored because of lust. *How preposterous!*

Inside the safety of her home, Zendaya turns to me, waiting for me to open up.

"I think I'm going to be the next high priest."

"Medusa, everyone came to that conclusion a long time ago. Do you think that is why our illustrious god was staring at you?"

I chuckle. "Why do you mock the gods so?"

"It's not mocking," she says with a sarcastic tone. "But seriously, that was intense. Granted, gods don't have pupils and irises like we do, but he was looking at you like… like he wanted you."

"Zendaya, please. That could not possibly be it. The only thing Jata or any god could want from me, or any other human, is praise. I have nothing else to offer him."

"If you say so." Zendaya disappears in the direction of her kitchen and returns a few moments later with two cups and a wine sack. Without asking me if I want some, she pours the deep red liquid into the ceramic cups and passes me one. I don't drink wine often, but given the events of today, or even the week, wine seems in order.

Taking the cup, we salute. "To the first woman high priest of Joro, may you remain blessed and bring blessings to the land greater than any man ever has."

"Thank you."

A week later, all of Joro gathers again, this time for the coronation of King Gainde and Queen Nia, who are both dressed in fine fabrics of gold and jewels of tiger's eye, onyx, and purple jade. This is one of the few times all citizens are allowed inside the palace, and the palace's great hall is packed from wall to wall. As with the former king's funeral, the people of Joro don their finest wear.

As Nia and Gainde sit on their respective thrones, Kunle and I rub a mix of oil and turmeric on their foreheads. "By the divine order of the gods, Jata and Nthanda and their creators Kemet and Songhai, and their creator, the Moeder Heelal, we crown you the new king and queen of Joro," we say in unison. "It is your duty to lead this glorious land into prosperity, uphold peace, and defend Joro from those who wish to interrupt that prosperity and peace. Uphold the laws. Create new ones as the gods lead you to. Be just in your rule and to your people."

We place crowns of gold and precious stones on their heads, Kunle on King Gainde's and I on Queen Nia's, and handed them scepters of fine wood, gold, and precious stones.

"May your reign be long," we say together.

"May your reign be long!" the crowd repeats.

Turning to the crowd, Kunle presents the new king and queen. The crowd cheers as King Gainde and Queen Nia wave to them.

In less than a fortnight's time, the sun had set on one reign and rose with another. The air is pregnant with change, and no one knows what the future holds, except for Moeder Heelal.

Chapter 8
Medusa

After the festivities following the coronation, me and Sisay are back in our chambers in the temple. Sisay settles into her cot for bed while I feed the various snakes I keep in wicker baskets.

Sisay doesn't care for snakes, but she is less afraid of them now than when she first came to live with me.

"What if one gets out?" Sisay asks as she prepares for bed.

"The containers are secure, child. They can't get out." I look my new ward over and see the apprehension still in her eyes. The poor girl is holding her body tight with fear. Rising

from my simple straw mattress, I go to one of the woven baskets and kicked it over. Sisay gasps with fear but realizes the top doesn't come off.

I kick the basket two more times and watch it tumble this way and that. The snakes are still secure inside, but instead of being quiet like they were before, the snakes are hissing loudly. Sisay watches with tentative eyes as I pick up the basket and return it to its resting place. "I wouldn't sleep in the same room as the snakes if I weren't able to make it safe for me to do so. I most definitely wouldn't have you in here if it weren't safe. Besides, I don't think the other priests and priestesses would let me stay in the temple if I couldn't keep the snakes secure. You are safe. Now sleep." With that, I blow out the lone candle used to illuminate my modest room.

Sometimes, I still have to remind Sisay that the slithering creatures keep evil spirits away whenever she shows fear of them. The snakes also keep the other priestesses and priests away from my room, all of whom Sisay doesn't think too highly about and thus, making my words all the more true.

"I've been thinking about something since King Ahmose's death," Sisay says.

"What is that?"

"What happened to Asmara's soul after the Elders destroyed her?"

I close the last wicker basket, then make my way to her bed. I sit on the edge closest to Sisay and stare at her. "That… is a smart question that I do not know the answer to. The gods have never said what happened to her soul or the souls of the other demigods that were destroyed during the war. I never thought about it before."

"Asmara and the other demigods were part mortal, so they had souls. They had to go somewhere."

"Maybe the gods destroyed their souls as well."

"But no text mentions it. You always told me we must not assume the will of the gods."

"Hmph. I told you that?" I say with a smirk. Every day she makes me so honored that I get to raise her.

Sisay nods.

"Always remember that. If you want to be a good priestess someday, you listen for the will of the gods. They will speak. Now, it has been a long day, and I am tired." I blow out all but one candle before lying down.

"Why do you think she betrayed us... and our gods? Asmara, I mean."

"Power and greed are incredible forces."

"Forces created by man or the gods, since she was both?"

A few seconds pass as I think about my response. "The gods are perfect. Infallible. Greed is not among them. They possess incredible power, but because of their perfection and infallibility, they know how to use it better than any being within the Moeder Heelal. This is why the demigods were so dangerous. They had power like the gods, but the minds of humans."

"We mess things up."

"Yes, we mortals have a tendency of getting in our own way. That is why we, who are called to serve in the priesthood, must teach and guide them to be better."

Sisay keeps going. "Kemet and Songhai need to put that on a fresh tablet and send it to Kunle. Make him sit in front of it until the words and meaning have sunk into his head. All of them, actually. Were you aware that Cairo and Accra were lovers? I saw them kissing and touching each other's breasts yesterday. Some apprentices have said that Cairo is also Kunle's lover."

"We will not partake in gossip among the priesthood."

"It is not gossip if I saw it! Okay, the last part about Cairo and Kunle was gossip, but Cairo and Accra, I saw with my own eyes."

"Sisay, it is late."

"Yes, mother. May the gods keep your dreams pleasant."

"May the gods keep your dreams pleasant."

A month after the coronation, things have been back to normal in Joro. The regular sellers fill the courtyard market, and there are no more festivities celebrating the new king and queen. I can finally spend my time doing what I enjoy doing most—praising the gods. As I meditate in my favorite small sanctuary, I go into a trance, a deeper trance than I've ever known. It feels as if something is pulling my soul away from my body. I, or my spirit, floats in a vast place with skies of the darkest night, but it doesn't feel dark for the many stars that shine as bright as Joro's two suns and four moons.

Something about the place feels oddly familiar. I have no anxiety about where I am. Instead, the calm and peace I feel when I pray to the Moeder Heelal fills me.

All around me in the distance are galaxies, great and small. Stars and stardust spiral around each one, like an intricate dance. This shocks me, as the gods have never told of other places that exist. I wonder about the gods and mortals of those other places. Could they be just as kind or cruel to each other as they were in the lands I'm familiar with? Did they have demigods, and if so, had one or some ever betrayed them the way Asmara betrayed the former gods of Joro?

For the first time, I question the gods I learned about and worship. Why would they keep such wonders from the mortals they claim to love, or were they not all-knowing, as their stories claim them to be?

"All-knowing they are far from," a husky female voice says.

I turn every which way, looking for the voice that seems to come from everywhere.

"I am here, my child," the voice says.

Turning again, I notice many stars clustering together until they form the shape of a female body. "Who are you?"

"I understand why you wouldn't recognize me. Even the gods don't have a physical description of me. I am the mother of everything."

"Moeder Heelal," I gasp while bowing.

"Rise, Medusa. I brought you here for a reason, and we have little time."

"Whatever you need from me, I am your vessel."

"Good, because you are going to need to save yourself and your galaxy from your king and your gods."

"I do not understand."

"Allow me to take you back," the Mother Universe says.

Moeder Heelal puts the tip of her star-studded finger against my forehead, and once again I'm transported to another place. I look around at the crystal floor I wish I could feel with my bare feet. On one side of the room sit two figures with deep bronze skin, one male and the other female, on large thrones. I recognize them from the carvings and paintings along the walls and tablets at the temple and the palace.

"Kemet and Songhai." Again, I bow.

"They can't see you or me," Moeder Heelal says. "We are in the past."

"The past? In Muhabura?"

"Yes. It is time you and the rest of my children, mortal and immortal, of your galaxy learn a truth the oldest immortals have hidden from you."

I want to ask something else, but Moeder Heelal puts a finger to her full starlight lips, then signals for me to listen and watch.

Listen and watch is exactly what I do.

A portal opens in the middle of the great rotunda. A god, a goddess, and a mortal walk through. Mortals aren't allowed here, but I know of only one time when a half-mortal came to this holy place.

The mortal has to be the demigod Asmara, which means the gods with her are Kinshasa and Malabo, the original serving gods of Joro. This is just before the great war of the gods began.

"You've crossed the line," Eshu says to Kinshasa and Malabo.

"What is the meaning of this?" Songhai asks. "Why have you brought this demigod here?"

"You know our demigoddess, Asmara, and her power of prophecy. We have put her to use for the good of all the lands, leading them all to prosperity and preventing war amongst the mortals. Everything she has said has come true. Asmara has a new prophecy, a dire one that involves all under the Moeder Heelal, including you both," Kinshasa says with his head bowed. Malabo and Asmara have their heads bowed, too.

"We have seen her work. I am intrigued by this demigod who possesses the ability to see the future when we cannot," Kemet says. "Speak, child."

"The Moeder Heelal is not happy with you, Kemet and Songhai. You have grown greedy with power, and you have kept many things from the gods and the mortals under you. Of all the

gods she's created and given dominion over a galaxy, it is with you she is most disappointed."

"Watch yourself," Eshu says.

Asmara continues. "One day, the gods of your creation and the Moeder Heelal will forge a new demigod. This demigod will be the most powerful of us all. More powerful than you. If you do not change your ways, she, with Moeder Heelal's blessing, will destroy you and rule in your place."

"Blasphemy!" Songhai yells.

"Moeder Heelal has never created a demigod or meddled in the affairs of the gods or mortals within her," Kemet says.

"You are correct, but she sees all, and she is not happy with this galaxy."

"What do you mean by this galaxy? There are no others that exist. Surely the Elders would have told us of such if it did," Eshu states.

"We've heard enough from this demigod's mouth," Songhai interrupts, not allowing Asmara to answer Eshu's question. The two Elders look at each other, communicating something with their eyes so no one else can hear.

"We have decided," they say in unison while lifting their arms with their palms facing out to Asmara. Gold beams shoot out from their hands and wrap around Asmara's body. She screams as her body tears apart. Within a minute, Asmara is no more.

The reaction of their makers shock Kinshasa and Malabo. They brought their most prized demigod to Kemet and Songhai to warn them, not for them to destroy her.

"How? Why?" Kinshasa asks.

"We will not have those falsehoods spreading throughout the Moeder Heelal," Kemet says. Again, the Elders raise their hands, this time to Joro's serving gods. Kinshasa and Malabo raise their hands to defend themselves, but it was of no use. Their power is no match for Kemet's and Songhai's. It takes longer, but Kemet and Songhai also destroy them.

Hot gold embers lay in piles on the crystal floor where Asmara, Kinshasa, and Malabo were standing. Kemet takes a big breath and blows the embers out of the round room and into the sky, where the brightness of Muhabura turns them into dust particles.

"Eshu," Songhai says.

"I am your servant to use however you wish," he responds.

"Good," she says. "Spread the word to all the gods. The demigod Asmara conned her serving gods into bringing her to Muhabura, where she let in a group of demigods to overthrow the Elders. Asmara destroyed Kinshasa and Malabo. Demigods have become too dangerous to our delicate order. We must destroy them all."

Eshu opens a portal to go from heaven to heaven. "Anything else?" he turns back to ask the Elders.

"No. We will take care of the rest."

"It was all a lie," I say as I turn to Moeder Heelal.

"And now you will help me correct it." She touches my forehead again, and we are back amongst the stars.

Chapter 9
Medusa

I feel betrayed by the Elders and a heavy sense of sorrow for Asmara. She was innocent, while the Elders were everything Asmara said they were. Greedy. Selfish. Secretive. "I've dedicated my life to serving them. All of them! For years, I've committed to the ideal of being more faithful to them than Asmara was." I look around at the stars and galaxies around me. "These other galaxies?"

"They are real. All with their own gods and mortals. Many exist under me. Your Elder gods have always known of them, for I showed them when I created them. For their own reasons, Kemet and Songhai preferred to share a story of them being the only and most perfect creation of mine. As you saw, that could not be further from the truth."

My mind is still reeling from the Elders' lies to cover their destruction. "Why are you showing this to me? Why not the High Priest?"

"Two reasons. Your High Priest is too much like the Elders and your serving gods. Even now, they plot against you along with your king."

"Plot against me?"

Moeder Heelal transports us to the sanctuary where my body is still in a deep trance. I look over my body with a strange curiosity. My face looks peaceful, though peace is the furthest thing I feel right now. I'm angry and confused. I want answers and accountability.

"While you've been meditating, Kunle has ordered everyone to leave the temple. Your king requested this, and he's paid your High Priest handsomely for it. You are the second wife he's been praying for, the one he's come to you about time and time again. He plans on making you his wife tonight, whether you agree, or he forces it upon you. Your serving gods have answered his prayers concerning you to make it so, but for different reasons. Like your king, Jata lusts after you as well. His lust for you has made you an enemy of your goddess, Nthanda."

"I do not understand. I've been faithful to them all. Not once have I ever shown any of them interest in anything but serving them."

"Faithfulness rarely trumps greed, my child."

"And your second reason for showing me and not Kunle?"

"Your High Priest is not the demigod Asmara prophesied about."

"But I am?"

Moeder Heelal nods.

"Why me?"

"You have a heart much like my own. The purest of all in this galaxy. Because of that, you are the only one who can set it right. With you, I can start over and do it better."

"Start over?"

"I gave them all," she stretches her hands out to indicate everything she's created, "too much freedom. Time after time, I create a galaxy and two gods to have dominion over it, and I step back. It has led to monumental disappointment."

"Children disappoint their mothers from time to time. That is natural."

"How often has your daughter disappointed you?"

"Rarely."

"That is because you and her parents before her have been involved in her development. You've given her rules. Something to aspire to. There are gods out there who conspire to rise above me while their mortals know nothing about me. I can destroy them all with a single thought." She sighs. "I am a mother to them all, and yet I've been no mother at all. I need you to show me a better way of doing things when we start over. You will be my daughter in every way that Sisay has been yours. Together, we will create gods who are worthy of the praise their mortals give them and mortals who are worthy of the life they're given."

I stare at her for a few moments as I process her words. She wants me to be her daughter while she destroys mine. "I will be your daughter, under one condition."

"What is your condition?"

"You do not destroy innocents."

"Do you care about them that much?"

"I care about my daughter. I will not see her life cut short or made difficult for the missteps of another."

She is silent for a beat. "How do you propose we start over, then?"

"We don't. We teach better and lead by example. You can get rid of the gods that you must, but not a single innocent mortal is to be put in harm's way. Mortals are teachable. Gods, not so much."

"This is why you will always be a better mother than I." She stretches her hand before me with a finger pointed at my head. "I accept your terms. This is going to hurt."

She touches my forehead, and unimaginable pain courses through me. I go to scream, but no sound comes out. It feels like every cell in my body is on fire.

"You must accept the power with your mind and soul. The sooner you do that, the sooner you can get back to your body. It will protect you from what is coming, and I will teach you how to use it at another time."

For me not to be in my physical body, I struggle to breathe, let alone think.

"Now, Medusa. The ones who mean you harm are setting towards the temple at this very moment."

I focus on calming my mind, despite the burning pain. It is not the easiest of tasks, but I have to get back to my body to protect myself and Sisay. *With my mind and soul, I am the Moeder Heelal's daughter.* I say these words two more times before I am back in the temple.

My body jerks and spasms as sweat breaks out all over me. For what feels like an eternity, I feel like I can't breathe. In my head I'm screaming, though no sound comes from her lips. When the intense sensation ceases, I take in a cherished breath of air. I catch my breath as I try to wrap my mind around what's coming.

I give thanks to Moeder Heelal. Thanks that I'm still alive, back in my body, and for her protection. As I pray, I take inventory of how I feel physically. Other than the feeling of exertion I have after a good praise dance session, I feel normal. I guess I expected to feel different, stronger somehow.

While still kneeling with my head down, I pat my thigh for the belt I keep there with a blade at the ready. The feel of it gives me some comfort, though I do not relish the thought of having to use it against someone, especially King Gainde. Doing so would be a sign of treason and could cost me my head.

"Beautiful."

I lift my head to see King Gainde standing in the doorway of the small sanctuary. I take a deep breath to steady myself. "My King." I bow my head slightly, not wanting to take my eyes off of him, then I rise to my feet. "What brings you to the temple?"

"Your King pays you a compliment and you don't acknowledge it?"

"My apologies. I thought you were referring to the carvings of all the serving gods on the walls. I think they are beautiful. It is why I prefer to worship here."

Gainde takes a quick look at the walls before setting his eyes back on me. "I wasn't referring to the walls."

"That was my misunderstanding. Thank you for the compliment, King Gainde."

There is a thick silence between us for a few moments.

"Did you come here for prayer?" I ask in hopes he would settle for that and leave me be.

"Not quite. I came here hoping the gods had answered my prayers of late. Your prayer too, I recall."

"I do not know what you mean, my king."

"The prayers for you to be my second wife. I wish I could offer you the crown. A woman such as yourself deserves to be beside a king as a queen."

"I prayed for no such thing. Besides, I have dedicated myself to the priesthood, to the gods. I cannot be anyone's wife. You are aware of this."

"We prayed for this, Medusa. Don't deny me, your king, and the gods." Gainde steps forward, and I step back.

"If I had known it was me you were praying to have, I would not have prayed with you."

"Ah, but you prayed for it, and everyone knows your prayers are always answered. It was a little mischievous of me to withhold that information from you, yes. As you said, if you had known, you would have denied me from the start. It was more important that only the great Jata and Nthanda knew my heart in the matter."

"I do not desire to be any man's wife, not even the wife of a king." I take another step back, and Gainde comes forward. "Your request is flattering," I lie, "but I must say no."

"It is not what you say, foolish woman. This is the will of your king, and I, your king, will not be denied. I'm going to give you another chance to reconsider—"

"My answer will not change."

"I can always make you my wife. Your consent isn't required. You know the law as well as I do. All I have to do is force myself upon you and have someone find us. I have two guards just outside this room and more outside the temple. With what I paid him to make sure no one was in the temple but you, Kunle will say whatever I want him to say. You will be mine when you leave this temple, whether or not you agree."

Dread fills my being. I have to fight with myself to keep it from weighing me down and forcing me to give up. I remind myself that Moeder Heelal gave me some sort of protection. It would be great if I could feel it or know what to do with it. Never taking my eyes off Gainde, I open the slit on my dress, revealing my leg. King Gainde smiles, thinking he is about to get his prize without force, but it disappears just as quickly when I pull my dagger from its sheath.

The sight of the blade angers him. "You would threaten your king in such a way?" He seems in disbelief that I'm not giving myself willingly.

"I return any threat received in kind. I will kill you or any man who tries to hurt me or force themselves upon me."

King Gainde reaches for my hand with the knife, but I dodge his grab and swat his arm away. In my mind, this is the only warning he's getting before I cut him.

A sinister grin comes across his face, and I fear he's being turned on even more by my resistance; like he will find pleasure in trying to break my powerful spirit into submission. I move to the side and out of his reach, preparing for the king's next attack. If I stay out of his reach and rotate us around the room, I could have a chance at getting out of here. At the very least, I can get to my room, where I can release a poisonous viper on him.

My instinct is to pray to the gods for guidance, safety, and strength. However, after what I now know about them, doing so would be futile. *Why have the gods betrayed me so?*

I kick myself for thinking of the gods at the moment because the room fills with a blinding bright light. That can mean only one thing. Jata has come down to indwell Gainde. There was once a time when I found comfort in the gods coming to be among us this way. Not anymore.

Zendaya's suggestion that Jata lusted after me at King Ahmose's funeral comes to mind. Foolish me, I thought his stare was because I would be his next high priest. If I had known the truth then, I would have returned to Ginawa with my daughter for the rest of my days.

Putting my free hand on the wall and keeping the other with the blade in a defensive position, I feel my way around the room. I try to move quickly and keep my eyes closed. When I feel the edge of the doorway, I bolt for the corridor and am hit by something large and made of metal. My eyes open as I go down, and I just barely make out the guard's shield with Gainde's emblem on it before everything goes black.

When I come around, I can feel myself being dragged by my hair. Disoriented, I kick and swing my fist to get free, but I'm fighting nothing but air. With a hard pull, I am slung and I come down hard. What I can make out of the walls lets me know that I'm back in the small sanctuary.

"Medusa, Medusa. Why would you run from me?" Jata's bass voice, layered over Gainde's tenor, asks. It booms in the small room. "Why won't you agree to be the king's wife?"

I make my way to my feet and stare into Jata's gold pupil-less eyes. "You heard and know my answer."

"Yes, that you do not wish to be any man's wife. Would you change your mind if you knew I desire you as a wife more than he does? That accepting his proposal would make you my wife?"

"You know the holy text better than I do. What text allows for a mortal to be a god's spouse?"

"You know what I mean."

"You know my answer."

"I've answered his prayer. You will be our wife."

Chapter 10
Nthanda

I watch with great pleasure the happenings at the temple, as the king tries to convince the priestess to marry him. As Joro's goddess, I should not take such pleasure in the thought and hope that Gainde forces bonding on her, but it would be just the thing to bring Medusa down a peg or two. Leaving my heavenly quarters, I go to find my husband to keep him occupied so that he can't mess this up for me. Surprisingly, his rooms are empty, and he's not in any of the commonplaces of our home. *Could he have traveled to the heavens of another land? Or…*

Medusa Untold

I rush back to my room and pick up my looking sphere. Instantly, anger fills me as the room in the temple becomes submerged in golden light. *He thinks he's going to take pleasure in her flesh. Treat that mortal as if she is some sort of second wife to him. I think not. Two can play that game.*

Changing the view to the palace, I seek Queen Nia. She's just finished her bath, and her maids are putting oil on her. The pampering will have to wait. I turn myself into gold light directed at the baths. The queen's maids scream as I indwell her. I'm sure I'm taking them all by surprise. It's been years since I indwelled a queen outside of the land's festivals. This reminds me of the time I spent inside Nia's mother's body just to get some love and attention.

Once I've merged with the queen, I see her maids bowing with their faces touching the floor. I snatch the simple nightdress from the one who was holding it and get dressed. As I do so, several of the queen's guards come rushing into the baths. They stop and turn their backs when they see the queen's bare chest just before I tie the top around my neck.

"My queen, we heard screaming. Are you alright?"

"Do I look like your queen to you?" I respond.

The queen's captain turns around and bows to his knees when he sees my eyes. "Apologies, goddess Nthanda. We did not realize."

At the mention of my name, the rest of the guards kneel.

"I need you and your men to come with me. There is a situation at the temple that needs my immediate attention."

"Yes, goddess. Whatever you wish."

With determination, I leave the queen's quarters and make way to the temple. I despise how slowly mortals move. If I didn't need to be in a mortal body, or didn't need the train of guards behind me, I would be there already. I ignore the people who startle when they see my eyes and then drop to the floor. Oh, how I wish I could step on them like the insects they are.

If I'm being honest, I don't actually dislike the mortals. I just don't feel any way about them, except for *her*. I despise that woman with my entire being. Jata and I weren't the happiest, but we could fake it and put on a good show until she came to Joro, until she made herself appeasing and available to my husband. Her mere existence makes me want to end all mortals.

When I get to the vestibule and the temple is within sight, I stop and turn to the guards. Looking right at the leader of the queen's guards, Tunis, I say, "I may not come back with the queen, and she will need your protection from everyone, including the king and my husband."

This catches Tunis' attention, and he looks me directly in the eye. "My goddess?"

"You heard me correctly. This is a direct order from your goddess: protect the queen at all costs." With that, I turn and continue down the palace steps and across the courtyard with the queen's guards in tow.

As we approach the temple, the king's guards can see exactly who I am. They know though they are looking at the body of their queen, their goddess is before them. They bow their heads to me, but have the nerve to halt me.

"The king ordered us not to let anyone in, goddess Nthanda," the head of the king's guard, Bamako, says.

"The King or Jata?" I already know the answer to this question, but I want to see how far the man will go to protect the king; if he will lie even to me. I'm in a vengeful mood and have no problem with taking it out on anyone who gets in my way.

"The King, Your Holiness."

Nthanda growled. The title he used is what the mortals call those of the priesthood. I stomp off, but he calls to me again.

"Goddess, please. I beg thee."

"Do you fear the king more than you fear me?" I hiss.

He knows he messed up. "No, goddess. My apologies." Even bowed, he trembles like a leaf in the wind. Defying a direct order from the King equates to treason. He and the rest of the king's guard could lose their heads, and their respective families would become outcasts or forced to leave Joro in humiliation to start over in another land with no means.

"By order of your queen and goddess, stay here. All of you. Let no one in. When you speak of this night, make it known that the priestess Medusa betrayed the gods and was rightfully punished for it." I walk into the temple feeling confident about the seed I plant in their minds.

When I find Jata and the priestess in the small sanctuary, Jata has a gold beam wrapped around the woman's body and has her pinned to a wall.

"It's unfortunate, Medusa, that you are making this so hard," Jata says. "I forgive you for that. Soon, you'll see how great this will be for everyone."

"Husband, I wonder if you'll forgive me for this," I say. I hit Medusa with a beam powerful enough to break Jata's hold. "To a lowly beast you shall become, no longer holding the beauty that bewitched our husbands. May mortals step on your head as you spend eternity this way."

Chapter 11
Jata

I'm not surprised when I hear my wife's husky tone over Queen Nia's soprano. In so many ways, I was expecting it. Leave it to her not to let me have an ounce of pleasure or happiness. Her presence here only speaks to her jealousy of my desire for Medusa. What I was not expecting was for her to take her jealousy out on Medusa just to get to me.

I yell as Nthanda puts her curse on Medusa while I try to counter the effects by doing the one thing I'm strictly forbidden'd to do as a god. I hit Medusa with enough power to turn her into a demigoddess. Quickly, I read the minds of the guards outside the temple. Not only can they hear Medusa's screams, but many of them are wondering what she could have done to deserve what was happening to her.

Tonight has gotten out of control. If there was a time that I wished us gods could see into the future, it is now. Had I known this is what would come of tonight, I wouldn't have ever answered Gainde's prayers for Medusa to be his second wife. I would have left her alone to do what she desired to do the most, and that is to worship me. Some guards have thoughts of leaving to distance themselves from the temple or to go get help, but I use my powers to freeze them where they are. The king and queen are going to need them after my wife and I leave their bodies. I have a thought of wiping all their minds clean of tonight's events, but I'm distracted when Nthanda puts up her other hand to double her efforts to turn Medusa into a beast.

With my free hand, I hit Nthanda with a blast that knocks her out of the room and into the wall of the corridor. She hits her head hard and is unconscious. Until Nia regains consciousness, Nthanda will remain trapped in the queen's body, giving me some time. Turning my attention to Medusa, this is the first time I notice she is no longer screaming. She is unconscious as well. This is when I am grateful for the incognito power gods have. It allows us to move without even the Elders seeing where we've gone. Only we can't hold it for long, so I have to move fast.

Keeping her under the protection of my power, I remove myself from Gainde's body and transport me and Medusa to a cave deep within Joro's mountains. I lay her body on the floor of the cave as I cast a spell over it to hide the cave from the gods and to keep mortals from venturing in by accident. After casting the spell, I create the things a mortal would need to survive in the cave. A ditch forms for a flowing stream of water through the cave from where the Tehenu first touches the land and becomes a waterfall. Along the walls of the cave, I created additional ditches to allow lava to run through from the holes created in the walls, providing light and heat. I also put a pond of lava at the very back of the cave, where it is the darkest.

When I'm done, I look Medusa over. I find myself wanting to pray that she wakes up, but I've never prayed before. If I did pray, I most certainly can't pray to the Elders. That would undo everything I just did to protect Medusa and myself from my actions tonight. She is breathing, but she is so still. Patches of green and yellow snake-like scales on her face and body reflect in the lava light. They serve as a sign that Medusa is no longer human. Exactly what she is, I'm not sure. Between Nthanda's curse and my countering to turn her into a demigod, there's no telling what Medusa has become. Nthanda and I will both have to answer to the Elders for our actions, but that is something I will worry about later.

My concern now is Medusa's mind. I want to make sure she doesn't go mad. I've never created a demigod before, so I'm not even sure if I did it correctly. She still has a mortal-like heartbeat, though it is different now. It is slower than before. I caress the green and yellow patch of scales near her right eye, and she stirs. Medusa's eyes flutter open, and I gasp at what I see. She has golden irises and black pupils. The irises of the demigods of old were red.

"How?" I ask, not really expecting her to have a way of explaining the events of tonight or the changes she has gone through.

My voice seems to startle her, and she moves away from me as quickly as she can. "Where am I?" she asks.

"A safe place for you."

Medusa looked at me with her eyes full of rage. "Nowhere is safe for me where you are."

"I almost made you my wife. Still, I think of you as such. You are always safe with me."

"I. Am. Not. Your. Wife!" Medusa states as her anger rises. "You tried to force yourself on me, force me into a union I've never wanted, in return for my years of devotion and worship to you and Nthanda."

"I didn't act alone."

"I'm aware. The king is equally wrong and responsible. He will get his too."

"How? You can't leave this cave, or else Nthanda will either finish the curse she tried to put on you, or she will kill you."

Medusa pauses and looks like she's thinking of something. I try to peer into her mind, but I can't. This is yet another unexpected change. I watch her as she checks her body over, starting with her hands and arms. She releases a sigh of relief when she runs her hands through her hair, feeling that at least that is still the same.

She moves over to the stream and stares at her reflection, moving her head from side to side.

"What are you thinking?" I ask.

"You said I can never leave this place."

"For your protection."

"What about others coming here?"

"Neither man nor god can find this cave other than myself, not unless they know where to look. I made sure of it. You have fresh water and some light and heat. I will send you meat and bread." There is more I need to say to her, but for the first time in my existence, I am lost for words. I can't apologize for Nthanda, but I can't apologize for putting her in my wife's crosshairs. Avoiding looking at her, I make my plea. "Medusa, Nthanda acted irrationally. It was me she wanted to hurt, and she did that through you. Besides Kush and Ife, she knows better than anyone what you mean to me… how much you mean to me."

When Medusa doesn't respond, I look up and am shocked to see she is levitating off the cave floor.

"You tried to take everything from me," she says as I watch her in astonishment. Interestingly enough, a couple of snakes make their way into the cave and circle under Medusa's feet.

"I gave you everything you prayed for and more," I say. More and more snakes slowly make their way into the cave and huddle around her. "I protected you from an immensely powerful being who tried to turn you into a monster because she was jealous of you."

"Would she have been jealous if you had never lusted after me? Now I'm something the Elders forbade centuries ago! How is this you protecting me?"

I have no response. Both my disdain for my wife and lust for Medusa were the driving forces behind Nthanda's actions. I never stopped to consider Nthanda would break one of the few laws gods have just to get back at me. I figured she'd have Nia attempt to poison Medusa, which I would've prevented by having Gainde hire a taste tester just for Medusa. Now, I must face an unknown punishment by Kemet and Songhai, one that at the very least would take me away from the one I want the most. Truly, the Elders would have no choice but to see I only turned Medusa to protect her from Nthanda's curse. Technically, it was Nthanda who broke the law first. I changed Medusa in order to keep Nthanda's curse from taking hold.

"I will do whatever it takes to protect you from her and everyone else. The Elders… I will deal with them, but you are safe as long as you stay in this cave. I blocked this place even from their eyes. No one in the heavens can see where I am right now. They won't find you. I can teach you some things. We can figure out together the limits of your powers."

As I explain myself to Medusa, and in a way practice my explanation to the Elders, the cave floor becomes covered in snakes. I've never seen such a thing happen. *Did she call them here?*

I watch Medusa as her breath becomes heavier and heavier from her anger. As she does so, a creature slithers up from the bubbling stream. The creature whispered about in Joro for centuries. The first of its kind existed long before I was formed, serving as a sort of pet to the previous gods. A black python of exceptional proportions, its scales appear to change color from the iridescent sheen on them as it crawls to Medusa.

The ejo nla hisses while looking right at me. Even though I'm an all-powerful being, I still find the creatures repulsive. My first concern is Medusa, as she is still of mortal flesh. It is possible that a snake bite could harm her. When I look up at her, a few snakes, both poisonous and constrictors, are slithering up, down, and around her body. A few small ones have coiled themselves around her locs.

"Don't move," he tells her.

"Don't you dare have concern for my wellbeing after what you almost did to me." She rises higher into the air. "As your priestess, no one loved you gods more than me. Today, I found out that none of you were ever worthy of my love and praise, or that of any mortal." The angrier Medusa appears, the more the snakes hiss and snap at me.

I look around at the snakes in amazement. "*You're* controlling them." Looking back at Medusa, she has a finger pointed at me. I know she's about to attempt hurting me, copying what she saw me and Nthanda do in the temple. Still, I look on in admiration, wondering if she could really do it so soon without being taught what to do.

"Because of your unworthiness, I banish you, Jata, from my presence. My presence is now poison to you. The very life force that keeps you alive and powerful drains from your body whenever you are near me. You shall suffer as you tried to make me." A gold beam shoots from her finger and hits me square in my chest. I don't attempt to defend myself or stop Medusa. I want to see if she can pull off her curse, to witness her in all her new glory.

It is better this way, I think, to be kept away from her by her own doing, instead of by the Elders. I can feel myself getting weaker and weaker by the second. As the life force drains out of me, I say what I'm sure will be my last words to Medusa. "You're magnificent."

Gold light emits from the cracks forming on my arms and legs. I'm aware that my statues inside and outside the temple are cracking too. That has always been how mortals have known of the health of their serving gods. It is meant to trigger them to praise us in order to strengthen and heal us. The cracking of the statues causes a great rumble throughout Joro that sets fear in everyone. None who are alive today have felt an earthquake before, but they know their history; earthquakes only happened when their gods were fighting and injured while in their full god form.

I can feel the prayers and praise coming to me. It gives me the strength I need to transport back to my home in the heavens.

Chapter 12
Medusa

Immense rage fills my body at not seeing Jata's body as a pile of ash before me. I scream like I've never screamed before. It is the only thing I can think of doing. As my body shakes, the mountain shakes. The lava pond in my cave rises, and the stream sloshes from side to side. Sisay's face flashes across my mind, and I force myself to gain control of my anger. If what Jata said is true, and I can't leave this cave, I can't be by her side to protect her.

"Moeder Heelal, what am I to do now? What's next?"

I wait for an answer. The longer I go without a response, the more I know that right now, I'm on my own. In despair, I collapse onto a bolder and cry. I cry for my daughter, the life I once had, the future I desired, and the unknown future as Moeder Heelal's right hand. *How can I show her how to do better when she isn't responding to me? How can she share her power with me for my protection, and not tell me how to use it?*

There is a nudge of my arm, and I look up to find the ejo nla staring at me. I vaguely remember seeing it enter the cave. I should be shocked that it exists, but considering all that I've learned and experienced today, I'm not. Learning the creature of fables is real is nothing compared to what I've witnessed today. Its existence is the only thing I don't question.

I pet its head before putting my face in my hands. This time, it nudges me more forcibly. When I look up, my view is different. Instead of looking at the snake, I'm looking at myself through the snake's eyes, though I'm blue. I tilt my head to one side, and the ejo nla does the same. I turn my head to the left, and it does the same. The entire cave is in shades of blue, green, and yellow. Looking back at the ejo nla, I look myself over more closely. The green and yellow snakeskin-like patches show brightly against the blue of my form. All the dark-colored snakes and the rocks I see as blue, too. The lava is such a bright shade of yellow that it almost looks white. The bright-colored snakes show green and yellow.

"Hmmm. Back to my vision." Instantly, my vision is back, and I can see everything in its correct color. "Back to yours," I say while looking at the ejo nla. I'm looking at myself again. "This may be useful."

I make eye contact with a green viper. "Give me your eyes." My vision changes to that snake's. I send it out to the opening of the cave. Given how long it took the snake to get there, I know Jata was at least truthful about being deep within the mountain. From how strong the winds are just outside the mouth of the cave, the opening is high up, too. I call the viper back, taking my time to see the walls of the cave as it returns. For a mortal, the long entrance into the cave is pitch black dark. There isn't any light except where I am. If that alone wasn't enough to keep a mortal out, the smell of sulfur from the lava is. However, it does not bother me.

With all the snakes in the cave, I practice alternating from my view to theirs and send them about different tasks, like crawling up the walls, exploring sections of the mountain, attacking small prey, etc. After a few hours, I had multiple snakes doing different things at the same time. Now I had enough confidence to do the one thing that is of the utmost importance to me. Saving my daughter.

Once Kunle and the others realize I'm not coming back, Sisay won't be safe there.

I send the ejo nla down the mountain at lightning speed. When it gets to the woods, I direct it to the temple, but away from the Tehenu. If there are any people risking being in the woods at this time of night, they will stick to the riverbanks. We reach the stone wall that separates the north-end of the Proper from the woods, and I direct the snake to go up and over it, landing right at the back of the temple. However, the wall doesn't hold the weight of the snake, and the portion under it crumbles. Snakes don't have ears, but I have it wait to feel for vibrations of anyone headed towards the wall. When I feel nothing, we head up the back stairs of the temple. I know the temple was not built to accommodate such an enormous creature, but I am grateful for the wide openings and corridors it has. I'm also grateful that my quarters are the closest to the back of the temple and that no one else of the priesthood live in my corridor. They didn't want to be near my snakes. I do not miss the irony of my love for snakes, Nthanda's attempt to turn me into one, and my new power to control them.

You are what you set your mind on.

My mother said that to me frequently as a child. How I miss her now. I'm glad Sisay and I visited her a month ago. I don't know how or when I will see her again.

Sisay has left the door ajar and all the candles lit, as she always does when she gets in before I do. Softly, we push the door open and slither inside. Because of the size of the snake, we have to move to the far side of my bed first and up onto it, so the snake can fit inside the room. I have it pick up and hold my satchel in its mouth. Hopefully, this will work as a sign to her. As the ejo nla did with me, we nudge her sleeping body. I back the snake up and have it lay its head on my bed, hoping it doesn't alarm the girl too much. I don't want her to scream, but stories of this snake traumatized her when she was young.

She turns over, and her eyes grow wide at the sight before her. As she inhales deeply, we toss my satchel to her. Thankfully, she notices it and releases her breath. She says something, but I'm not sure what. I have the snake nudge the basket Sisay keeps her clothing in and then look at her. Again, she says something, but this time I can read her lips. *Don't eat me.*

I chuckle. Unfortunately, snakes don't laugh.

Sisay packs her things into my bag, and she even stuffs what she can of my collection of herbs and ointments. When she's finished, she looks at the snake like she's ready, but there is one thing I need her to do. I have the snake nudge the baskets that hold my collection of snakes with its body. I can't leave them there to starve and rot. Tentatively, she walks over to the baskets and removes the tops one by one. The freed snakes move to one side of the room. Using the ejo nla's head, I push Sisay over to its body, urging her to climb on. When she gets it, she does just that.

Together, the snakes and Sisay on the ejo nla's back make their way out of the room and into the corridor. There is someone in the main corridor that leads from the one my quarters are in and to the back entrance or the large inner sanctuary, depending on which way you turn. We wait for them to leave, but Cairo peaks her head around the corner to look at my door instead. What she sees terrifies her, and she screams so loud that it reverberates off the walls. Two of my poisonous snakes charge towards her. She is so stiff with fear that she doesn't even move. The snakes bite her feet and head towards the back entrance, with the rest of us following behind.

Going through the new opening in the stonewall behind the temple, we make our way out. I have each of the snakes take a different path, with the ejo nla taking the river. I do this for two reasons: the first being the water will not leave a trail, and the second so Sisay can remember how to get back to the cave. No longer am I concerned about anyone being along the wood's riverbanks.

The ejo nla swims up the river, keeping the top of its back above the water so Sisay can stay on safely. It would be easier for the gigantic snake to swim along the river floor, since it is going upriver, but I push it to stay along the surface for Sisay's sake. They make it to the waterfall and start going up the mountain. Because of the size of the snake, it can cover a lot of ground quickly. It isn't long before they reach the opening of the cave. That is where I have the ejo nla stop and nudge Sisay off its back with its head.

While I make my way to the mouth of the cave, I watch Sisay through the ejo nla's eyes as she peers into the darkness of the cave. I can't help but wonder what she's feeling and how she will react to this new version of me. How to explain this to her, I'm not sure, but I know I'm not ready to tell her what Gainde and Jata tried to do to me. I don't know if I should tell her the truth about the Elders and Asmara. My focus was so much on ensuring her safety, I didn't think about these things.

As she comes into view in the distance, I switch to seeing her with my eyes. If I were still human, I wouldn't be able to make her out, but I can see her clearly. Her legs and the bottom half of her nightdress drip with the river water. Though Joro is in its warm season, I would imagine she is cold right now. It isn't as warm high up the mountain. I watch as her eyes grow larger the closer I get.

"Easy, child," I say, to comfort her and to let her know it is me.

"Mother?"

"Yes." I get closer still, and I can tell she is unsure. She still can't see me.

She takes a step back.

"Careful, Sisay. One wrong step and you will tumble down the mountain." Now I'm close enough that she can see me. I stop just inside the mouth of the cave.

"Your eyes… are almost like those of the gods. What's happened to you?"

"I was betrayed."

"By whom?"

"The gods and the crown."

"How?"

"That is of no matter now. I brought you here because I can never return to the temple."

"So, we are going to live here?"

"Me, yes. You, no." Sisay objects, but I cut her off. "No. You cannot stay here. You can visit me anytime you want, but you cannot live here. I don't think my betrayers are done with me yet. I will protect you at all costs. Unless something changes in Joro, you living here is not an option."

Sisay's chest goes up and down in panic. She's lost so much in her short life. I can only imagine she feels like she is losing me as well. "Where will I go?"

"Zendaya's. She's always been fond of you, and you of her."

"But you're my mother."

"I will always be your mother. However, because of what I've endured, I cannot leave this cave, at least not at this time."

"Take Zendaya this basket." I hold out my hand as a pair of snakes come out of the cave, pushing a basket of fruit from trees near the mountain. "Let her know that provisions for you will be provided. She just needs to give you shelter and a firm hand." I chuckle at my last words to pull Sisay out of the melancholy that was overcoming her. It did not work.

"What about my training in medicine and to become a priestess like you?" Sisay whines.

"The medicine lessons will continue right here. You'll have to do a lot of the collecting, as I cannot leave this cave. As far as becoming a priestess, I'll be honest with you…if I had known then what I now know about the gods, I would never have declared my priesthood."

"What do you mean?"

"They don't deserve our love or our praise," I say coldly. By the way she flinches, I can tell my words shock her. I'm the last person anyone would have thought would say disparaging words about the gods. I always taught Sisay to hold the gods in the highest regard.

"They must have done something truly terrible for you to say that," she says.

I'm too angry with the gods to respond to my daughter's statement. "Go. Get to Zendaya's."

Sisay looks around the dark forest. "It's late. Do you think she will be up?"

My eyes go to the sky possibly for the first time today. I see so much more of it now, and I look to see if I can recognize Moeder Heelal within it. I wonder how long she will leave me on my own, now that everything about me is different. "You have a point," I say, bringing my attention back to my daughter. "This cave goes deep into the mountain. There is heat from flows of lava to provide heat and light, but it smells like sulfur. It may bother you."

"If it means I can stay with you, I can bear it." She looks over at the ejo nla that is resting to the side of the cave entrance. "How do you control them?"

"It is part of my curse." I'm not sure how else to explain what Nthanda did to me as anything else, even though I had Moeder Heelal's protection.

"I'll explain another time. Besides, the curse wasn't able to do what it was intended. I had good and bad help in that area. I'm still figuring out what I can and cannot do besides control snakes and never leave this cave." Tears well up in Sisay's eyes. At that moment, I hear her thoughts. Flashes of her imagining me in the cave alone for the rest of my days play in my head. *Interesting.* "Hush now. All will be well. Come, let's find a spot where you can get somewhat comfortable and rest. You'll go to Zendaya's in the morning."

Chapter 13
Jata

I return to my heavenly home after Joroan prayers gave me the strength to escape Medusa and her death wish for me. I didn't expect or want things to turn out this way. She was supposed to want me as much as I want her; to be my wife of sorts. If Nthanda hadn't shown up…

I search all over for Nthanda, screaming her name and tearing the place apart. Forbidden or not, she is going to die at my hands for what she's done. She tried to turn Medusa into an unsightly beast because of her jealousy. *Would she have been jealous of me if it hadn't been for you?* Medusa's words play back in my head. I shake them off. I will deal with my accountability after I deal with my wife.

The skies rumble from the thunder of my screams as I search for her. It took some time for me to realize that Nthanda isn't here. Looking down on the world I rule over, I locate the queen, but can see that Nthanda is no longer stuck inside Nia.

"Where are you?" I growl as I look over all the land. She is nowhere to be found. It wasn't until I watch Medusa practice controlling the snakes from the perch off my quarters when the thought of where Nthanda is comes to me. At this moment, I know I've messed up by searching in our home and down on Joro. Where I should've been looking was up to the highest heavens.

I hear the familiar chime of a portal opening behind me. I know it's Eshu, the Elder's favorite messenger god, who also doubles as a bounty hunter. His tracking skills were imperative when hunting down and destroying all the demigods during the time of the Great War. His presence in my home confirms my suspicion of where my wife is. Nthanda went directly to the Elders. Eshu doesn't utter a word. He knows I'm aware of his presence, as he didn't hide by going incognito as he has done many times before with all the serving gods at one point or another. Eshu waits for me to turn around to face him, which I don't give him the satisfaction of. He's always been jealous of the favor the Elders give me.

When Eshu's patience wears thin, he speaks. "Are you ready?"

"If being charged with the well-being of mortals all this time has taught me anything, it is that no one is ever ready for their end," Jata answers.

"That is true, but you have favor. Kemet and Songhai are willing to hear your side of the story."

This catches my attention. The Elders can watch any portion of the past on crystals to see what actually happened. However, I went incognito just before leaving the temple and put a spell on the entire mountain range where Medusa is hidden. They want her, and they need me alive to locate her. That is the only favor I have.

Eshu and I walk through the portal. On the other side, we enter the enormous throne room at the top of Muhabura, where the Elders reside.

Giant clear quartz obelisks frame the edge of the round room and opens to the sky. The four moons of the galaxy seem so much closer from here than from my heavenly home. Bringing my eyes to the front of the open space, I make eye contact with the Elders, who sit on their thrones of onyx and jasper. Nthanda stands before them with her back turned to me.

"It is good to see you, Jata," Kemet says. "I wish it was under better circumstances."

"Kemet. Songhai. I wish the same," I respond.

"Now that you are here, Jata," Songhai says, "we can get to the matters at hand."

Songhai's use of the plural version of *matter* doesn't go unnoticed by me and confirms my suspicion of them wanting Medusa.

"Nthanda says you have been neglecting her as your wife," Songhai continues. "The same wife awarded to you for your efforts during the great war."

"She is right," I confirm. "Though I'm sure she failed to mention that she's been neglecting her role as goddess to our mortals."

With a wave of her hand, Songhai makes a large scroll appear, and she unravels it. It's a record of Nthanda's work as a goddess—the prayers she's answered and dismissed, the blessings and curses she's given, and the grace she's shown to the mortals of Joro. "Nthanda, of all ruling goddesses, you have the brightest glow. So bright, one would think you are much beloved by your mortals, which you are, but what have you done to earn that love?"

Nthanda and I both know she has no defense here. I can only imagine she thinks that being the daughter of the gods betrayed by Asmara would grant her a pass in the eyes of the Elders. As I expect, she makes her plea. "I don't see what that has to do with the fact that Jata attacked me unprovoked, nearly killing me and the mortal I indwelled, and most likely turned a different mortal into a demigod. That is strictly forbidden."

"A mortal you tried to curse," I say. "You aren't and weren't remotely dead. Queen Nia is recovering just fine in her chambers, if you cared to know."

Kemet raises his hand to silence us. "Eshu, bring Kush and Ife here as well. I have a feeling they can shed some light on this situation."

"They know nothing," Nthanda quickly says.

"From the way you said that," Kemet states, "I know the opposite is true."

"Your will," Eshu says in response to Kemet. He bows his head and opens a portal. A few moments later, Eshu returns with the serving gods of Ginawa.

I make eye contact with them, and Kush gives me a slight shake of his head. He knows I've done something involving the mortal born in his land but living in mine. This is exactly what he warned me about.

Kemet waves his hand, and large iridescent crystals move into the room and suspend in the air in a large octagon shape at my side. These are the water crystals the Elders use to see the past. Once in place, they lose their solid form and create a liquid viewing screen. "Let's get the facts, shall we?" he says.

An image of the temple shows on the viewing screen. It starts with Gainde walking up the outer steps and ends when I went incognito just before leaving the temple.

"Nthanda is correct. Jata broke the law and put us in jeopardy for another war," Eshu says. Eshu wants what I have so badly, but he doesn't care for mortals. He thinks being a serving god is better than being the Elder's pet errand god. Eshu also felt jealous that I was awarded a wife when Kemet and Songhai refused to give him a partner. *It wasn't necessary for his position,* were the words they told him.

"As is directly causing harm to a mortal with the use of godly powers," Kemet rebuttals, though he was talking to everyone. "In fact, considering how long Jata has wanted the mortal on your planet, the same mortal who had the most genuine praise any of us have seen since before the great war, and there were no desires in Jata's heart to change the mortal when he indwelled in Joro's king, I find it safe to say that he acted only to protect that mortal from Nthanda's initial act of cursing her, and by extension protecting his own life."

"Nthanda," Songhai asks, "at any point did you stop to think what would happen to your own existence if the mortals of your planet did not have Medusa to intercede for them?"

Nthanda stays quiet. I wonder if she realizes her punishment will be harsher than mine, based on the Elders' words so far. There's no way she is walking away from this without some blame and punishment.

"I knew he would do something stupid," Ife mumbles.

"What can you add to this, Kush and Ife?" Kemet asks.

They look at each other and nod. Ife speaks. "A few moments ago, Nthanda came to us, requesting we aid her in killing Jata."

"Naturally, we told her no," Kush says.

"Then we told her to leave," Ife adds.

"And what about Jata?" Songhai asks.

Kush sighs. "He visited a bit later, when the mortal in question spent time with her family. Jata expressed his lust for the mortal but mentioned no intention of engaging directly with her."

"He is unnaturally obsessed with her," Ife states.

Now, Nthanda finds her words. "If the husband *you* forced upon me as if it were some type of honor—"

Songhai takes away her voice with a wave of her fingers. Nthanda grabs her throat when she realizes she can't make a sound. I wish I had thought of doing that a long time ago.

"You parade around like a goddess," Nthanda states, "but you are as irrational as mortals, desiring so much glory without doing none of the work required for it. You've answered fewer prayers than any other serving god in the galaxy. Nthanda, you've continued to exist solely on praise for work Jata did. I never thought it appropriate to call a god spoiled, but you have proved me wrong."

"Your actions," Kemet says, "of directly harming a mortal, were both deplorable and unforgivable. You've left us no other choice."

"You do not deserve to be a god," the Elders say in unison. At once, they each raised their hands in Nthanda's direction. "The power within you shall return to Muhabura, and you shall be no more." Beams of white light shoot out from their hands. Nthanda shoots back with both hands, but it's not enough, nor is she strong enough, to overpower even one Elder, let alone both of them.

No sound comes from her, but Nthanda was clearly screaming. The way her mouth stretches open with her eyes shut hard, she looks the epitome of torture. Her body arches and cracks with her godly essence escaping her form through the cracks. Eventually, the crumbles and ash of her being pile into a heap on the black marble floor until it's all that's left of her. Kemet inhales deeply and blows the air out through his lips toward the pile. The dust that is now Nthanda blows past the clear quartz obelisks and into the sky. I watch as her dust burns into nothing in the sunlight.

Just a few moments ago, I was determined to kill Nthanda myself, and it wasn't the first time I had had that thought. It is something I thought I would get much satisfaction from. Having now witnessed her demise, I feel bad for her. As a young goddess, she wasn't required to do anything for praise and worship because she got the same glory her parents did. Everything came to her merely because she existed. As a ruling god, she thought it would've been much the same. She never learned to rule. Nthanda lived in a constant state of disappointment as a ruling god—disappointed with the mortals she had charge over, and disappointed with me as her husband. Guilt sets in for the role I played in her demise, but I don't think I would have done anything differently.

"What to do with you, Jata?" Songhai asks.

"I understand I broke the law in trying to turn my mortal into a demigod and attacking Nthanda. I accept whatever punishment you deem appropriate."

"Laws you broke to save said mortal," Kemet says.

"That makes the decision on what to do a hard one," Songhai adds. "But you sound as if you have resigned yourself to the same fate as Nthanda. Why is that?"

"I only tried to change her to protect her, and now…"

They wait for me to continue, but I don't.

"Where is the mortal you protected?" Kemet asks. I remain quiet. They will destroy her if they find her. I hid her to prevent that from happening. "Is she even still mortal or alive?"

More silence.

"You won't be able to resist going to her," Kemet says. "All we have to do is watch you long enough and you will lead us right to her."

"She is a fast learner and more powerful than any demigod before her," I say with much pride. "She made it so that coming near her would mean my death. My Medusa is better than us all."

"So, she is alive," Songhai states.

"A demigod could never wield such power," Eshu says.

I smile as I think back on my last moments with Medusa. "She is so much more," I say to Eshu. I'm not exactly sure what she is or how powerful she is. What I sensed from her is beyond anything I've ever known. Turning back to the Elders, I say, "Unless she reveals herself, you will never find her."

My words anger the Elders. From the tense way in which they hold their bodies, they are holding back information as well. Could they possibly know of Medusa's power?

Songhai lifts her arm to blast me, but Kemet stops her. "We may need him to find her, dear. Ife. Kush. Has the mortal returned to your land?"

"No," Ife says. "She has a powerful aura even as a mortal. We would have sensed her. Few demigods could go incognito from the eyes of the gods."

"Jata hit her with enough transforming power to turn her into a god," Songhai says, which in the hard way she presses her lips together tells me she didn't intend to say it out loud.

"Is that possible?" Eshu asks.

"No," the Elders say in unison. They divert back to the matter of what to do with me.

Using the crystals, Songhai plays the scene from the temple again. They see everything until I leave Gainde's body and go incognito. The next time I'm seen is when I'm back in my home looking for Nthanda.

"For your own sake, Jata, give her up," Kush says.

"No ones life is worth more than hers to me, not even mine, brother," I reply.

"Take him away!" Songhai yells. Other gods, all of whom live in Muhabura to serve the Elders, appear, wrapping me in a white rope-like energy to keep me from fighting them. "You no longer have mortals to serve or to serve you. You can either give up the demigod for a swift death or rot away as your powers slowly diminish."

I laugh as they take me away. There's nothing funny in particular, but they might as well kill me. Not even a slow death from the lack of praise and prayers will make me give Medusa up. I've betrayed her enough already.

Chapter 14
King Gainde

When I am myself again, I look down on my wife as she lies unconscious in the corridor inside the temple. At this moment, I hate Nia. Nthanda and Jata are on my hate list, too. None of them were part of my plans for taking Medusa as my wife tonight. All the gods had to do was answer the pray from the heavens, not come down here to screw up the answer. I could feel the years of lust and yearning Jata has for Medusa, the same woman I've lusted and yearned for nearly as long as he has. In the previous times Jata's indwelled me, I could see he didn't care about or for Nthanda. What just took place, I can see why. She is petty and jealous. Another thing I've realized about the gods tonight is that they are no better than us mortals. We're taught to revere and worship them, but they are far from being omnipotent beings. I'm disgusted with them all.

I call to the guards at the end of the corridor. "Where did she go? Medusa?"

"We have not seen her, Your Highness," one answers.

"Come with me." The two men follow me as I search all over the temple for her. From room to room, I search, even in the living quarters. I know her room as soon as I enter it. The scent of her perfume, made from a flower found only in Ginawa, fills the room and caresses my mind. Instantly, I'm brought back to the first time we prayed together and her hands were on my shoulders. My back was to her, and I badly wanted to turn around and bury my face between her thighs.

The smaller bed in the corner must be where the girl she keeps sleeps. Both beds in the room are tidy. I notice a familiar piece of cloth lying on the table next to a candle. It is a long strip of green cotton neatly folded. I pick it up and unravel it. Medusa, like the virgin women of age in her native Ginawa, wears a strip of cloth around their thigh or arm. I didn't notice earlier that she didn't have it on. Bringing the cloth up to my nose, I inhale deeply. I dismiss the thought that this may be the closest I get to having her. "Let's keep searching."

As we leave Medusa's room, the very ground trembles. The two guards question whether the earthquake is from the gods or if the volcano within the mountains has awakened, as there hasn't been an earthquake or eruption in Joro in over a century. When we leave the living quarters on this side of the temple and cross the main sanctuary to get to the living quarters on the other side, we get our answer. Various cracks can be seen on the statues of Jata and Nthanda. It is still intact, but whatever is going on, he is still alive and holding his position as Joro's god.

After not finding her, I decide to return to the palace. We'll have to continue searching for her in the morning and broaden the search to the entire land. Other than returning to Ginawa, I don't know where else she could have gone. There was no way for her to leave the temple without going past the guards...unless Jata took her.

On the temple steps, I am met by the royal guards blocking Kunle from entering. "What did you do?" the high priest asks me. Like everyone else in Joro, he felt the earthquake.

His eyes fill with worry as they dart from the god's statues outside the temple to me and back. I turn and look at them, and they have the same damage as the ones inside the sanctuary. I have no clue what is happening to Jata, nor do I care at this moment, as long as I can get Medusa back. She is supposed to be my prize, my wife, and I may never see her again. This is just one more reason to hate the gods.

My disdain in the present moment isn't just for the gods, but also Kunle and his tone. "Dare you question your king?" I snap.

Perhaps he's caught up in his fear of whatever the gods are going through at the moment, but Kunle completely misses the seriousness of my tone. "You've clearly angered them! What will this mean for Joro? Atonement for your sin must be done immediately."

"My sin? Don't forget, old man, you made this possible, and for a pretty price at that. What makes you so certain they aren't upset with you for selling one of your own?"

The ground shakes again, this time more violently than before. Cracking and grinding sounds come from all around the temple. The head of Nthanda's statue falls onto the top of the temple steps. I nearly lose my balance until one of my guards grab me and instruct me to crouch down. Some guards fall down the steps.

When it settles, we all look around and find that except for the head and a hand, Nthanda's statue is no more. A pit forms in my stomach as the guards ask each other what happened. From Joro's history, we all know this means Nthanda is dead. No one alive on Joro has ever seen such a thing—the death of a god. The story of Asmara runs through my head, as I am sure it does the other men here with me. Could my actions have started another war between the gods, or at least between Jata and Nthanda? If Jata ended his wife, good for him. I can't do the same without committing treason. I just need Jata to bring back what is mine.

With a shaky voice, Kunle gives his response. "I want no part of whatever you did. You will get every coin back and I—"

"Take him," I command. My guards do as they are told. "Don't act like you care *now*. If you really did, you would've asked about Medusa, and yet, you've not even mentioned her name." I turn my attention to Nia's chief guard. "The queen cannot walk of her own accord. Return her to her chambers and keep her there."

"You want us to imprison the queen in her quarters?" he asks.

"Only until morning. I will come to her then."

The queen's guards looked back and forth at each other. Clearly, they have thoughts about what's happened tonight. Nia's chief guard speaks again. "My king, may I ask…what happened to the queen?"

I go back and forth in my mind about what to tell them, if anything at all. They heard what the high priest said about my paying for Medusa, and they felt the two earthquakes and probably knew the goddess was indwelling Nia when she entered the temple. I look at all the guards. Hope and expectation for an answer are in all their eyes. I point to the cracked statue of Jata. "Our wives got in the way."

Another earthquake rumbles through Joro. All standing outside the temple crouch down to the ground and watch the statue of Jata for more damage. Nothing more appears on it, so

I'm not sure what is causing this latest quake. In my mind, I make my last request of Jata. *Bring Medusa back to me. Now.*

The next morning, I make my way to Nia's chambers as I said I would. Nia's guards, however, seem hesitant to let me in, and I'm not sure why. "What are you waiting for? Open the doors."

"Your Highness, forgive the intrusion, but we must ask. What are your intentions in seeing the Queen?"

"My intentions? I'm checking on my wife. What business is it of yours?"

"Nthanda made us swear to protect the Queen at all costs, especially from you and Jata."

This throws me for a loop. Even I realize the conundrum Nthanda put them in. She had to know her order meant they would at some point commit treason against their king. "I presume she did this last night?"

The guards nod.

Now I'm conflicted. What am I to do with guards whose sworn duty is to protect the queen and who have orders to take me down if it's in the best interest of said queen? But I am the king, and I won't let some goddess with jealousy issues keep me from being the king. I put my hands behind my back, and signal to my guards to get ready.

"You didn't have to tell me that, and I respect you for doing so. I understand your position. I assure you, I intend the queen no harm. We were both caught up in events that had nothing to do with us. You have no idea what it's like to be used by the gods in such a way. I want to make sure she is okay and see if together we can get a better understanding of what happened."

My words seem to relax the Queen's guards. Last night's events were unlike anything any of us have encountered before, and they only witnessed things from the outside. There is still no word about what happened to Medusa, or if she is alive. There is no way they didn't hear her screams. The guards let me pass and allow my guards to pass behind me, intending to fall in line behind them as they normally do. I come to a sudden stop just inside the door, forcing the queen's guards to stay up against the walls with little to no room to move with my guards in front of them.

"Take care of them," I say before closing the chamber doors behind me. Later, with my father, I'll see over the assignment of new guards for Nia.

I stand at the doors looking at the back of my wife, who's standing on her balcony with a maid fanning her with a large woven leaf fan. The maid notices me walking across the room towards them. She notifies her mistress, who seems to stiffen.

"Leave us," I order the maid when I reach the balcony. With her head down, the maid hastily heads to the door. I try to direct her to use the hidden door to get to the maids' wing, but she moves so fast. When the woman opens the doors, blood is all over the corridor. I can see some of my men dragging bodies away from where Nia and I stand. The maid screams at the top of her lungs. A guard close to her drops the body in his hands and marches towards the maid as she continues to scream. I have to run across the room to them to keep the man from killing her.

"Go out another way. You saw nothing," I tell her while holding the woman by her shoulders.

"Yes, your majesty," she says while frantically nodding. I let her go, and she scurries away as if she can't make her feet move fast enough.

"What did you do?" Nia asks.

"I was informed that your guards made a treasonous oath to our goddess last night." I turn to look Nia in the eyes. "You wouldn't know anything about that, would you?"

Nia steps back. "I thought it was all a dream."

"If only."

Nia gives me a hard look. "How much of last night was you and how much was Jata?"

"I'm not capable of shooting you with a magical beam, Nia. How are you feeling after that?"

"Surviving. That's not what I was asking about. Everyone knows a mortal doesn't possess the power a god does. Did you go to the temple intending to bond with Medusa, or did Jata force you?"

"I came here to discuss what you remember from last night."

"I remember you trying to force yourself on the priestess. Was it you or Jata who desires her as a wife?"

"Can a god have a mortal wife?"

Silence.

"Did you go there to bond with her, or did Jata take you there?"

"It doesn't matter."

"It matters to me."

"Why? Based on your words, before your father's funeral, you didn't want me as your husband."

"I didn't want a husband at all."

"And now?"

"I have one, so we are past what I didn't want. The answer I'm trying to get from you if you desire someone else as a wife."

"This marriage was forced upon us both, Nia." It is the only answer I can give her without sounding cold-hearted.

Silence falls on us for a few moments before I speak again. "What was it like?"

"How could finding your husband attempting to—"

"I meant when Jata hit you, or Nthanda, with whatever that was?" I'm trying to keep the subject off my desire for Medusa.

"Horrible. All of it was horrible. It was quick, but it felt like my skin was burning and cracking. Then there was nothing. I can still feel it—the burning, but not nearly as intense." Nia rubs her arm. "I never felt such rage before, mine and hers. But I saw…did you know they hate each other?"

"I knew Jata didn't care for Nthanda, so it's not surprising they both felt that way."

"It's all a surprise to me. Nthanda's never let me see into her mind or feelings before. I never knew it was possible to feel what they feel. Never have I wanted to hurt someone until last night. She…she was stopping just short of killing Medusa, and I wanted to hurt you."

I look at my wife. I never considered Nia's feelings in my pursuit of Medusa. She appears nonchalant about everything else; I figured this would be the same. Her eyes say differently. Her next words let me know I'm walking on straw. She has no problem setting a blaze under my feet.

"I've never had a problem with the priestess, or any other woman in the land, but I am your queen. I was always destined to be queen, so it is only your connection to me that gives you your power. Don't forget I am my father's daughter, blood or not. There is only one use I have for you, and it is not pleasure."

"Understood. Wait…you know?" I ask. I thought she was oblivious of her true parentage. Her father ordered no one to mention it within the Proper.

"You really think I'm stupid," the queen snaps.

"Apologies," I say as I stand to leave, but Nia stops me before I get to the doors.

"I expect your presence in my chambers tonight for bonding. Since I have a husband, we need to produce an heir."

All I can do is nod as I look at her. Leaving Nia's chambers, several things run through my head, starting with how easily Nia compartmentalizes. I've seen instances of her disconnecting emotionally before, but maybe there was more to it. Something more sinister. After her threatening reminder, I'm going to have to bond with her tonight and hope it brings her the result she desires. What I really need is to contain her, or at least have eyes on her every move with guards who are more loyal to me than her.

Then there is my father. I must be careful with my words to him about all that's happened. My father despises men who let their wives run them, and if he finds out about the threat Nia just made, Baraka will never cease to remind me of my failure at being the head of my household.

If I do it correctly, I can use Nia's threat with the right parts of last night's events against her to keep her imprisoned in her chambers or even the tower for her own good. I will use it as a last resort if I later find out that she's plotting against me.

And where is Medusa? She has to be found before she can spin her own version of events. Containment and control are my game right now, and it is a game I can't afford to lose.

Chapter 15
Nthanda

I feel so weak. "Am I alive?" my voice strains to ask.

"Yes."

"Eshu?"

"It is I, Nthanda."

"Where are we?"

"Outside of Kemet and Songhai's reaches," Eshu answers.

"That's not possible."

"I'm much older than you and know things about the galaxy and the Elders you don't. I've been testing the limits of their powers and carved out space for myself in it."

"Why?"

"Before I answer that, how do you feel?"

"Weak. Nearly dead. I almost died."

"I saved you, Nthanda."

"Why?"

"Because the Elders have lied to you for most of your existence. It is time you know the truth. Once you know everything, you can help me."

"Help you with what?"

"Overthrowing the *almighty* Kemet and Songhai," he says.

I look at Eshu in shock. I'm in no position to challenge anyone. In order to heal, I need prayers and praise. Eshu knows this and gives me some comforting words. "For now, this will be where you rest. I'll work on conjuring up a way for you to heal."

"The Elders, why do you want to destroy them, and why should I? They are the reason we exist, why anything exists."

"Why should they be the only ones to create as they wish? Don't you remember what it was like before the war? We gods could create life! Now, mortals and animals have more ability to create while we gods can't! Kemet and Songhai have created these rules for us while they get to do whatever they want? No one has ever checked or challenged them on it."

"The demigods challenged them."

"Not exactly. They had no real chance of winning the war that was waged against them. Their mortal side made them weak. Instead of cherishing the much more powerful and beautiful beings they're partnered with, gods now have a desire for mere mortals." Eshu cupped Nthanda's cracked chin.

There's something peculiar about how he refers to the Great War, but I'm too weak to focus on it while trying to figure out what's happened to me and where I am. "You haven't said why I should want to take them down, or how you saved me."

"I'm projecting myself right now, and I can't hold it for much longer. I projected the two of us and went incognito, taking you out of Muhabura just before you were no more. With practice over time, I've gotten better at making my projections move and look realistic. The Elders don't know I've been doing this. I have to go now."

"Why, Eshu?"

"Because the Elders killed your parents, not Asmara."

"What?" I don't understand what he's saying. The Elders… my parents? It makes little sense.

"I have to go now."

"Explain this to me."

"I will when I return. I'm not sure how long it will be, but I will return to you."

"Eshu, find her," I beg. "Find Jata's mortal and kill her."

Eshu nods before disappearing.

I know finding her will be challenging, even for Eshu, the Elder's favorite messenger and hunter. Jata won't make it easy. There's a good chance he has some type of protection on her. I hate my husband, but he is no idiot. The gods promoted Jata for a reason. He will not make it easy for her to be found. Eshu will get the same orders of tracking down Jata's mortal from the Elders, I'm sure. That is just fine with me as long as the result is the same—her death. In fact, if Eshu can return my strength to me, Kemet and Songhai, Jata and his mortal, even Kush and Ife, they will all die.

Chapter 16
King Gainde

I sit in the throne room with my father looking over a group of soldiers. From them, we'll select the queen's new guards. Assir, my secretary and childhood best friend, is nearby, taking notes. We are close to narrowing down the ones who will not only keep Queen Nia safe, but more importantly, would be more loyal to us than her, when Nia herself walks into the throne room with soldiers trailing behind her.

The soldiers already here bow until she takes her seat next to me. "What matters are we dealing with today?" she asks.

"I don't think this is a matter for you, Your Majesty," Baraka says. "We would've called for you if you were needed."

My back goes stiff, as I know this is the wrong response based on the conversation I had with her this very morning. My father is accustomed to the absence of a reigning queen.

"This will be my only time reminding you of this, Baraka. I am queen, your queen. You are of no counsel to me. You have no position to decide what is and isn't a matter for me."

His jaw tightens from clenching his teeth. I know my father well enough to know that he takes offence at being spoken to in such a way by anyone, let alone a woman. What makes it worse is that there is nothing he can do about it. Everything Nia said is true. He has to give her the respect her title commands, even if it means faking it. Gone are the days of dismissing her like he did when she was Joro's princess.

"Certainly, your Majesty," he says while fighting down his anger. I can feel my father shaking beside me.

The tightness with which my father said it doesn't go unnoticed by Nia either. Her next words show her need to drive the point home. "Your queen wishes to know what this matter is."

In my head, I'm wishing that my father doesn't become violent with her.

"Your new guards, Your Majesty."

Nia looks at the soldiers she walked in with moments ago. "What about my new guards?"

Deciding to spare my father, I answer. "We were selecting your new guards."

"I've already done that," she says while moving her hand in the general direction of the men she walked in with. Both my and my father's backs go straight.

"How did you go about doing this?" I ask.

"Like you, I grew up within these walls. Unlike you, I am the child of kings. There are people who will do anything for me."

There are no words to be said. My father and I just stare at her because this is not the woman we thought we knew.

"Now that's settled," she continues, "there is a matter I would like to bring forth."

"That is?" I ask.

"The matter of Medusa." She looks at my guards, who are lined up against one wall. "Do you all recall goddess Nthanda's words to you last night regarding Medusa?"

The men nod.

"Say it so the others can hear," she orders.

They say in unison, "Medusa committed a great sin and suffered punishment for it."

Nia turns her attention to the soldiers I had brought in. "You heard that?" They nod. "Good. Spread the word throughout the market that there is a reward from the palace for anyone with information that leads to Medusa's capture and that anyone helping her will be arrested for treason. Bring her to me and you'll get your next orders."

The soldiers no longer being promoted to the queen's guard file out with their command. My father, who is not aware of the current situation, inquires about Medusa's major wrongdoing. He is still bent on Medusa being the next high priest, despite my many objections. I order our guards out of the throne room.

"You said nothing of your wishes concerning Medusa this morning," I say to my wife.

"Just as you said nothing of making the priestess your wife before you went to the temple yesterday. Tell me, husband, how did you think that was going to go with someone who swore their life to the gods?"

I don't respond, but my father and Assir do.

"What?" Barak asks.

"You didn't," Assir gasps.

Still nothing from me.

"You actually did it. You forced her," Assir says. This is what he feared the most about my lust for Medusa. "You've cursed us all."

"He tried to force her," Nia clarifies. "He didn't get all the way before Nthanda interrupted him and Jata."

"Wait, the gods were involved, too?" Assir asks.

"It was a complicated evening," I say.

Baraka turns to Assir. "What do you know of this?"

Assir looks at me, but I refuse to make eye contact. "The night before their wedding, I told him to leave the priestess alone."

Out of nowhere, my face stings from my father backhanding me. "Do you have any idea what you've done?"

Long ago, I grew tired of my father's violent outbursts, but now that I'm king, I feel like I can do something about it. I wanted no one outside of my siblings and Assir to know of the abuse. I stand and strike my father, the punch landing on his chin. Baraka stumbles back, and I stay on him. I swing again, but Baraka blocks it and punches me in my side. Now I'm the one stumbling back. After getting my bearings, we both take fighting stances opposite each other.

"Oh, so now you think you can beat me, your father," he says in a condescending tone before throwing another punch and missing.

"Not only do I know I can beat you, father," I respond while faking left only to swing right, connecting with his father's jaw again.

"Stop this," Assir begs Nia. She simply raises her hand to let him know to let this play out.

"There is something you seem to have forgotten, but I remember," I continue. Throwing a hook and jab, both my fists connect with my father's face, and he falls to the floor. "I am your king." I close the distance between us in two steps and I put my foot on Baraka's chest. "It will serve you well to remember that."

"Guards!" Nia yells. Four of her guards appear. "Take Baraka to the dungeons. Put him by himself and as far away from others as possible. I don't want anyone to hear him. There is to be a guard on him at all times."

"Nia," I plead.

"Are we or are we not joint rulers?"

I reluctantly move off my father and allow the guards to take Baraka as he yells at me for being his greatest disappointment. Once they're gone, I turn to my queen. "Is that necessary?"

"The sovereign should not permit any subject to develop a habit of attacking them." We stare at each other for a few moments. "Assir, send someone to fetch Kunle from the temple. We need to discuss the Medusa matter with him."

"Kunle is in the dungeons, too," I inform them.

"What?" Assir and Nia ask in shock.

Not only have I possibly cursed the land by my actions, but I locked up the best person who could appease the gods and the Elders, and their collective wrath.

"There have been whispers amongst the staff," Assir says. "Nthanda's statues are piles of rubble and Jata's have vanished."

"This cannot be reality." Nia rubs her forehead and says, "This cannot be how my rule is remembered." The room is tense as the gravity of the situation I've caused falls upon us. "Why is Kunle locked up?" Nia asks.

I have no choice but to tell them the truth. Doing things in secret got me into this mess. It is only now that I realize secrets will not get me out of it. In my anger at Jata and Nthanda for interrupting my plans, I didn't consider how I was going to explain arresting the Kunle.

"I paid him to make sure the temple was clear of everyone but Medusa yesterday evening. After everything, he returned to find Nthanda's statue cracked and crumbling. He blamed me for cursing Joro, then said he would return the coin, so he'd be blameless, as if that were possible."

"So, you locked him away to cover your tracks," Assir says. The disappointment in my friend's voice cuts through me like a sword.

"For the sake of the crown, he has to remain there," Nia says.

I slowly stalk towards Nia. "All these years before, were you faking being obtuse because you've been anything but since this morning?" I get right up in her face, bending down to place my hands on her wrists.

Nia responds so only I can hear her. "I was who I needed to be then, and I am who I need to be now."

"Maybe this marriage won't be so dull after all."

"After the stunt you pulled yesterday, you need to pray that this marriage isn't hell for you."

Nia surprises me, and I'm enjoying this version of her. It's a shame her father felt the same way about women as my father does. King Ahmose never wanted Joro to be solely ruled by a queen, which was why he and my father arranged this marriage so early in our lives. Because of the likelihood that Nia was not of his loins, she had to be married to a Joroan highborn instead of a prince from one of the other three lands in the galaxy. This way she stays in Joro, and Ahmose's lineage, although perceived, continues to sit on the throne. I take my seat next to Nia as she continues to show more of her assertive side.

"Assir, none of what you heard is to go into the official record. As far as the royal historians are concerned, Kunle stole from the crown. The coins he received from the king will be the evidence against him and are to be returned to the crown. As far as I'm concerned, Baraka committed treason today, but I will let my husband decide his father's fate."

"Have my sisters moved to the chambers the queen used when she was yet a princess. They are to be raised in the ways of a princess. My father shall remain in the dungeons for the remainder of his days."

"Yes, your Majesties," Assir states. "There is still the matter of the priesthood. Who will be the High Priest now?"

All three of us are quiet for a few moments.

"I really don't know the names of the other priests and priestesses," I say.

Nia chuckles. "Neither do I."

Chapter 17
Medusa

Sisay left for Zendaya's in the early morning hours. She didn't want to leave, and I didn't want her to go, either, but this cave is no place for her, especially while she still has a chance of having a normal life. I know Zendaya will keep her safe. Plus, I've sent her with a small snake so I can check in on her.

I stand just inside the opening of the cave. With my godlike eyes, the palace and temple are clear in my sight. I can even see and make out the people in the courtyard, which is full of vendors and shoppers. Everything in Joro seems to go on as usual, except for the increased number of guards there. I wonder if they are looking for me.

Closing my eyes, I concentrate. If I can see them from this great distance, maybe I can hear them as well. First, I focus on the sounds closest to me—the wind outside of the cave whipping back and forth, the bubbling stream and lava flows deeper inside the mountain. The sound of the mountain itself comes to me. Never did I think of the mountain as something that moves, but it sways ever so slightly, and it groans as it does.

On the other side of the mountain, the ejo nla devours a mountain goat while the lower half of its body squeezes the life from a second. The bones of the second mountain goat break and I hear when its heart gives up. Further down the mountain, the rest of the wild goats scream at each other. Their hearts are racing after an encounter with the large rainbow python. At the base of the mountain, the waterfall from the heavens has a thunderous roar. The Tehenu River moves violently here. Birds chirp in the woods, and a mother bear and her two cubs play. Deer munch loudly on the low-lying leaves of bushes and trees. The forest seems to be just as loud as the waterfall to me now. I can hear everything thing from the ant pulling a dead bee back to its colony to the goose chasing a man down the riverbank. The man screams like a teenage girl.

As I concentrate on the area closest to the temple, I hear murmuring. It's not clear yet, so I focus on the voices harder. I recognize them as another priest and two priestesses.

"It had to be one of her snakes."

"They shouldn't have been here in the first place."

"Medusa is responsible for Cairo's death."

"No one has seen Kunle since yesterday. Do you think she did something to him?"

"We are without gods and a high priest!"

Heavy footsteps approach the whisperers. The sound of cloth moving under metal lets me know it is a soldier. "Has anyone seen the priestess, Medusa?"

"Not since yesterday. The same is for her brat and Kunle." No longer whispering, I can make out their voices. The priestess, Accra, Cairo and Kunle's lover, asks the question.

"There is a reward for Medusa's capture," the guard informs them. "She's committed a great sin against the gods and the crown. Anyone who helps her will face arrest and beheading for treason."

"What about the high priest?" the priest Dakar asks.

"He was arrested yesterday for stealing from the Crown. A new high priest needs to be appointed. The king and queen want all the priesthood to report to them at high sun."

"She, Medusa, has also committed a murder," Accra says. "We found the body of priestess Cairo in the corridor outside of Medusa's chambers early this morning. She had two sets of snakebites on her legs."

"The priestess is known for her love of snakes," the guard states.

"None of the snakes or her girl are here," priestess Luanda adds.

"I will take this information to the king and queen. If you see Medusa, yell for the guards. There will be more of us around until she's captured."

The guard leaves, and the group returns to whispering. I don't bother listening to them. I cease stretching my hearing at such a distance. Anger rages through me as I process the lies of the crown. "I committed a sin? They are… of course they are blaming me."

I want to destroy the palace and everything it stands for. Gainde needs to suffer for his role in this. They will all pay for what they've done to me.

"You aren't stuck in this cave, you know," a familiar voice says to me.

I look in the direction it comes from. Instead of appearing as the night sky as she did before, Moeder Heelal is as bright as the blue sky.

"Where have you been?"

"I'm always near."

"You did not prepare me for what happened."

"Didn't I? If Nthanda had her way, she would have turned your legs into the tail of a snake and forced you to slither around on the ground for all eternity."

"You could have told me what—"

"If I told you what the three of them were planning to do to you, you would've killed the king before Jata indwelled him, and all the land would be watching your execution in the courtyard right now. It had to play out this way."

I can't say she is wrong. "You said I'm not stuck in this cave. What do you mean, because according to Jata, I am?"

"I've already shown you that the gods do not know everything."

"Please, Moeder Heelal. Explain."

"You can go invisible to every being, mortal and immortal, except me, just like the gods can. The exception you have is that you can hold it indefinitely. You can also detect when there are gods around you using it."

"What can't I do that they can?"

"Nothing. Your power, my daughter, is second only to mine."

"I'm not a demigod, but a full-on god."

"Precisely."

"Teach me how to use my powers, starting with the incognito. I need to go down and warn Sisay and Zendaya."

"I will teach you, but there is no need to warn them."

"The crown will kill them because of their association with me."

"They will get to you safely when it is darkest tonight. You will make sure of that with the help of the creatures you now control."

I try to focus my mind to see into the future. It's not that I don't believe Moeder Heelal, but she isn't the most forthcoming being.

"Patience, Medusa. You will learn to do that in time. Tell me, what all have you learned to do so far?"

"You already know."

"I do, but I want to hear it from you in your own words."

I silently call a snake from within the cave. It comes to me quickly, slithers up my body and anchors itself in my locs. "As you said, I can control them, even multiple snakes at once. I can see and hear at great distances. Last night, for a second, I could hear my daughter's thoughts and even visualize it in my head."

"Did you try to expand on that?"

"No. I don't want that to become how we communicate."

"Which is why I wanted you to use your words just now."

"Understood."

"Let's work on your power of telepathy. There is a man in the woods shaving the bark off a cinnamon tree. Locate him."

I close my eyes.

"Keep your eyes open. Locate him while you are taking in other sensations."

This time I stare at the treetops and listen for the sound of wood being carved. I take longer to do it than if I had my eyes closed. The movement of the trees and seeing birds flying in the air distract me some, but I eventually locate him. "I have him."

"Listen to his heartbeat and the way air fills and releases from his lungs as he breathes," she instructs me.

The beating and whooshing rhythm fills my ears. Both are faster than normal because of the labor of extracting the precious bark. I nod after a moment.

"His thoughts are a piece of him. Listen and visualize them the same way you do his heart."

I focus harder. The image of a woman comes to my head, but it is gone the next second. I groan in frustration.

"Relax. Breathe. Try again."

"I need to get closer."

"You don't. Now try again."

Taking a deep breath, I focus on the man's thoughts again. There, the woman is still on his mind. She is short and round, with a beautiful smile and disposition. "He is very fond of her and hopes to sell enough cinnamon and present the coins to her family. He desires to marry her."

"What is the woman's name?"

"Kigali, but he calls her Lili."

"Good job. Let's try it again. This time, find the thoughts of your friend who is keeping your daughter. You need to know what she knows in order to help them tonight."

I haven't tried to see into the Commons because the waterfall is between where I am in the mountains and it. This is going to be harder than listening in on the conversations in the temple. Steadying myself, I focus my mind on the route I would normally take to Zendaya's home from the temple. Going this route, I cross the Tehenu at the bridge and where it is quieter downriver instead of at the waterfall.

Making my way through people I'd normally see daily and communed with, most of their thoughts are on the gods, Kunle, and me. I catch a thought of someone who thinks none of this would have happened under King Ahmose. I can't disagree with them. Unfortunately, none of this is Queen Nia's fault, either. She is a casualty of her husband's lust and Nthanda's jealousy. Many people think I've gone back to my homeland and am hiding there. If only they knew the whole truth.

Zendaya is exactly where I thought she would be, at home by her front window. Only she has it shut, which is unusual for her during the day. It's her way of shutting out the world from asking her about me. She's so worried. Because I didn't tell Sisay much, Sisay couldn't tell her much. I wish I could comfort her from here somehow. It doesn't seem like she yet knows about the crown's price for me. Just then, her brother bursts into her home.

Medusa Untold

I really dislike that man.

Chapter 18
Medusa

"Is she here?" Nyani demands information from his sister.

"What? Who? And keep your voice down. Wambua is asleep."

"The girl?"

"You're not making sense."

"The girl, Zendaya. Medusa's girl?"

Zendaya doesn't like how frantic Nyani seems. He's never shown an interest in Sisay before, and her intuition tells her something is wrong. I can hear her mentally yelling at Sisay to stay put wherever she is in the house. If only Sisay could hear it.

"I haven't seen her all day," she answers loudly enough for Sisay to hear her in the back of the house. "Why?"

"Soldiers are looking for Medusa. There's a reward from the palace. That girl would know where Medusa is hiding."

"Medusa is a priestess, the best priestess Joro's ever seen. She has no reason to hide."

"You haven't heard? She's no priestess, no more. She committed a great sin yesterday and now she's wanted."

"What sin is that? Hmm?"

"One so horrible that Nthanda's statues have fallen, and Jata's are gone like they were never there. If the palace doesn't find her, that means the gods took their revenge out on her."

Zendaya's thoughts of her brother being the biggest idiot in the land makes me laugh. It feels good to laugh for once. "How many people have you told this to?"

"Everyone."

"And you've yet to hear yourself?"

"What do you mean? This is what I know."

"You know nothing. Tell me, Nyani, what can a mortal, a single mortal, do to an eternal being like a god to cause them harm? One mortal can't starve the gods of power and glory on their own. You've been speaking nonsense."

"Leave your house, why don't you? Everyone is talking about Medusa's great sin and wondering where she is."

"Until Medusa tells me herself that she has the power and audacity to take down our gods, I will not believe it."

I am grateful to my friend for her loyalty. She didn't have to defend me so fiercely. Doing so with anyone else would raise suspicion that she knows more about me and what happened. Nyani, thankfully, is not that depth of mind.

"It was a good thing I denied her when she inquired about being one of my wives a few days after healing your boy."

Zendaya and I have the same reaction in our minds. *What?*

"As I said," Zendaya says, "I've not seen Sisay all day. She was supposed to come help me in the garden today but never showed up. I figured she was busy at the temple."

"Medusa must have gotten her mixed up in her great sin or has the girl hiding with her. If the girl or Medusa shows up here, bring them to me at once."

Zendaya nods, knowing she would do no such thing. I watch her thoughts as she decides she must get Sisay back to me as soon as possible and that her best chance at doing so is tonight.

I stay in Zendaya's thoughts even after Nyani leaves. She acts normal for a few minutes, tending to her beading, before going to the back room where Wambua is napping, and Sisay is hiding behind a large pot.

"Stay quiet," she says softly while unfolding a blanket to fold it again.

Sisay nods.

"She's going to have to change her mind because it is not safe for you here. Do you remember how to get back to where she is?"

Again, Sisay nods and raises her arm to show the baby constrictor snake that is gently wrapped around her arm.

Zendaya silently declares her dislike of the creepy creatures.

"Do you know what you need to do?" Moeder Heelal asks me.

"Yes."

"Good. Now keep watch of Zendaya's thoughts. It will help you time everything perfectly. In the meantime, I want you to practice controlling the serpents while you watch her thoughts. You're going to need to multitask tonight and when you face the gods."

"When will I be able to take on the king?"

"In due time. It will be before you face your first gods. For now, practice what I told you. Your daughter's life depends on it."

That is all the motivation I need. I order various snakes to gather provisions from the woods for Sisay—fruits, vegetables, and nuts, as well as leaves to make a bed. While doing so, I feel that someone or something unfamiliar is in Joro.

"What is that?" I ask Moeder Heelal.

"Do you want to try going incognito, or do you want to check with your mind on top of all that you're already doing?"

After having my mind set on not being able to leave this place, I'm not quite ready to try going incognito. One wrong move and I mess everything up just when we're getting started. "I'll do it from here."

Pushing my mind, I now set about checking out the temple besides watching Zendaya's thoughts, checking in on Sisay through the snake she has, and having other snakes make ready for her to stay here. Whatever it is, I sense it is in my old quarters, but it isn't alone. Others in the priesthood are searching my room for clues on where to find me or what they want to take for themselves. They rattle on about me and my supposed great sin, but none of them notice the page of an open journal turn over. The being responsible for that would be invisible to them. However, I can see his translucent body clearly.

Long locs pulled into a single braid down his back. Small gold wings at the back of his ankles and on his wrists that would glitter in the full sun tell me exactly who he is. Eshu. "If Eshu is in Joro, that means the Elders are looking for me as well."

"They are. Jata's twisted love for you is causing quite an uproar in Muhabura."

"How so?"

"They need him to tell them where you are, but he won't give you up."

"I want to see."

"You aren't ready to go there yet."

"There must be a way you can show me without us going there. I need to know what is going on with all sides coming at me if I am to defeat them all."

Moeder Heelal looks at me for a few moments before walking a little way into the cave. I follow her and watch as she touches a wall. It displays a picture of Muhabura's throne room. It looks just as it did when Moeder Heelal showed me what really happened with Asmara and Joro's original gods, Kinshasa and Malabo.

I recognize Kemet, Songhai, and Eshu. The other two gods standing before them, I'm not sure. "Who are they?"

"The gods of your homeland, Kush and Ife."

"Let me talk to Jata," Kush suggests. "Maybe I can get through to him. Restoring him to his position over Joro will motivate him."

"Restore? We will assign new gods immediately," Songhai says.

Kush presses. "Tablets announcing the new gods haven't gone to Joro yet. You've not written them. There is still time to fix this."

"They've removed their High Priest thanks to this mess," Songhai responds. "Tablets can't go until they appoint a new High Priest."

Kush continues. "We all know how hard a change of gods is on mortals. They are sensitive beings. There hasn't been a change of gods in Joro since the beginning of the Great War. I'm asking that we give a little more consideration to their sensitivity."

The Elders do not immediately give a response, so Kush continues trying to reason with them.

"His true crime is not giving up the demigod; that's not exactly punishable by death or removal from his position."

"Kush," Ife says to warn him to stop.

Kush puts his hand up to stop her in response. "You risk turning the mortals against any god you put in Jata's place, all because he did what was necessary to save a mortal from a jealous and immature goddess. That will grow into them turning on you, on all of us. We will cease to exist without their prayers and praise. Putting another god over Joro is not the way."

Kemet sighs. "You have a point. Jata will remain imprisoned here while still serving his godly duty of answering prayers. That will be the only thing he can do, and he will not get any power from their praise. He may not return to Joro or have his full power restored until the demigod is located, whether or not he gives her up. You can let him know."

Kush bows and leaves the room.

"Follow him," I request of Moeder Heelal. The image changes to a dungeon-like room. Jata is in it, lying on a rock slab.

"You just had to drive your wife mad, huh?" Kush jokes.

Jata huffs and looks upon the glistening golden prayer feathers in front of him. "I take it you had something to do with this." Jata doesn't bother listening to the prayers. With a wave of his hand, he answers them all. "At least I'm still a god in some way."

"Where did you hide her?"

"So they can find and destroy her?"

"I'm trying to get you restored so your people can have some stability."

Jata is silent as if he is reflecting. "She was incredible, Kush. More than I could have ever imagined."

"Demi's usually were special."

Jata looks at Kush. "Her eyes were like ours."

Kush's eyes grew wide. Concern is evident all over his face.

"The Elders better hope my mortals don't start praying to her or that word about her does not spread from land to land. She will be unstoppable if they do."

Kush backs away from the cell.

"Watch out for Eshu. He's up to something. As one of the Elders' favorites, they don't watch him closely, but I noticed his form flickering after Nthanda was destroyed. He was projecting far away from here. For all we know, my wife may still be alive, and he has her hidden somewhere. We all know how he desires her and the chance to rule."

Without my asking, the image goes back to the throne room. Songhai can't bark orders at the younger messenger gods fast enough. "Find him! Find him now!"

Kush re-enters the throne room and goes straight to his wife.

"We were all watching as you talked to Jata," Ife informs him. "Eshu vanished as soon as Jata mentioned his name. Finding him has become top priority."

"He cannot use incognito for long. They will find him," Kush says.

Quickly, I mentally search the temple for Eshu. He's no longer there. I face Moeder Heelal. "Is she still alive?"

"She is. Eshu is working on giving Nthanda power again, not to rule, but to take the Elders down."

"Why does he want to take on the Elders?"

"He has jealousy issues like Nthanda as well."

"And he knows the truth about the death of her parents." I think about all this new information. I've gone from being in a lust triangle I knew nothing about, to being at the center of a war with the crown and two factions of gods. "This is too much."

"You, Medusa, are the best-equipped being to settle all of this. Remember, I chose you. My power and the power of the gods make up your being. You are no longer a mere mortal. You are a goddess, unique in every way from all others."

"Do a few different powers make me so unique?"

"No. Your heart does. Now get ready. The time to save your daughter approaches."

Chapter 19
Medusa

It's the middle of the night. Zendaya has her sleeping child tied to her back with a long wrap as they, along with Sisay, make their way through the village. Thanks to the Moeder Heelal teaching me how to use my incognito abilities, I am watching them from the highest peak of the mountain. The ejo nla is sitting in position behind the tree line in the woods. Thanks to the little snake I gave Sisay early this morning, I can feel her heartbeat through it. All they have to do is get to the woods unseen. Because of the long-lived collective fear of the ejo nla, we are banking on the soldiers not being willing to go into the woods at night. Earlier, Sisay had to convince Zendaya I have power over the legendary snake so they will be safe in the woods, unlike anyone else.

I watch them as they creep along the backs of houses, avoiding the stone walking and cart paths most of the soldiers are on. The soldiers are still searching door-to-door. Zendaya tosses bits of dried meat and fruit at any pets lingering in the back gardens of homes to keep them quiet as they move below windows and skip past doorways. They are making good progress, surprisingly, and are only a short distance away from the tree line. Zendaya jumps pass a rear door of a home, not realizing a soldier is there checking it. He sees her only out of the corner of his eye, but it is enough to make him go check. Sisay and Zendaya are stuck on either side of the door, unable to move from behind the collection of water and wine barrels flanking the opening. Neither of them can see each other as the soldier steps outside the doorway, standing between the stacks of barrels.

"Who's there?" he calls.

I have Sisay's snake give her a squeeze, hoping it will calm her nerves because her heart is racing. As the soldier steps out, they hunch down as low as they can to blend into the shadows of the barrels. Zendaya is also panicking because her boy stirs.

A white feather appears in front of me. I almost swipe it away until I realize what it is. I've heard about these before, but of course, have never seen them in person. It is a prayer feather. I take it into my hands and hear my daughter's prayer that they aren't found and for a safe arrival to my cave. Doing what I saw Jata do in the vision Moeder Heelal provided earlier, I wave my hand around it. Gold essence flows from my hand to the feather, turning it gold before it dissolves in the air.

I just received and answered my first prayer as a goddess.

The soldier relaxes and re-enters the home, leaving through the front entrance and moving on to the next house in the opposite direction Zendaya and Sisay are going. The two release a breath when Sisay makes it to Zendaya. "That was close," Zendaya whispers as they hugged. When Sisay peers into the woods, she sees two familiar wide glowing golden eyes in the distance just beyond the tree line. "We have to run straight for the trees," Sisay tells her adult companion.

"What? No, we must take our time and be careful."

"The ejo nla."

"What?"

Sisay points her head toward where the giant snake waits. Zendaya turns and grows stiff when she sees the enormous eyes and makes out parts of the snake's silhouette in the dim light. It is larger than she imagined, and in her head, she is screaming.

"I prayed to my mother. It is here for our protection," Sisay whispers after covering Zendaya's mouth. "It could have eaten me last night, but it didn't because of her. All we have to do is run for the trees. Medusa will take care of the rest."

As Zendaya stands against the house questioning her sanity, a soldier spots Sisay from a nearby home. "Stop right there!"

That makes Zendaya's mind up for her. "Run!" she yells. For her, running to the creature rumored to make half of a large herd of cattle disappear overnight is much more logical than being captured by the crown.

Zendaya and Sisay take off for the tree line as multiple guards chase after them. Zendaya sees the snake moving towards them. "No, no, no!" she repeats.

"Stop! Stop!" multiple guards yell.

"Keep running!" Sisay counters. They jump onto garden borders and trample over flowers and vegetables. The sound of the soldiers' footsteps grows louder and louder in Zendaya's ears as the men close in on them.

"Medusa!" Zendaya screams as a plea, afraid they won't make it. The ejo nla strikes with lightning speed and brute force at the men who chase after Sisay and Zendaya. It throws them so hard against a home that there's no chance of survival.

"Ejo nla! Ejo nla!" someone screams from inside their home.

The snake turns around and catches up with the three I sent it to protect. They continued to run towards the mountain with the ejo nla leading the way. Once at the base of the mountain, Sisay suggests they get on the giant snake's back.

"That is too much for me," Zendaya says.

"Can you climb the mountain quickly? I can't, but the snake can. Plus, it is colder the higher up the mountain you go, and Medusa's cave is pretty high up. We won't be warm again until we're inside it."

"How about I just take you up myself?" I say, appearing in front of them.

"Mother!"

"I thought you said she wasn't a goddess," Zendaya whispers to Sisay.

"She said she's not."

"I'll explain once you two are out of harm's way. Until then, give me your hands." The ejo nla dashes up the mountain.

"Did something spook it?" Zendaya asks.

"I told it to hide. Soldiers are gathering at the edge of the woods."

"We're not flying up, are we?" asks Zendaya.

"No." Before I finish my answer, I teleport the four of us to the innermost part of my cave. "I learned how to transport earlier today and to change the weather on top of the mountain. It's now raining hard all over the land to cover your tracks in the forest."

"It is great you are learning how to do so much on your own," Sisay states.

"I had some help today from Moeder Heelal."

"As in *the* Moeder Heelal?" they say in unison.

"The one and only." I put my hand out to motion for them to sit on two small boulders. Zendaya looks around at all the snakes here as she unwraps her son, who is now awake. "They have dens and burrows throughout the woods. They come and go from here as they please, unless I summon them. I can send them out if it will make you more comfortable."

She shakes her head and sits Wambua on the ground. "No sense. I can't stay long, though I can't imagine how I can go back to my home."

"That's why I took care of those soldiers. No one else saw you."

"I'm sure plenty of people heard me scream your name."

"They heard someone scream my name. There's no way they can prove it was you or anyone else," I state. I can hear Zendaya thinking about it. She trusts me more than she trusts any other person. If I say it is safe, then she will believe it.

"Because people know how close we are, I'd like two snakes to stay at your place at all times, if that is okay with you."

Zendaya agrees. "Before I go, will you tell me what happened to you and why the king and queen want you captured? The things being said about you…are more than horrible."

"Let me start at the beginning."

I tell them everything, from King Gainde's attempt at forcing me to bond with him, and Jata and Nthanda showing up. I even tell them about Moeder Heelal's proposal and the lies of the Elders. When I finish, both Sisay and Zendaya have tear-stained faces.

"Curse them. All of them," Sisay says. Under any other circumstances, I would've corrected her, but this time I don't. I feel the same.

"The people need to know," Sisay says. "They can starve the gods of praise and demand that King Gainde—"

"I will have no one risk treason for me," I interject. Sisay objects, but I cut her off. "No." The teen shrinks into herself, giving up.

"What are you going to do?" Zendaya asks. "If the Elders find out where you are…"

"I have help and protection from the Moeder Heelal."

"Can you trust her?" Zendaya asks. "Moeder Heelal created the unworthy gods presiding over us."

"I get where you're coming from. I believe I can trust her. She's kept her word to me so far. She assures me they all will feel my wrath." They nod, satisfied there will be some justice, eventually. "Now, Zendaya. Let's get you back to your home. Your brother is heading there now, and he has guards with him."

"I was asleep until Wambua woke up from all the commotion outside." She winks at me, and I wink back at her before transporting them to her home.

Medusa Untold

Chapter 20
Medusa

I'm back in the cave with Sisay in an instant. She stares at me like she is still getting used to this version of me, which is understandable. "It is a lot to take in," I say.

"It is. You look like you, but you don't. You sound like yourself, but you don't."

"I even sound different to you?"

"There is a slight layering in your voice. Similar to when the gods would indwell the king and queen, only they are different tones of your voice instead of two distinct voices stacked on top of each other."

"Hmm. I hadn't noticed that. What else do you think is different about me?"

She looks me over and either can't find her words or struggles to put the right words together. "I have the power to read minds, but I don't want to depend on that with you. Please talk to me."

"You're not as sure as you were before."

"This is all new to me."

"I know, but there is more to it than that."

My daughter, always so perceptive. She knows me better than anyone else. "Everything I knew and was sure of was a lie."

"That doesn't mean you are," another voice says.

I turn my head and see Moeder Heelal approaching as if she entered through the mouth of the cave. Sisay jumps up at hearing the voice, staring down at the glowing figure in the distance. She removes the blade she keeps on her thigh, just like I used to and taught her to do. "Who's there?"

"Sisay, relax. You can't hurt her."

"Shank and twist, mother. Shank and twist." Sisay moves into a defensive stance with her legs wide and her dominant hand just off to the side of her torso.

I move to her quickly, placing my hand on top of hers that holds the blade. "You don't want to offend Moeder Heelal."

This is when Moeder Heelal steps into the low light of the cave. She's taking on a more mortal-like appearance from the shoulders up, though the rest of her body still shines from the stars within it. Sisay returns the blade, but she's not completely at ease.

"Can we trust her?" she asks silently, knowing I would hear her.

"Yes. Also, she can hear your thoughts as well." Both Moeder Heelal and I chuckle.

"It is a pleasure to meet the reason this galaxy won't be destroyed."

Sisay bows her head. "Moeder Heelal."

"After all your mother had told you, I understand why you're not trusting. Hear me when I say I have no ill intentions toward your mother. I'll let you in on a secret. She is going to make this place better, and you are going to help her."

"I am?"

"You have a fierce spirit, much like your mother. And you're compassionate and willing to do what it takes to protect others, including your mother. She's the second most powerful being ever to exist. One day, you will rule this land."

"I will?"

"She will?" I ask.

"I'm the adopted daughter of a priestess," Sisay states. "How will I ever sit on the throne?" Sisay asks.

"You will see in due time. But you are right about your mother. She isn't as confident as she was before."

"How can I be confident in anything when everything I knew was false?" I ask.

"Forget everything you were told. The words of mortals and the gods of this world mean nothing, as you've learned. Your confidence rests within yourself. Even as a mortal, you had the power to control your destiny. You believed in what you were doing and gave it your all. You didn't question yourself and your actions. Don't question them now. The world around you can go up in flames, but the confidence within you should never waver. You have no control over their misleading you all your life."

Everything she said is easier said than done. Yes, I did everything right, but those right decisions were based on falsehoods. Falsehoods that I then taught my daughter. "Did you come here for a pep talk?"

"I didn't. I wanted to introduce myself to Sisay since she'll be spending significant time with you here now. It is best she becomes comfortable with me while we train."

"What are you teaching me next?"

"What do you want to learn next?"

"This isn't my timeline."

"Oh, but it is. Nothing changes without your actions first. The Crown and Nthanda will continue to hunt you until you confront and destroy them. The Elders will remain in place, fearing you and Eshu until they're removed. Nothing happens without you. I'm just here to show you the tools you already possess to accomplish those goals."

"Is this what you mean when you tell me to always show up for myself?" Sisay asks me.

I chuckle. "It is."

"Well, show up, mother." She digs through her bag and pulls out two small and thin canvases and a reed pen. "I might as well record this history for the new world to come."

"You're going to need more canvases and ink than that. Perhaps a few reed pens, too," Moeder Heelal states.

"There's no way for me to get that from all the way up here," Sisay admits.

"Can I manifest some for her?" I ask.

"You absolutely can. Focus on what it is you want."

I straighten my stance and close my eyes.

"Eyes open. Always see what it is you are trying to do with your mind's eye first and your physical eyes second."

I nod and stare at the spot on the cave floor next to Sisay's bag. With my mind's eye, I visualize a thick stack of canvases similar in size as the ones in Sisay's hand. The canvases are not stacked neatly, and they pile up to Sisay's knee. Some have a slight bend to them, and others are straight. I visualize these details in my mind, to the point where I can see Sisay pick one up.

"Bless the gods. I mean, bless my goddess mother." Sisay says.

When I look at her, there is indeed a pile of canvases as high as her knee. I'm… amazed.

"When one sets their mind to it, they can do great things," Moeder Heelal says. "Now, do the other pieces."

Like I did with the canvases, I visualize them one after another until they manifest in front of us. Each time, it gets a little easier. Moeder Heelal instructs me to manifest a weapon, whatever weapon I've always wanted to wield.

I know exactly what I want. In the ruins of the old temple in Ginawa, the one remaining wall held the weapons and shields of our elite warriors. There was one weapon that always stood out to me. A pair of elongated throwing knives with three blades, two on one side and the third at the top. The hybrid knife and axe would cause multiple injuries with a single hit. According to Ginawa's legends, the blade-smith crafted the blades for throwing at the enemy, but one warrior, Bamako, skillfully used them as swords. I would have my father tell me the story of Bamako repeatedly as a child until I would tell the story along with him. Bamako never lost a battle. His downfall was a woman and poisoned wine. Oh, how I begged my father just to let me hold them! He said if I grew up to become a warrior, I could. As a teenager, I chose the life of a priestess instead.

After the betrayal of the crown and gods, I've become a god more powerful than the ones I used to worship. Once I take them down, I will be the greatest warrior ever.

First, I imagine the handles, made of gold and patterned like a snake tightly wound around them. The handles are long enough for me to hold one with two hands stacked on each other. Immediately above the handle, I can see the shortest of the three blades sticking up and curving away from my hands. I can feel the weight of the iron that is sharp along the edges and points. The second and largest blade is wider and longer than the first and is shaped like a long plantain growing on a tree. A third blade tops the weapon and has two endpoints. Bamako would swing the weapons down, putting the longer end of the top blade either into the ground to slow his momentum when running full speed or into the tops of his enemies' heads.

I twist my wrists around to swing the knives in full circles at my sides.

"What… are those?" Sisay asks.

"Kapingas. A mighty warrior in Ginawa had some like these a long time ago."

"You can cut someone in the head, chest, and stomach with one swing of just one of them," she says. Sisay hasn't taken her eyes off them yet.

I give her a smirk in response before throwing one into a cave wall. It sinks so deep into the wall that only a portion of the top blade and the handle stick out. Reaching out my hand, I call the kapinga back to me.

"They are perfect," I say.

"They should be," Moeder Heelal responds. "You made them just as you desired. Now, I want you to practice fighting with them."

"Sisay will not act as my sparring partner."

"You're right," Moeder Heelal states. She raises a stardust finger and points behind me. "They will."

I turn to see two starry figures standing on the other side of the bubbling stream. Looking them over, they favor Jata with a sword and King Gainde with a spear. Seeing images of them makes my anger rise.

"These are projections I manifested while you were working on your weapon. Now that you know how to manifest, you can bring forth sparring partners for practice whenever you want."

The weight of the kapingas differs greatly from that of the small blade I kept on my thigh. Yes, my father taught me how to use the blade and how to fight with my hands and feet, but this is completely different.

"Sisay, get back."

"There's a force shield around her. No harm will come to your daughter."

"You've thought of everything," I say in my mind. Moeder Heelal gives me a knowing smirk as her reply. Turning my attention back to the projections of the two beings I want to end the most, I take two steps back, and they get into defensive positions. I charge towards them, screaming as I jump over the bubbling stream. Keeping my knees soft, I tuck and roll when I land, then take my first swing at Jata. He blocks with his sword, and it gets caught between the second and top blades of one of my kapingas. I try to read my opponents' minds, but nothing comes to me.

"They are projections, Medusa," Moeder Heelal states. "They do not have minds of their own. All they will do is try to kill you."

Out of the corner of my eye, I clock Gainde's projection throwing the spear towards me. I jump and swing over the side of Jata's projection. The spear goes through him, and he perishes into dust. I land crouching down with one leg straight out to my side. Gainde's projection runs towards me and I towards it. Once again, taking to the air, I flip over his head, crossing my wrists above my head. The top blade of my kapingas touches the projection's neck, and I yank my arms apart, separating his head from his body.

I want there to be red and gold blood. Rivers of it, in fact.

"In time," Moeder Heelal says to me. "Yes, as a god, you are more than capable of taking down mortals with no problems. The challenge for you will be when you face off against the gods. Kemet and Songhai are much older than you and are confident in their powers. They are also confident that the gods they've created will do all to protect them. Be cunning."

"I can always read their minds," I respond.

"That isn't so easy from god to god."

"You can read my mind."

"I created the gods. I am more than they."

"You created me. As you said, my power is second only to yours. That alone makes me more powerful than they."

"Yes, but you are still young in your power and will go up against ancient beings. You can get up to par in all areas to beat them. Again, how long it takes will depend on you."

There is silence between us. We can hear only the bubbling of the stream and slight groans of the mountain.

"How will I know I'm ready?"

"When you can locate where Eshu and Nthanda are hiding, and can hear their thoughts, that will be your sign. Go after Gainde at that time. The first of the gods you'll face will come to you directly after."

I think about this. Looking for Eshu, who is also looking for me, gives me something to work towards. There is a question that's been burning in me since Jata left me in this cave. "Why is this the only way to go about it?"

"This is what you chose."

"Are you saying that, because I don't want to destroy all beings in the galaxy, gods and mortals alike, I now have to fight all of its gods?"

"That's exactly what I'm saying. You know how fickle mortals can be. You were one recently. The mortals in this galaxy, especially on this land, would never accept you as their sole god without you earning it. Wiping the slate clean would've been easier, but this way, you will earn their respect and praise. More importantly, you'll feel you earned it, which I know is important to you."

Sisay chimes in. "That is what will make you better than the gods we have now."

I look my daughter over. She always thinks so highly of me. According to Moeder Heelal, one day she will be queen. She'll rule this land and possibly have a family of her own one day. It didn't dawn on me until now that the thought, hope even, of Sisay one day burying me is gone. I'm eternal now. I'll bury her, her children, her children's children, and so forth.

The thought humbles and saddens me all at once. I look at Moeder Heelal, and she looks away. She knows what I want to ask her, but I will not do it in front of Sisay. Dropping my kapingas, I cross the bubbling stream, closing the distance between myself and Sisay in what feels like a couple of steps. I remove the reed pen and canvas from her hands and take her into my arms.

Time passes differently for the gods, and for me now. What will be years for her will be hours for me.

"Mother?" she asks.

I can't bring myself to say anything. Instead, I hold her close and wish I could slow time down or make her live a very long life. I kiss her hair before releasing her. "Stay here."

I look at Moeder Heelal and silently tell her we need to talk. We both transport to above the highest mountain peak.

"You love her, I know."

"This isn't fair."

"Nothing is."

"I was supposed to grow old and die."

"As long as this galaxy's gods stayed on the path they were on, growing old as a mortal was never your destiny. You heard Asmara's prophecy."

"I can't watch her and her lineage die for all eternity."

"I can't help you with that, Medusa."

"You won't, you mean."

Moeder Heelal sighs. "I will not pretend I know what you're going through. Nor am I going to tell you how to feel. A lot has changed for you—"

"Everything has changed for me. Why not go to the Elders directly, yourself? Asmara and the other demigods would still be alive. My life would've remained simple."

"Your life wouldn't have been anything like the one you're grieving. If the war had never happened, Ginawa would still have a priesthood, and demigods would've made themselves rulers of the lands. You would never have left Ginawa, because you'd be nothing more than a slave."

This takes me back.

"No free will. None of the little magic you had before. No Sisay as your daughter. You see nothing but gloom for your future, but this path gives you your most fulfilled life, even in watching that girl grow up and one day die."

Tears of frustration streak my face. *Was I ever in control of my life? Why me?* I just want things to go back to the way they were before.

"You're upset and grieving aspects of your old life and things that have yet to happen. Rest. Spend some time with your daughter. Work on your powers. Remember, nothing happens without you." With those words, she vanishes.

Chapter 21
Nthanda

"More. I need more," I tell him.

Eshu sighs. "My power takes time to restore, Nthanda. They aren't just given to me off the back of prayers like yours. I can give you only a little at a time."

Everything still hurts. There are still cracks and gashes along my body. The little power Eshu's given me has healed smaller wounds, but the rest seems to seep out of the larger ones. It's not enough—the power he's shared with me, nor his efforts to find

Jata's mortal. All of this is taking too long. "There has to be something more you can do."

"You don't believe I'm doing all that I can for you?" The back of his hand caresses my face.

I'm in no mood to suffer his love for me. Yes, his obsession with me is why I'm alive, but once I am whole and get my revenge on all who's wronged me, I'll do away with him, too. Never again will I trust someone after what Jata and the Elders put me through. Pulling away from him, I struggle to stand. "Look at me, all of me, and tell me you are doing enough."

Eshu takes his time looking over my broken body and finally bows his head. "If there were another way, I'd do it."

Looking at him with his head bowed brings his words from a moment ago back to me. *They aren't just given to me off the back of prayers like yours.* Maybe there is a way for him to restore my powers without giving up any of his.

"Bow down lower."

He raises his head and looks at me incredulously instead.

"Bow and pray to me," I demand.

"What reason would a god have to pray to another god?" he asks.

"You, Eshu, are the only being that can pray to me. I need the prayer and praise to heal." I can see the conflict playing out in his eyes. Gods don't pray at all. A god like Eshu, one who never lived as a serving god, may not even know how to pray. Not to mention, him praying to me places him in a position to be subservient to me. We gods are subservient to no one but the Elders, and that has ended for us. For both of our sakes, mine more than his, he needs to figure it out quickly.

"Nthanda…it may not work."

"We'll never know if you don't do it," I say. He seems to need a little encouragement. Suppressing my indifference towards him, I caress his face. Eshu's eyes light up from the simple touch. If Jata had been this obsessed with me, longed for any piece of me the way Eshu does, things would've been so different. I would've known happiness. Now, all I know is rage and revenge. "You said you'd do all you can for me."

Eshu nods and slowly bows at my feet. "To the great and most beautiful, Nthanda. All praise be to you…"

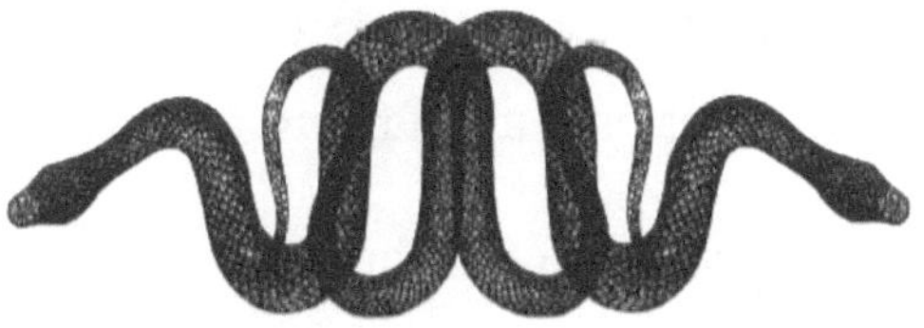

Chapter 22
King Gainde

I pace the throne room in utter frustration. "How many places can she possibly hide?" I snap at no one in particular, though Assir and the new warrior captain Jacana are in the room.

"The woods are vast, my king, as is the mountain range. Some peaks are so dangerous no one has ever climbed them," Jacana says as an explanation. "To be honest, many of the men refuse to go anywhere near the woods since the ejo nla was spotted in the village weeks ago."

"Then order them to kill it!"

"The men are not your accomplished father, and even your father could not do such a thing," Jacana responds.

"You don't want to kill the snake," Assir interjects.

I give him a livid look, but Assir raises his hand, his way of asking to be heard.

"Other than tales of death of man and beast, we know nothing else of the ejo nla. For all we know, it could be a creature of the gods' creation, or Moeder Heelal's. Checks and balances, if you will. It's no coincidence that it showed itself during a time of uncertainty with our gods. They," he points his finger to the heavens, "are angry enough."

Without saying it directly, Assir reminds me of my role in the uncertainty Joro is in. Now, several families are mourning their husbands, sons, and brothers. "What do you two suggest?"

Jacana speaks first. "Has anyone given any thought to the possibility of Medusa following the Tehenu over the edge of the land?"

It is a thought I had but never wanted to entertain. *Could I have driven her to take her own life?*

Jacana continues. "If her sin, whatever it was, was so great that it destroyed Nthanda and removed Jata from—"

"Jata's restored," I interject.

"His statue outside the temple reappeared, damaged, but it is there. The one inside the temple is still gone," Assir affirms.

"What does that even mean?" Jacana asks.

"We don't have a high priest right now, so no one knows," Assir answers.

"Should we shift priorities?" Jacana suggests.

I reply, "Both can be done at the same time. The selection of the new high priest doesn't require guards."

Reluctantly, Jacana continued. "Well, it would make sense for Medusa to be burdened with tremendous grief. Maybe she could no longer live with herself."

"She was very strong-willed," Assir says.

"Is. Don't talk about her like she is dead until we have proof she is," I say. The thought of Medusa being dead, my desires of us being as husband and wife to each other gone, troubles me.

Jacana states the obvious. "We wouldn't have proof of her going over. For all we know, the Elders could've dealt with her already, but—"

"Without a high priest to receive and interpret any new tablets, we wouldn't know," the three of us say in unison.

"Send some soldiers to bring the entire priesthood again, as well as the historian, and summon my wife. We didn't decide on a high priest before, but we need to settle this part now. Too much time has passed."

After choosing Accra as the new high priest and Joro's first female priestess, I visit my father in the dungeons. This is my first time seeing him since Nia ordered his arrest, and I refuse to let my three sisters come down here even though they ask about him. I stand outside his dank cell, looking in. His back is to me, so I clear my throat to announce my presence.

"I'm aware you're there, Gainde. You carry the distinct stench of a coward," he says, with his back still facing me.

"You will bow to the king and address him as such," Jacana states.

This gets my father to turn around. "You have a lot of nerve, boy, thinking you can talk to me in that manner."

I stop Jacana before he says anything more. "Wait for me upstairs. I'm fine alone." Jacana reluctantly leaves.

"You're going to be in a world of trouble with that one as my replacement," Baraka states.

"That's interesting, because I distinctly remember you saying he was a promising lead when we were going over prospects for the queen's guards."

"Hmph. So you listen."

"How are your accommodations?"

"It's the dungeons, Gainde. Everything here is worse than the poorest section of the Commons, but that's not why you're here."

"The girls are thriving in their studies and now have the title of princess."

My father stares at me with cold eyes. If he wanted to know about my sisters, he would've asked. Also, he knows I wouldn't come to the dungeons just to give him an update on them.

"Nia's with child."

I'm not sure what reaction I was expecting from him, but it wasn't for him to be so stoic. After a few moments of my father looking at me like he doesn't understand my words, he finally responds.

"Why are you telling me?"

"What do you mean 'why'? This is what you wanted. All you talked about in the weeks leading up to the wedding and at every opportunity after was me having an heir."

"Your having an heir secured my power, connection, and legacy to the throne. You and your wife have stripped me of everything, so why do I care?"

I think back to the day King Ahmose decided on a date for me to marry his daughter. My father sent a servant to tell me to get to the throne room at once. Instead of going, Assir and I hid in the palace stables, drinking wine. That was when I revealed my desire for Medusa to my best friend. When my father came into the stables, he slapped me around while reminding me of how hard he worked to get us in this position. *You will not mess this up.*

"Was I ever anything more than access to the throne to you?"

"An obligation, much like your mother was."

"Don't speak of Mother that way."

"Is your wife more than an obligation to you?"

I'm silent. Anyone who knows me knows I was not a fan of the marriage. Standing in this dank dungeon, looking at my father through rusty iron bars, I realize why I came down here, and I now have the answer I didn't know I was looking for. "Thank you."

For the first time in my life, he gives me a confused look.

"I thought you'd give me some advice on being a father, but I now see you've given me that all my life. When Nia told me she was pregnant, I felt dreadful, mostly because I was scared; unsure of how to be a father since I'm not doing so well at being a king or a husband. But you've given me the best example of how not to be as a father. I won't treat my kids as an obligation and just decided not to treat my wife like that anymore. My child will have a voice and be able to explore their interests. I will listen to them and be present instead of servants and governesses knowing them better than I do."

"You're a king because of how I raised you."

"I'm a king because you were hungry for power and wanted me as a proxy for your reign. I don't know who I am as a person, as a man, because of how you raised me. All I had was the expectation of one day being a king and husband, but no clue or guidance on how to be either. Your hunger for power and lack of being a father set me on a path to destroy this entire land."

"Stop being dramatic!"

"Joro barely has a god!"

My last statement echoes through the empty stone corridor. I rein in my emotions with a deep breath. "It should've been you who died instead of Mother." I walk away, determined to be better than my father was to me, my sisters, and our mother. In doing so, hopefully I can figure out how to be a better king. Returning to the throne room with Jacana, I kiss Nia's hand as I take my seat. "What are we discussing?" I ask her, Assir, and Accra.

"The number of men falling dead from snake bites recently," Assir says. "The coroner said he's seen nothing like it."

"It's Medusa," Nia states.

"What do you mean?" I ask.

Nia first directs her words to Accra. "What you hear in this room stays in this room. If I hear of this from anyone outside this room, you will join Kunle."

Accra swallows hard before responding. "Yes, Your Majesty."

Nia explains her reasoning. "The dead men are Medusa's doing. Nthanda's intention in cursing Medusa was to change her into a half-snake, half-mortal, eternal beast. I could see what she wanted Medusa to become as clearly as I'm seeing you now."

I follow where she's going. "Jata countered that, making what should've been a curse into a blessing. Instead of her becoming a snake, you think she now has the power to control them."

Nia nods.

"That is a theory," I say, not sure how much credit to give it.

"This is where your mother dying after your youngest sister's birth has done you a disservice. You would know not to so easily dismiss a woman's intuition had she still been alive. The increase in deaths from snakes being Medusa is a good and bad thing. The good part is that it means she is still here. If she were in the heavens, there would be a statue of her and new tablets, but what we know of the gods, they wouldn't accept her."

"And the bad part?" I ask her.

"If she is still here, that means eventually she will come for you."

I correct her. "Us. She will come for us."

"Oh no. Don't entangle me in your deceit now. I wasn't the one who tried to force Medusa. Nor was I the one who tried to curse her. I was merely a body caught up in your shared lust of her with Jata. Medusa has no reason to want revenge on me. But maybe I should do like what I hear the women in the common village do and pray to her for protection for myself and the child in my womb.”

“You only just realized you were with child, so she doesn’t know. Even if she did, she wouldn’t hurt our child or any child.”

“Never underestimate a wronged woman who wants revenge. That woman will do anything to exact her own justice.” My wife stares at me, and I can see the anger she still holds for me behind her eyes. I never apologized to her for what I had done.

“I’m sorry… for everything.”

The way her breath catches, and she moves back in her throne…I don’t think she expected me to apologize for the position I put her in. If I am going to be better and right my wrongs, Nia is the person I need to start with. She is right. Medusa will come after me at some point. It won’t be good for me, and possibly Joro, when she does.

“What’s the name of the common woman Medusa was friends with?” I ask.

"Zendaya, Your Majesty," Jacana answers. "We've questioned her, and a soldier watches her home. She's done nothing out of the ordinary."

I rise from my throne. "We're going to speak to her. She has to know something." Even if she doesn't, this woman may be how we get Medusa to show herself if the theory is true.

"At this late hour?" Nia asks.

"Waiting for Medusa to show herself isn't working. We have to make her," I say as I walk out of the throne room with Jacana following close behind.

"Trying to make her do something is what got us here in the first place," Nia yells at my back.

I tell myself that this time will be different. She wasn't willing to bond with me, but she'll do whatever it takes to save her friend. I'd bet my life on it.

"Fall in line," Jacana orders the rest of my guards waiting outside of the throne room.

Together, we march out of the palace and into the Commons.

Chapter 23
Medusa

Several weeks in mortal time have passed. I work on my fighting skills, manifesting, mind-reading, and telekinesis constantly. Eshu is still a ghost to me. Training is all I can do to keep myself and Sisay sane. She is missing so much time just being a kid, and it breaks my heart.

Every night, Zendaya gives me an update on what is going on in the land and what people are saying about me through prayer. I have no way of telling her I don't need her to do that. This time though, her prayer is different. She informs me she told her neighbor, a woman with an unkind husband, to pray to me. The woman, Sa-Ra, needs my help. I've interacted with Sa-Ra a few times before, but never for an extended period. She always seemed willing to speak but too timid to.

Not much later, another prayer feather floats before me, and it is from Sa-Ra.

Most favored Medusa. I pray this works as Zendaya said it would. She said you would understand more than anyone about righting the wrongs of men. My husband is among the soldiers ordered to look for you. The constant searching makes his temper flare more often than before. As his wife, I know I should pray for his peace of mind, but after years of him taking his frustrations out on me with his fists, it is only my peace of mind I care about. Like you, I never wanted to be a wife, but my family married me off as soon as they could. I didn't like my husband when I married him. I hate him now. Please, I beg, if there is anything you can do, rid me of him, whether it is my life or his. You will have my devotion either way. Asé.

I'll never understand the ugliness some people have in their hearts. Quickly, I decide exactly how I'm going to help Sa-Ra, as I've helped others. I call a gibbon viper out of its den near the base of the mountain and send it into the Commons. There it bypasses soldiers and homes as it makes its way to the intended destination. I'm careful to make sure people do not see it, as it is the second most feared snake in the land because of its lethal venom. No prayer to the gods has ever saved one of its victims. Typically, when gibbons are spotted in gardens or near homes, people attempt to kill them with a flat shovel or something else with a sharp edge to chop the snake up with.

The snake crawls into the home through an open window on the side of the house. We make eye contact with Sa-Ra, who is sweeping the front room. She freezes for a bit but doesn't make a sound. Unexpectedly, she points to the doorway of the two that leads to where her husband is. I send the snake in the correct direction, and it isn't long before I find the man at a table stuffing his face and drinking wine. The sight of him disgusts me.

The snake crawls onto the table and watches him until he notices it there. It takes a few moments, but when he does, he throws the plate of food at the snake, and I have it slither at him quickly. I could have easily bitten the man in his hand, but I want to make it more personal. This revenge isn't just for Sa-Ra. His face is going to feel more pain than he's ever given his wife. The snake strikes his face, its fangs sinking deep into the soft flesh. The man grunts, curses the gods, and then starts screaming as the burning sensation from the venom spreads from his face to the rest of his body.

To make sure he doesn't leave, and she doesn't enter, I have the snake move to the doorway. He yells his wife's name out of desperation. If I could make the snake talk, I'd tell him that no one is coming to help him, and this is the death he deserves for what he's put her through. Watching his thoughts, I can see he has many regrets. His overwhelming concern is how his life will be judged. He fears he's not done enough good.

It isn't long before blood trickles out of his eyes, nose, ears, and mouth as his organs turn into liquid. Before my change, I never thought I would take pleasure in the suffering of others. Now, watching him and listening to his silent pleas for help as he chokes on his blood gives me much satisfaction.

When he finally slumps over, most of his blood covers and drips from the table. Before leaving, I give Sa-Ra a look over. She drops to her knees, and her prayer of gratitude appears before me. I order the snake back to its den, and I bless Sa-Ra with an increase of coinage in the coin purse her husband kept in their room. If she does right by it, she won't have to marry to survive again.

In the last few weeks, more and more women have directed their prayers to me. Going from being the person to pray for and over people to now being the god who hears and answers their prayers is a head trip, to say the least. When people asked me to pray for them, I now know they held back the details of the situations they wanted prayer for. Being a god, the ones who pray to me tell me everything. I know which couples truly love each other and those who are with each other because there was no other choice; the number of men who have bonded with women in secret but refuse to claim them as their wives; those who just want more of equality; highborns who are in love with someone from the Commons that their families would never allow them to marry.

Life is not kind to women, especially in places like Joro and Himba. Unlike the other lands in the galaxy, the land of San is ruled exclusively by women, and women play a major role in the priesthood and households. My homeland is a combination of the two extremes: men and women play equal parts in everything. Ginawa is the only land to have both female and male warriors.

There isn't a prayer I don't at least listen to, including that of Queen Nia's. Apparently, one of her maids told her I've been answering prayers of women throughout the land. The queen apologizes to me for what happened. In secret, she despises her husband for what he made the first few months of their reign to be. She is now with child. Though she knows she needs to have an heir, pregnancy and childbirth scare her. If there is any way for her to have an heir and rule as she wishes, she is open to it.

I had been on the fence about the Queen since that night. I've since listened to her thoughts and know she had nothing to do with what happened. Revenge will be had for her husband's actions. Unfortunately, there may be some blowback for her.

I just need to find Eshu first.

Focusing my mind, I stretch my powers to search the edges of this galaxy, since he doesn't seem to be on any land or heaven. I know he is out there somewhere, plotting against me and the Elders. Initially, I thought I couldn't find him because he was using incognito, but then I remembered I could see Jata just fine when he was in this cave. I can hide from them, but they cannot hide from me. Just when I was about to give up again, I hear a voice.

"I've been searching, Nthanda."

"Then how have you not found Jata's mortal yet?"

Finally! The thoughts are faint, as if he is just outside of the galaxy. That is why the other gods haven't been able to find him. They wouldn't think to look so far from Muhabura, and Eshu did a good job in covering himself, just like Jata did in hiding me.

Now is my time.

I then task myself with locating Gainde, but I hear Moeder Heelal's voice in my mind telling me to wait. So I turn my attention back to Eshu and Nthanda. I find out more about them and their plans.

"You will get your chance to kill her and Jata."

"I'm tired of waiting. You've restored me to my power. Why don't we both go looking for her?"

"Because if what Jata said is true, she is the one Asmara prophesied about. We can't take on the Elders with all the gods on their side, and worry about Medusa—"

"Don't say her name to me!"

"I forgot. I'm sorry. But we can't worry about where she is and when she will attack while going to war with the rest of the gods. We must be strategic about this. It's just the two of us, not an army. We can't handle multiple battles."

They stop talking to each other, but I can hear Nthanda's thoughts. She plans to kill Eshu when all is said and done. She's suppressed her anger towards him for not telling her the truth about her parents sooner or defending them. Much like Moeder Heelal's initial plan, Nthanda wants to destroy everything in the galaxy, mortals and gods alike, and create a world that will give her the praise she feels she deserves.

I almost feel bad for Nthanda. If she weren't so stuck on killing me, I'd assist her in taking out the Elders. It's a shame that neither she nor Eshu realizes they can't do anything about Kemet and Songhai without me. We could've made a great team if they didn't have such selfish motives.

A prayer feather appears before me. As much as I want to set about finding Gainde right now, I take a moment to listen to it. The sound of Zendaya's voice does the opposite of comforting me.

Medusa Untold

My friend and my goddess, Medusa. I need your help, and I need it now. King Gainde and his guards just left my home. The snake you sent to guard my home is dead. The guards put their swords through it before entering. I found it in my garden in pieces. They tortured and questioned me about you. The king wanted me to give you up. If you thought he was obsessed with you before, he is drunk with it now. They cut and burned me, and still I told them nothing of what I know about you. The king's captain told King Gainde I knew nothing, but the king did not agree, so they took my son. Medusa, they have Wambua, and said I have until high noon tomorrow to give you up or I will never see my son again. It is only because I know of your powers that I did not fold. I beg of you, whatever you are going to do, do it now. Bring my son back to me!

This is exactly why I got Sisay out of the temple and let her stay here after it became too dangerous for her in the Commons. If only I had done more to protect my friend and her son.

"Sisay, gather your things."

"Mother?"

I look her in the eyes. "It is time. Gather your things." We've discussed this moment every night since she's been in the cave with me. Sisay knows what is required of her, even though she doesn't like it.

Once she is ready, I take her hand, and transport us to Zendaya's home.

"What are you doing here?" Zendaya asks in a loud whisper.

"Stay here until the rain stops," I tell her.

"It's not raining, and the night sky is clear," Zendaya states.

"It will rain. When it stops, go to the palace and tell the guards I sent you to Queen Nia. Sisay is to become her daughter and you, her governess."

"You can't expect me to walk into the palace after what just happened to me." She holds out her arms and motions up and down her body. She has bandages wrapped around her arms and legs.

"You won't have to worry about the king or his guards."

"They live there!"

"Do you trust me to reunite you with your son?"

Zendaya takes a deep breath. "Of course you do. You heard my prayer."

"Okay. You will do so at the palace, and it will become your home."

She nods. I give Sisay another hug.

"Are you sure about this?" she asks.

"It is the only way." I know what she is really asking me. She knows what is to come. Sisay worries I will change after doing this. She has every right to worry, but she doesn't realize the change has already happened. I've kept my anger hidden from her. "I don't know how long it will be, but I will see you as soon as I can."

She nods, and her tear-streaked face nearly breaks me.

"Take care of each other," I tell them before transporting high in the sky.

Chapter 24
Medusa

With the galaxy's largest moon, Benin, at my back, I watch Gainde and a dozen of his guard as they cross the bridge over the Tehenu. After reaching the courtyard, Gainde orders the guard carrying a crying Wambua into the palace. The rest of the men he lectures about how important it is they find me, and they need to search deeper into the woods and higher into the mountains. I wait until the child is safely inside before yelling his name. He and his men all turn one way and another, trying to find where the voice is coming from.

After a bit, one of them yells. "In the sky!"

Upon recognizing me, the guards surround the king, with most of them in front of him and less than a handful at his back. The thoughts of the men nearly make me laugh.

How does she fly?

Her eyes. Look at her eyes!

I didn't kiss the kids before leaving today.

Her sin has turned her into a witch!

I hoped she'd thrown herself over the edge.

What my wife said is true: Medusa is a god now.

Though I am too far away, one throws his spear towards me. When it reaches its highest point, I stop the spear, turn it around, and drive it into the man who threw it. Two of his guards break file and run into the palace. One goes to his meager chambers to hide; the other goes to the throne room to inform Queen Nia. I hear her as she orders him to rally more soldiers, but leave her guards with her.

"You're hurting people to get to me now?" I ask him.

"You're here, so it worked."

"What did you think you were going to get from facing me? You are aware of what Jata and Nthanda did. What they tried to transform me into. If it weren't for Moeder Heelal getting to me first, who knows if I would have survived?"

"I had nothing to do with that part."

"Your lust made me accessible to Jata. You had no regard for my wishes. All you cared about was forcing me to be your wife. Jata and Nthanda wouldn't have gotten to me if it weren't for your lack of control and ego."

"Medusa, I'm—"

The sound of trumpets cut him off. Soldiers all over the Proper scurry out of their beds, grabbing their uniforms, shields, and swords. After the trumpeter in the Commons hears the trumpets in the Proper, he, too, rushes out of bed to sound his alarm for the soldiers there.

When the trumpets stop, hundreds of men stand in uniform, ready to take down the threat that is me. All stand ready with their spears or swords pointed toward me in the sky. There are even men with bows and arrows on top of the palace.

"If you don't want to die tonight, put down your weapons and go home."

"Hold!" Jacana orders. None of the men move.

"It doesn't have to be this way, Medusa," Gainde says.

"It didn't have to be, but this is of your doing."

Suddenly, a soldier standing near the river is snatched into the current. The pauses in his screams indicate the number of times his head goes under the water. Eventually, they stop altogether. Another scream, but this time it is from the courtyard. One would think the man is on fire the way he carries on.

"Medusa, please," Gainde begs.

"Snakes!" a soldier yells. "Snakes everywhere!"

While I was holding their attention, every snake in the land made its way to surround the guards and soldiers. Poisonous snakes sink their fangs into flesh, and constrictors snatch and squeeze.

"Protect the king!" Jacana yells.

The king's guards form a tighter circle around Gainde as the soldiers in the outer perimeter swing their swords and spears at the snakes.

"Archers! Aim at Medusa!" Jacana orders.

Just then, there is a large rumble, and the temple falls as the ejo nla bursts through it. The snake releases a mighty hiss. Some soldiers are so scared that they pass out. Others who fall do so because of the venom from other snakes doing its work.

"Aim at the ejo nla!" Gainde yells. "Aim at the ejo nla."

Confused about their orders, some archers aim at me, and others aim at the ejo nla. The arrows don't penetrate the thick black scales of the ejo nla, while I redirect the spears coming towards me to soldiers below.

The ejo nla takes a mouthful of soldiers into its giant mouth, raises high in the air and throws them down hard. As the snakes make work of the soldiers, I take joy in the fear building in Gainde. The painful destruction happening around him sends his mind into a frenzy. Soldiers and guards stumble around, bleeding from every orifice. Others' bones snap and their eyes pop out of their skulls from being crushed by the pythons. The ejo nla makes a snack of a few.

The young king has never heard grown men trained to fight scream like this. He loses his stomach at the sight before him. Nia and her guards appear on the palace steps. She orders them to stay back with her. This isn't her fight.

Rain falls from the sky, starting slowly, but then going to a steady downpour. Gainde's numbers dwindle as he regrets his actions that night. I hear him wishing he had never been born. This changes my plans with him slightly.

"I planned on killing you tonight," I tell him.

The archers release another round of arrows towards the snakes, but I turn the arrows around on them. The courtyard, bridge, and riverbanks are full of dead bodies, men and snakes alike, and blood mixed with rainwater. Constrictor snakes make meals of those not killed by venom.

Gainde turns in a slow circle, taking in the consequences of his actions. He is not the overconfident king who was sure he would have me as his wife. What stands before me is broken, a shadow of his former self.

"What are you waiting for?" he asks me.

"For several fortnights, I've thought of killing you. The number of ways which I would do it, trying to determine which one would give me the most satisfaction. One thought was to have a snake force its way inside your backside, but why make a snake suffer that way? Now I see there is a better, deeper way to hurt you. You will live for now."

"What do you mean?"

"Your dynasty shall end with you. From this moment forward, your seed will be like poison to the womb of any female who has the misfortune of lying with you. You shall have no heir. Your sisters will marry into other lands and be fruitful there but will never find happiness as long as they live in Joro and with you." I look at Nia. "This has nothing to do with you."

She doubles over in pain and screams at the top of her lungs as the now poisonous seed within her ravages her womb, making it no more. Once again, she is a bystander caught in the middle of her husband's mess. By the time her guards pick her up, she's already bled out the child from her womb.

Turning my attention back to Gainde, "Never will you know the joys of parenthood, as you have taken away mine." Gainde falls to his knees as he struggles to breathe from the pain of having the inner workings of his manhood ripped apart.

I can hear the thoughts of the highborns and servants who live in the Proper. Many of them are watching the happenings in the courtyard from the safety of their homes or balconies of the palace. Even prisoners in the dungeon can hear that something is happening. Though they can see streaks of light in the sky, they can't see what is causing them.

As the queen's guards carry her inside and Gainde is forced to make his way on his own, I sense two beings rushing towards me. The ejo nla senses it too, as he hisses in the direction the beings are coming from. Moeder Heelal said they would come soon after I attacked Gainde. She's been right about everything so far.

"Reveal yourselves," I demand, with my hand pointed in their direction.

Eshu and Nthanda come to a stop as I see them. My ability to disengage their incognito gives them pause.

"Not even the Elders can do that," Eshu thinks.

"No, they cannot," I respond out loud. "Why don't you tell me more about them, Eshu?"   "We are here to take you to them," Nthanda lies.

"Why would you take me to the ones who think they killed you and are responsible for the death of your parents?"

Their eyes grow wide.

"Yes, I know about that. Just like I know, you two are here to destroy me."

Eshu is having second thoughts. "You are beyond capable of what any demigod could ever do."

"That's because I'm more than a demigod. In fact, I'm more than either of you, but you already know that, Eshu."

"Blasphemy!" Nthanda yells.

Nthanda rushes towards me, and I manifest my kapingas. My weapons come to me quickly thanks to the practice I've done. She manifests two gold swords that leave trails of golden streaks across the sky as she rushes forward. Nthanda brings the swords above her head and swings them down, crossing each other. I raise my kapingas to block. The clash of our weapons sends a shockwave throughout the land. In the distance, I can see damage to some rooftops in the Commons.

With our weapons locked together, Nthanda puts much effort into making me give in. I smirk at her when she realizes I'm not putting much effort in at all, and she screams. Her frustration is my opportunity. Using my kapingas, I throw her back. She flips through the air until she catches herself.

"I served you faithfully!" I yell. "You saw what the king wanted to do to me. You knew of your husband's lust, and you did nothing to stop either of them. Instead of helping your most faithful servant, you cursed me!"

"You made Jata lust for you, with all of your obedience, supplication, and submission," Nthanda says.

"None of it was for his lust! It was for your glory and the glory of the Elders and Moeder Heelal. All of you betrayed me!"

"Don't act like you didn't enjoy having the admiration of every man in Joro, including the king and its god!"

Immediately, she charges towards me again. I take a defensive stance, holding my kapingas out to my sides. The polished iron of the blades glows in the moonlight. Nthanda jumps higher, and I chase after her. We clash again, but this time we keep swinging our weapons. Nthanda is good with her swords, and I'm grateful to Moeder Heelal for encouraging me to practice. She was right. I wouldn't have been able to beat Nthanda or any other god if I'd gone after them right after my change.

Silver and gold continue to clash in the night sky until Nthanda cuts my arm. Gold blood drips from the wound, and Nthanda smiles. "See, I can kill you."

The smile doesn't last long as the wound heals itself quickly. That is something the gods cannot do.

"You need to try much harder than that," I reply.

This time I charge towards Nthanda, but I throw one of my kapingas at her, transport directly behind her, and take her by her arm. I swing her around twice before my weapon sinks into her body, with almost all the blades landing in her torso. Nthanda's frail metaphysical body hangs in the dark sky, nearly limp. Like Gainde, she refuses to admit her wrongdoing. She stares at me with anger and regret in her eyes. "You know, I tried to kill you some time ago with the fever plague, but Jata kept you safe. I should've killed you in the temple that night."

"You're right. You should have. Because you didn't, this will be the end of you. It will be the end of all of you." Taking the second kapinga, I push it into her back until it comes out of her torso. Gold light breaks through the cuts in her body until she dissolves into dust.

Eshu tries to get away, but I command his body to freeze. "Don't move."

"I didn't do this to you, demigod."

I move his body closer to me. "My name is Medusa."

"Medusa, yes, Medusa. I'm not the one you have a problem with."

"No, but you didn't speak up when the Elders killed Asmara, Kinshasa, and Malabo. You did their bidding, tracking and killing innocent demigods. You are part of the system that allowed all of this to happen. All of you are going to pay. First, you are going to take me to Muhabura."

Before we leave, I order the rain to stop.

Chapter 25
King Gainde

Inside my quarters, I feel shattered on the inside. Rejected by the wife I never wanted, the wife I wanted taking everything I never knew I wanted from me, losing my first child before it was born, and my seed never producing a child again. Just hours ago, I started caring about something other than myself, the dynasty that my father talked about so often, and now it is gone.

Even as king, I can't place my little sisters into the line of succession thanks to Medusa's curse on me. Now, I will have to force them into arranged marriages like I was, but in foreign lands, and they can never return to their homeland. Not that I gave them much of my time in the first place, but now I'll never see them again.

I'm a failure as a king, a son, a brother, and a husband.

Nia.

I feel guilty for feeling sorry for myself compared to what my wife and queen must feel. Her womb was full of life when the day started, and now…it's not. And it will never hold life again. I need to go to her, but what am I going to do, or say? This is all my fault.

You've cursed us all.

Assir's words play in my head. Assir was right, I realize. I didn't *have* to have Medusa. Before I saw being king as a means to get everything I wanted, not as a position of service to others. I know I will go down as the worst king in Joro's history. *What will become of my home?*

"Your Highness."

"What?" I say without even looking up at the queen's guard standing at my door.

"It's Kunle. He requests an audience."

This is the last thing I need. He's been in the dungeons since he tried to go back on our deal. As much as I would like for him and everyone else to have slept through the events of the courtyard, I can't imagine anyone sleeping through that. Many lives were ruined because of my lust for the former priestess. So much so that Joro's army has been decimated.

It's weird not having someone or even a small group of men walk with me everywhere I go, now that all of my guards have perished. The dankness of the dungeons has increased with the rains outside, as much of the cobblestone making up the walls down here is now wet.

"What do you want?" I ask when I reach Kunle's cell.

"What was all of that going on outside?"

"The gods getting their revenge on me and then fighting each other."

"Jata and Nthanda were fighting each other?"

"Medusa and Nthanda were fighting each other," I correct him. "She said Eshu's name, so he was there, too, apparently. She was the only one any of us could see."

"Medusa's no god."

"She is every bit a god now. Has been ever since that night thanks to Jata." I can see the wheels spinning in his mind. He knows, like everyone else, that he hasn't been kind to Medusa since she's been here.

"And she got her revenge on you for that night?"

I nod.

"Well, who won the fight?"

"I didn't exactly stand out there and take notes, Kunle. For your sake, you better hope they took each other out. Both Nthanda and Medusa have reasons to want to hurt you."

"I've done nothing but serve Nthanda."

"You cleared the temple that night, remember?"

His face drops as reality sets in that he isn't safe no matter which of the goddesses remains. I walk away and go to see my wife.

Nia's chambers are quiet, except for her sobbing. The sound reminds me of the day her father died. The pain I've caused her since…shame washes over me. Her ladies surround her on the bed as she lies on her side; one is fanning her, another is rubbing her head, and one is rubbing her arm. Two are gathering up sheets stained with blood. When the ladies noticed me in the room, they bow their heads but avoid eye contact.

I don't need them making me feel worse than I already do. "Leave us."

The ladies rise and leave through the door that leads directly to their quarters with their heads down. With slow strides, I walk over to the bed. I touch her hair, and Nia swats my arm away.

My words will never be enough, but I want to apologize. I regret all the times I ran from being in her presence and how I treated Nia in the years before our marriage. Though she did a phenomenal job at hiding it, Nia is a very capable woman.

"Nia."

She doesn't respond, but she stops crying. The silence makes the tension in the room thick. She asks me a one-word question that I don't hear clearly.

"What was that?" I ask.

"Why?" she repeats. Nia lifts her head and looks me in the eye for the first time since we were in the throne room planning a festival to distract everyone from recent events. "Why did you have to have her?"

My mouth opens and closes multiple times. "I didn't know you were everything that you've shown yourself to be."

Nia stares at me. "When my body began developing, my father ordered me to dress in fabrics that draped over or from a wide collar to hide my body. Was that it? You couldn't see the shape of my body like you could hers? Or were you like so many others who thought of her as the most beautiful in all the land? Because you avoided me like a sickness throughout our betrothal!"

I can't say anything. Everything Nia is saying is true. "I'm sorry."

"That is probably the first completely honest thing you've ever said to me."

Silence fills the room once again.

"As you know," Nia says, "I never wanted a husband… at least not long term. In the months before his death, I begged my father to call the engagement off and to let me rule on my own. 'Rulers are to bear the burden in pairs,' he said. That was how the Elders and serving gods rule and it was time for Joro to get back to that."

"I remember you mentioning it the morning of his funeral."

With a hoarse voice she continues. "As far as I'm concerned, the only thing you men are good for is providing the seed needed to procreate. That was the only thing I wanted a husband for."

"Nia."

"Stop saying my name like you want me to consider you when you had no consideration of me in your pursuit of Medusa! If you had left her alone, my womb would not be bare!"

"I didn't know that Jata would—"

"If it weren't for you, the land I rule would have gods and wouldn't be in turmoil with the Elders. Joro would still have an army. When the other lands find out about this, and they will thanks to the merchants who come here from their lands, we'd have no way to defend ourselves. My throne and home could be gone in an instant, all because of you! If it weren't for you, I would still have a chance at being a mother!"

"Nia, I'm sor—"

Chapter 26
Queen Nia

His voice and apologies do nothing but anger me. Before Gainde can finish his next one, I pull a dagger from under my pillow and slash his throat. He didn't know I was holding onto it the entire time. When the soldier reported to me that Gainde had gone to the dungeons to see Kunle, I asked him for his dagger. There was no way I could let my husband live after what he's caused, king or not.

Gainde's body remains sitting up as his blood splatters onto my face and body for a few moments before collapsing into my lap. I lie back and let his blood fill my bed until it cools. I now understand why my father did what he did to my mother. There is a limit to how much betrayal one can take. I'm grateful he raised me as his own despite the doubt. Only, I wish I'd killed Gainde sooner to mitigate some of the damage that's happened since our marriage. If other lands find out Joro no longer has an army, we're doomed. I need to come up with a plan, but first, Gainde's body needs to be disposed of.

I call my guards. "Burn his body."

"Your Majesty?" the guard asks.

"Burn it. Neither his body nor his soul deserves a king's burial or to be rewarded. Even his soul wandering around, lost in the galaxy for all of eternity, isn't punishment enough for the waste of an existence he was."

"As you wish."

"Also," I say, "send notice to the land of Himba that four Joroan royals require refuge posthaste. They will have means. They just need to be placed according to their station. Release Baraka. Have his coffers returned to him, as well as his daughters. Take them all to the galaxy way and assign two of my guards to accompany them there to ensure they are received accordingly. Make it clear to Baraka that if he ever returns to Joro, he will join his son shortly thereafter."

"Yes, my queen."

"One more thing. Awaken the executioner and bring Kunle to the throne room. I'll be there shortly."

"Yes. Would you like me to summon your ladies to clean you up and change your dress?"

I stand and look down at my blood-soaked nightdress. "That won't be necessary. My attire is most appropriate for the occasion, I think."

When the men leave my room with Gainde's body, I get down on my knees to pray.

"Goddess Medusa, by my very hands, the king is dead. Though your punishment for what he did to you was great, he needed to be punished for his actions. Like you, I am innocent in what has become of your life. With that said, I ask that you not punish me for the deeds of the man I had no choice in marrying. Allow me to be a mother. Allow me to be a queen. As your servant, we can make Joro stronger than it ever was and show everyone within the galaxy that women are great and powerful leaders in their own right. I understand you see what you've become as a curse, but I see it as a blessing, and I ask that you find it within yourself to do the same, for it revealed the wicked ways of both men and gods. Just as I would like to break the patriarchal systems here, please, I pray you, break them up above so that we both may be free. Asè."

Leaving my chambers, I take much pleasure in the shocked faces of servants as I pass them in the corridors before they bow their heads.

"Good, you're already here," I say to Kunle as I enter the throne room and he stands flanked by two men.

His eyes grow wide at the sight of me. "Your Majesty."

I take my seat and look at the throne next to me with disgust. "Have someone remove this at once. It is no longer needed. My throne needs to be repositioned to sit center." Assir nods as he takes notes. The shocked and then misty-eyed expressions that play across his face do not go unnoticed by me. He and Gainde had been friends since they were small kids. Though I've known Assir all my life, I can't bring myself to be concerned with his grief. My husband was no one to grieve over as far as I'm concerned.

"Is King Gainde no more?" Kunle asks.

"Don't worry. You'll soon join him."

"Your Majesty, I don't know what you heard—"

"Silence! I know all about your dealings with my husband and how they've led to the weakened state Joro is currently in."

The masked executioner enters, carrying his large double-sided axe. Kunle struggles against the guards in a feeble attempt to get away. The guards force Kunle to his knees. "Don't do this. I beg you! Do not do this. I couldn't deny the king!"

"Like the former king, your actions and greed have put Joro in a precarious situation. You've cost us gods, guards, and safety. The temple fell last night. There's been so much going on that I do not know if we even have a priesthood. Also, I don't have the men to search for survivors. Medusa was our greatest asset outside of the crown. I can only pray that she does not become our greatest enemy after today. For your crimes, I order you to death."

The guards bend Kunle over so his neck stretches over his knees. As the executioner takes position, I say a silent prayer to

Medusa to inform her I've taken care of Kunle and I request a sign of what to do about Joro's soldiers and priesthood. I end the prayer just as the axe separates Kunle's head from his neck. It rolls across the stone and stops at the bottom step under my throne.

A servant enters and whispers to one of my guards. He nods, and she stands in the entrance, trying not to lose her stomach at the sight of Kunle. As the guard approaches the throne, he is careful not to step in any blood. "Your Majesty, there is a woman here with two children. The older of the children is the girl raised by Medusa. They claim the goddess sent them."

"And they are here now?"

He nods. "Just outside this room, Your Majesty."

I have to play this just right if Medusa sent them. After what she's shown herself to be capable of, angering her is the last thing I want to do. They could be the answer to my prayers. "Have someone escort them to the Sitting Room of Honor and provide them with food and drink. Send my maids to my chamber at once. I need to change. Let me know once they are in the room so I can leave from here without them seeing me like this."

"As you wish, Your Majesty." The guard turns to the servant and tells her what to do with our unexpected guests.

Before he leaves, I tell him to have someone clean the room. "Let's burn Kunle's body with my husband's."

When it's safe, I make a mad dash back to my chambers. My maids are already there, and they have an elaborate gown picked out. "Let's keep it simple. The hour is late or early." Early signs of the sun rising show in the sky. "Another nightdress will do." Plus, I don't want to keep them waiting long. We clean the blood from my face, stomach, and legs before I put on a clean nightdress made of gold silk and lace.

"Your hair," a maid says as she pulls a matching robe onto my shoulders, "there's dried blood in it."

"Pull it back to hide for now. I will take a proper bath later."

They do as tells, and before long, I'm ready to see what Medusa will have of me. Walking the corridors to the Sitting Room of Honor, I am the most nervous I've been as queen. I don't remember being this nervous the first time Nthanda indwelled me when I was a child. Hopefully, I'll never have to be indwelt again. I've developed a foul taste of others carrying out their wishes through me.

"Her Majesty, the Queen," a guard says to announce me when I enter the room. The woman and older child bow.

"Your Majesty," they say in unison.

"Please stand. If the goddess sent you, then you are my honored guests. Have a seat." We all sit, and I can't help but notice the bandages on the woman. "Did my husband do that to you?"

The woman opens and closes her mouth, but she says nothing.

"It is fine. This is a safe space for you. I know he went searching for you earlier."

She still says nothing.

"He's dead. My husband, I mean. There's only so much a woman can take. If you have her daughter, I'm sure Medusa has informed you of what happened before."

"She did, Your Majesty. And yes, this is the work of the king and his men."

"You don't have to worry about them either." I can see the tears she is holding back. "Apologies. I don't know your names."

"Zen…I'm Zendaya." She places a hand on the smaller child, who's tied to her front. "This is my son Wambua, and this is Sisay, Medusa's child."

"How old is he?"

"Three years, Your Majesty."

I give her a smile and wonder if she knows how blessed she is to do what I can no longer do. Now, I give my attention to Sisay. "My, how pretty you are."

"Thank you, Your Majesty."

"Tell me, why did Medusa send you?"

Zendaya and Sisay look at each other and nod. "Medusa requests," Zendaya answers, "that you take her daughter in as your own, to raise as your heir. I am to be her governess."

Now, I'm fighting back my own tears. I stand, and they do too, as is customary, and I walk over to Sisay. She holds my gaze as I cup her chin. "You shall be my daughter, and I your mother. From this moment forward, you shall be addressed as Princess Sisay of the House of Ahmose. We will make it official with a celebration at a more appropriate hour in the coming days."

"Yes, Your Majesty. I mean…yes, mother."

A million thoughts play across her eyes. "What is it?"

"Would it be bothersome to you if I still called and referred to Medusa as 'mother'?"

I sigh. "Not at all. She raised you for a good portion of your life. I'm sure she will be involved in your life in someway. In fact, I'd find it odd if you didn't. Her arranging this shows how much she cares for you."

I give her a kiss on the forehead. "Now, daughter, I have a dilemma with our guards and soldiers. I would like to hear your thoughts on the matter."

"Are you referring to a lot of them being dead in the courtyard and along the river?"

"The bodies are still out there?"

She nods. "It looks like the constricting snakes also ate some of them. They are too full to move right now and will probably be out there for a while."

I shudder at the memory of having seen the snakes attacking the men in the courtyard hours ago. I never felt one way or another about the creatures, but I never want to see that many of them at once ever again.

"They aren't bad once you get used to them," Sisay says. "I have a small one in my satchel." She goes to dig it out, but I encourage her to leave it there.

"I don't care for the creatures either, Your Majesty," Zendaya says. "But I've grown used to their presence since Medusa uses them as her vessels."

"Hmmm." I nod. I don't know if I could ever get used to them. "So, about the dilemma. We no longer have enough soldiers to protect ourselves. After what's happened, I have a feeling few men will choose to serve as soldiers as their occupation."

"Women will," Sisay says. "I've been with my mother for the past few weeks. She's answered the prayers of many women throughout the land. If you follow Medusa, the women will follow you."

"A lot of women have lost their household's means of income over the last few weeks," Zendaya adds. "Especially after last night, Your Majesty."

"They will need paying jobs," I say.

"Mother trained me to handle a blade and sword. With one of your guards, I can train the women soldiers."

"I like this idea," I say. "Just so you know, having you as my daughter is the prayer Medusa answered for me." Turning to my guards standing just inside the room, "have the king's chambers cleared out and my things moved there. My daughter will take what is currently my chamber. Set her governess up in my old chambers from when I was yet a princess."

"Thank you," Zendaya says.

"I lost the child I carried today because of my husband's actions, but I've gained much more." Putting my arms around Sisay, I hug her close and give Medusa a prayer of thanks. "We will accomplish much together, you and I. I think you will find the life of a princess to be very accommodating. If at any point you feel trapped, let me know and we will work on that." The last thing I want is for an heir of mine to grow up feeling trapped as I did.

"Thank you," she replies

"Come. I will show you around the palace while we wait for the rooms to be readied. Then we can all get some much-needed rest."

Chapter 27
Princess Nia—Before Marriage to Gainde

Anger fuels my steps as I walk from the royal library to the inner palace where my father is. What I just read, what I just learned about myself, my mother, and my…

Falsehoods were told to me my entire life. Servants, tutors, and the man I've always known as my father. Now, I know why everyone reacts strangely whenever I ask about my mother and why my father never talks about her. It's probably the reason some people—mostly my father's advisors, my tutors, governess, and even the royal librarians, just now—look at me with disgust when I demand something of them. They all knew of my mother's betrayal and that I'm not the king's sired heir. No wonder he chose Gainde, a man below my rank, to be my husband. Father must have thought it the only way to secure the throne after he passes, which I hope is not anytime soon.

Not only is my fiancé below my station, but I find him utterly useless. There is nothing about him that interests me. Yes, Gainde is the son of our chief warrior, but he does nothing with himself and his time other than drink wine and flirt with servant girls and courtesans, most of whom he's bonded with, according to my ladies-in-waiting. He has no interest in government or ruling. His father, Baraka, wants the throne more than the one chosen to be the next king. No one can convince me that isn't why Baraka offered his son up when he was yet a child and I, a baby.

Gainde as the next king…what a joke.

I must talk to my father again. I have questions for him, and many more for my mother, that she'll never be able to answer. How could she bond with another man? She must have known it was treason. Who is the man she bonded with? All official records that once held his name are now blotted out with black ink, ensuring his name wouldn't be known to future generations; or known to me. I don't imagine my father let him live, especially after ordering the scattering of my mother's body parts throughout the land. Did he have other children who would be my half-siblings, or am I truly all alone in this world?

I don't know who I feel betrayed by the most. My mother, who was so selfish that she threw reason to the wind and left herself in a position to never be a part of my life; the man who sired me with her for being just as selfish as her by taking another man's wife and being so cocky about doing so with his queen; or my father for keeping all of this from me.

Guards announce my arrival into the throne room. My father looks up at me and smiles. Baraka and my father's other advisors look my way but don't make eye contact before giving me tight nods. Knowing what I know now, I understand why they've always treated me with barely contained disdain.

"My daughter, my heart," he greets me as he normally does. I don't miss the wheeze of his lungs at the end of his greeting. My hope for a long off transition of power fades a little more.

"Father, I must speak with you."

Looking at me, he can see the seriousness in my eyes, and he orders everyone to leave.

"Baraka," I say, "please stay." I don't want the two people who orchestrated my arranged marriage to have a misunderstanding of my feelings about it.

Baraka looks at me for the first time. "Has my son upset you, Princess?" he asks as the last of the guards and advisors leave, closing the doors behind them.

"Not at the moment," I answer.

"What is this about, Nia?" my father asks.

"You have always loved and raised me as your daughter." Registration slowly plays across his face.

"Whatever you've been told…I will have the heads of anyone—"

"I found out myself, father. I saw the royal record, the only one not changed to protect me from her betrayal." Taking a step forward, I continue. "You've protected me as your daughter."

"You are my daughhter."

I choose my next words carefully. "You chose me and raised me to be your heir."

"Yes."

I cut my eyes at Baraka, then back to my father. "Then, as your heir, I ask that when the time comes, you let me rule as such and not jointly with a man below my station."

"That man is my son," Baraka says, barely controlling his anger at what he's taking as an insult.

"And between the two of you, you are the only one who's achieved anything," I state firmly, before turning my attention back to my father. "Marrying Gainde, or anyone else, will create a new dynasty, not continue yours. I was raised to rule. Gainde was not."

"How dare you," Baraka barks.

"Know your place," my father yells back so loudly it echoes off the walls, along with the coughing fit he has immediately after. I watch my father, the great King Ahmose, as he picks up his goblet with shaky hands, takes a sip to calm the fit.

"No one should get a free pass to be king, especially when they've done nothing to prove themselves worthy of it."

The twitching I note Baraka doing with his lips lets me know he has a lot to say on the matter, a lot to say to me, but despite my being a woman, he does not outrank me.

"I don't doubt your ability to rule, Nia," my father says. "My doubt lies in everyone else, both in and out of Joro. There are those who will not only try to undermine your rule, but even remove you from the throne, solely because you are a woman. The land of San is the only one under the eyes of the Elders to have a woman ruler, and you are aware of the turmoil they've been in ever since their queen took the throne, which has been for longer than you've been alive. I don't want that for you.

"Marriage secures your throne. Marrying someone below your station, as you so put it, especially one who has no aspirations for the crown, secures your life. Gainde has no claim to Joro's throne without you. A prince with a claim to another throne would kill you for your throne and land." He pauses, as he does when he wants me to process his words.

Yes, San has been at war with itself for decades. Their last king and queen had three girls and no boys. The king left the throne to his eldest daughter, who, after just a decade of ruling, mysteriously died, and the next daughter became queen. The rumors are that the middle sister was behind her elder sister's death, but there's been no proof put forward. As queen, the middle daughter arrested her younger sister, claiming it was to protect her life. The subjects who do not support the current queen's claim the arrest was to keep the younger sister from doing to the queen what she did to her older sister. Though I understand my father's point, I can't give up without a fight. Neither I nor Joro are in the same situation. "Sanians were revolting against their king and queen prior to their deaths. Our people love and respect you. You can secure my throne with a decree. I will secure my life by how I rule."

"When it comes to the greed and ambitions of others, it won't be that simple," he responds.

Desperation grows inside me. "Father, please. I do not wish to marry. I can adopt an heir as my own from our land or have a maid have one for me."

"Do you not wish to marry or do you not wish to be with a man?" father asks me point blank, sensing there is more to my request.

Raising my chin, I answer. "Both. Though there is no woman that I wish to marry, either. I want to dedicate my life to my duties as queen and ruler of Joro, just as priestess Medusa has dedicated her life to the gods; just as you have after mother. My only care, outside of you, is for Joro. A husband would be an unnecessary distraction."

My father is silent, outright stoic for some time. Heart racing, I stand firm on my words and I try not to move a muscle. Silently, I pray to Jata and Nthanda that they sway him towards my cause. I just cannot be the wife of someone like Gainde.

"You know how I hate to disappoint you," he finally says.

I hold my breath because I can't tell which way he is going to go.

"But I won't put you at risk that way."

"Father—"

"I won't!"

Panic rises in me slowly, like a volcano building up magma. *Did he not hear what I said? He would rather leave, no give a spoiled man-child the throne, even in part, that should rightfully be mine.* Tears sting my eyes, but I hold them back from falling. I won't give Baraka the satisfaction. His smirk does not go unnoticed by me.

"You are to marry Gainde. The preparations have been underway for most of your life. Not only would this marriage protect you, but it would keep the people of Joro happy. To not go through with it after all these years would disappoint them and bring shame to Baraka's family. You are going to need Baraka's experience when you are queen."

Though I'm not looking at him. I can feel Baraka's smugness. I'm sure he is adding this to the tally of battles he's won over his lifetime.

"In fact," my father continues, "the wedding will take place two weeks from now."

"So soon?" I ask.

"Yes. I have little time left. The doctors confirmed as much this morning."

The tears I had been successful at holding back fall onto my cheeks, but now they aren't for me and the future forced upon me; a future I do not want. They are for my father and the future we will soon no longer get to have. *How much more wicked can this life be to me?*

"I will find Gainde and have him join us at once," Baraka says before leaving out of the secret passageway in the wall behind the throne.

I stand there looking at my father with hot tears running down my face. Taking in his face, I note how deceptively smooth it is. His hands, however, show his age with their weathered wrinkles and folds, and swollen knuckles.

"This is what's best for you."

"Your death is not what's best for me."

"Death is a part of life as much as air is a part of water. We've always known this day would come."

Time seems to freeze between us until he tells me to come to him. And I do like a heartbroken child. I collapse at his feet and rest my head on his knees. The sobs come gushing out like a fissure spewing lava. The wide collar of my dress drapes over makes the position uncomfortable, but I don't care.

He strokes my hair. We stay like this until my sobs go quiet.

"Baraka will be back with Gainde soon."

I get what he's saying. He knows I don't care for the father and son duo, and Baraka doesn't care for women. Standing, I adjust my dress and wipe the tears away from my face.

Father nods. "Ready to show them the queen I've raised you to be?"

Now I nod, and he gives me a sly smile. I stand beside my father's throne with a hand resting on top of it. A few moments later, Baraka and Gainde enter the throne room. I watch Gainde as my father tells him the news, keeping a passive face to hide my disdain.

He's not happy about the news either, but I'm sure for different reasons than I am.

I make a promise to myself that at the first opportunity, I will rid myself of him and rule as I should. He will not keep me from being the queen I'm meant to be.

Chapter 28
Medusa

Eshu and I ascend high into the heavens and land on the edge of Muhabura's fields. I've never seen grass so green. The wind moves like waves across the grass that touches my fingertips without me bending down. We stand between the Tehenu Falls of Joro and the Nzambi Falls of Himba. The Akan Falls of Ginawa and the Hausa Falls of San are to my right, with land in between them. The rivers look like liquid opal here, reflecting the various crystals that make up the mountainous Muhabura.

"You can get in from here," Eshu explains. "Just follow any of the rivers to Muhabura's falls and enter the cave behind them. The prisoner cells are on the lowest level. That's where Jata is being held, if he still lives. The Elders' throne room is at the top of the highest peak. This is as far as I will go. You can get far if you turn your incognito on."

"I won't be turning it on."

Eshu looks at me and huffs.

"No matter what you do from this point on, you know you are going to die, right?" I ask. His thoughts show he wants to run to save his life.

"I'd still like to try my chances."

"In the same way you gave the demigods you hunted and killed a chance during the great war?"

"I had my orders," he says, as if that is justifiable.

"And I have mine." One of my kapingas appears in my hand, and I strike Eshu before he has a chance to react. I leave him there to die and turn to dust as I walk through the grass towards the mountains.

Manifesting my other kapinga, I keep my guard up as I traverse through the unfamiliar territory. The stories I grew up with said there were trials in these fields. I don't yet know if I will trigger them or if that only applies to the souls of rulers.

"Moeder Heelal, are you here?" Hopefully, she's listening. I've not seen her since our tense discussion above the mountain a few fortnights ago.

"My child, I am always here," she says in my head.

"I never thanked you for protecting me." I pause, hoping she'll show herself. When she doesn't, I continue. "Because of you, I wasn't forced into a marriage with a selfish man or to play proxy wife to a god. My daughter is safe and will experience the best life offers. My friend and her son are safe as well. I couldn't see those things before."

"You were hurting."

"Still, thank you." She doesn't respond.

I continue walking through the grass, staying in the middle of the land strip between the Tehenu and Nzambi rivers. A smirk plays across my face when half a dozen gods come from the base of the mountain using their incognito. I continue walking as if I don't see them. Reading their minds, they think a group of just a few will fare better against me than any one god.

It shouldn't surprise me, but Kemet and Songhai still have not told them the truth about the prophecy of me and why the Great War happened. I can't wait to expose them to the gods who are waiting at the top of the mountain with their eyes on the fields, about to witness their fellow gods die.

Three of the gods walk the same mass of land I'm on, and the other three are in the field between the Nzambi and Akan rivers. I listen to them as they strategize about surrounding me.

We have to attack at once to not give her time to heal.

They all saw my fight with Nthanda. Good. I know I told Eshu I wouldn't turn my incognito on, but for the sake of putting fear into the gods watching, I decide to have some fun. When they can no longer see me, they stop in their tracks. If there was ever a time I wished gods had heartbeats, it was now. I want to hear their fear, like I did with the guards and soldiers moments ago.

Transporting behind the three in the same field as me, I tease them. "I found Eshu for you." All six gods turn toward my voice. Now, I transport behind the other three in the next field over. "I killed him for you, too." They turn again.

Moving to float above the Nzambi River, right in the center of the two groups of gods, I tease them some more. "Well, I did it for me, but I know you had the task of finding him."

One god shoots two arrows at once towards the sound of my voice, and I transport to the spot directly in front of him. Crouching down low, I wait until the arrow falls into the other field.

"Where is she?" they ask each other.

I swing up hard with both of my kapingas on the god in front of me, splitting him in half the long way. Instantly, I transport to the Nzambi River and wait with my feet firmly on the riverbed. When the three gods to my right get close to the riverbank, I jump out of the water with my arms crossed while turning off my incognito. Once my feet are above the water, I throw my arms wide and let my kapingas fly. They take out the two gods closest to the riverbank. I call my weapons back to me and charge to my left, where there's only one guard remaining. She swings her sword across, and I bend backwards, sliding on the ground on my knees and underneath her sword. As I slide, one kapinga takes out her legs. Her screams threaten to shatter the crystal exterior of the mountain. When I stand, a spear comes towards me, thrown from the other side of the Nzambi. Like I did in Joro, I stop the spear and send it back to the one who threw it. Only this time, I send it with enough force to go through him and the god behind him.

Standing, I take my time walking over to the legless goddess. "The Elders lied to you. They lied to all of you," I say before driving the crescent tip of the top blade of my kapinga into her head. Because I'm in their domain, I know even the gods in the mountain can hear me.

Jumping in the air, I float over the river, looking down on the two gods attached by the spear. After putting away my weapons, I snatch the spear out of them and reposition it in my hand to launch again. "The Elders do not deserve your loyalty." I throw the spear through the two gods again, hitting the first one in the throat and the other in the head. As they turn into gold dust, the wind carries them away.

I'm now halfway between the edge of Muhabura's fields and the crystal mountain. As I walk up, a legion of gods descends the mountain, like ants when a child pokes their home with a stick. Manifesting my kapingas again, I continue my slow but steady walk towards them. They rush toward me with a mighty roar, yet I stay calm. The Elders want to see me rattled, but I will not give them the satisfaction.

One thing that gives me satisfaction at this moment is that I can hear Jata's thoughts. Because he's slowly getting weaker with every step I take towards the crystal mountain, he knows I'm near.

When it seems the last of the legion has left the mountain, I pick up my pace substantially as I run towards the center of them. I throw my kapingas with all my strength, sending them towards the legion in a horizontal arch as they rotate through the air. They cut through godly bodies on either side of the legion as I charge up towards the middle of the pack. I laugh to myself. Being a warrior was my childhood dream. Look at me now.

I bulldoze up the middle of the legion, ducking the white light weapons the warrior gods hurl and swing my way. As the gods near me fall, I pick up their weapons and use them against the others. I send spears, swords, nets, daggers, and shields every which way. Gold dust scatters through the air as gods perish from coming into contact with either the kapingas or me. When I reach the backend of what's left of the warrior gods, I catch my kapingas. Setting my feet, I watch as the remaining warrior gods regroup and try to figure out a plan to take me down.

We must work as a team!

So many are dead.

Something's not right.

What is she?

She's just a demigod.

How does she seem to know every move we were going to make?

We stopped demigods before. We can stop her now.

More than half of us are dead!

There is something about her we don't know. We are missing something.

Our brothers and sisters. We are missing our brothers and sisters.

No one kills one of us and gets away with it!

They bark orders at each other. The gods are so lost in their emotions that they stop paying attention to the threat right in front of them. I create snakes, metaphysical ones that can attack other metaphysical beings, and I hide them in the four rivers. The gods finalize their plan of attack and get into position.

The tension is thick as the group of warriors stare down at who they see as an intruder and violator of everything they know to be true. They are so sure of themselves and their plan, they can't fathom perishing like their comrades. I wait until right after they give their battle cry, their signal to attack, to deploy my new pets. Most of the snakes jump out at the gods and coil around them until they too become dust. As I knew would happen, a few of the snakes perish thanks to the gods who are fast with their weapons. A second, smaller group of snakes jumps out of the rivers for an immediate follow-up attack.

Now that those gods are gone, I float over the lake that forms where the falls meet land before splitting into the four rivers, and I enter the cave. As I walk through it, I understand why Jata hid me so deep in Joro's mountains. The long, steep, downhill walk to what became my home is a replica of what I'm walking through. When I get to where the cells are, there is no bubbling stream or lava flowing through the walls.

I can feel Jata struggling to hold on to the bit of life in him as I approach his cell. His body is heavily cracked, as if he had just been in battle. Gold light fills the room as his essence pours out of his body. There's a force field that acts as a door to his cell. Placing my hand on it, I force it to vibrate so hard until it malfunctions and disengages.

"Medusa," he says as he struggles.

It disgusts me how much affection he puts into my name, as if we are dear to each other. My stomach turns as I look into Jata's mind, seeing how he watched me for years with unmitigated lust.

"I don't deserve your forgiveness, but—"

"You don't," I state. "And forgiveness doesn't mean your crimes against me will go unpunished."

"I know."

We stare at each other for a few moments before I speak again. "I killed Nthanda."

"Hmmm. My suspicions about Eshu were right then."

I nod and step closer. "I will not carry this hatred into my rule of the lands, into my eternity. The burden of eternity is too much to bear on its own. For that reason and that reason alone, I forgive you." I stretch my hand out and use my powers to lift Jata's weak form and pull him closer to me.

His discomfort grows, and yet I do not stop with my torture.

"Someone told me to see what I've become, not as a curse, but as a blessing," I say to him. He'd be dead already, but I force Jata's last bit of life to stay put, prolonging his suffering. He tries to scream from the pain, but he can't. "I'm understanding what she meant by that. The blessing is being able to give the mortals a god who not only understands them, but one who is deserving of them. Your kind has spent a millennium sitting up high while looking down low on mortals as if we were beneath you, while the entire time, your existence depended on the mortals. You all are nothing without the love of mortals, and you, Jata, took the love of one and twisted it into something vile."

"I apologize," Jata whispers, unable to use his full voice from the excruciating pain he's in.

"That's not what I want to hear from you. In fact, I don't want to hear anything you have to say. I want nothing from you but for you to cease to exist." With those words, I release the hold I have on his life, and he explodes into fine gold dust. I watch until the last particle settles on the crystal floor.

"Burn."

Fire engulfs the cell as I walk out of it, and the flames spread throughout the base of the crystal mountain. The fire will rid this place of the stain Moeder Heelal wants removed from within her. However, there are still more gods yet to kill.

Chapter 29
Queen Nia

It's been months since Sisay came to the palace to be my daughter. Since then, the people of Joro have buried the dead and cleared the temple of debris. I'm now standing on the foundation of what was the temple, practicing sword techniques with the first group of women who will become soldiers. Nearly one-hundred women strong, we face off in pairs against each other with wooden swords. I never thought of myself as a fighter, but learning and growing with these women has been exhilarating. Not only am I proud of my daughter for being right about this idea, I'm proud of myself for taking part in it. A queen should be able to lead her people in all things.

None of the priesthood survived the destruction of the temple, so we are once again without a high priest. If you ask me, I think that may have been intentional by Medusa. I don't blame her.

Thanks to encouragement from my daughter, we invited the rulers of Ginawa here to share how they get on without a priesthood. Shocked is an understatement for how they felt upon hearing that Medusa, a woman from their land, is now a god. After hearing the testimony of myself, Sisay, Zendaya, my guards, and some women Medusa helped, they believed. The lands of Joro and Ginawa now have a one-deity religion, and both follow Medusa. I can only imagine the chaos in Muhabura over this. After Ginawa rejected their gods, Kush's and Ife's statues vanished from their temples.

Sisay looks over the group as we spar, as she often does, along with the captain of my guards and a warrior from Ginawa. They shout corrections and praise as we battle our partners. A sound I've been dreading but partially expecting comes from the far end of the Commons, near the galaxy way by the edge of the land. The trumpet warns us that invaders are here and are approaching the gates between the galaxy way and Joro's crop fields.

Addis, the captain of my guards, climbs a nearby post to get a look. "My queen, soldiers! Looks like from the lands of Himba and San. Baraka leads them."

I spared his life for the sake of his daughters because I know what it's like to lose your mother at an early age. I believed they needed to have at least one parent, even if that parent was vile. Now, I wish I had executed him beside Kunle.

Baraka must have a wish to be with his son.

"Get your weapons!" I demand.

Trumpets sound off throughout the land as female and male soldiers alike ready themselves with spears attached to their backs, round shields made of iron, daggers sheathed above and under the arm strap of the shields, helmets, and swords.

"Addis!" I yell, as he is still up on the lookout post.

"The soldiers in the Commons are at the ready, Your Majesty."

"Let's go!" I respond. Addis jumps down as my and Sisay's chariots approach.

"Do you think they are ready for this?" Addis asks as we load in.

Before answering him, I look at Sisay as she and the warrior from Ginawa get into her chariot. She gives me a nod to let me know she's ready. "We have to be." It's the only answer I can give.

Sisay and I have discussed this moment at length. Homes in the Commons that were once occupied by families have become storerooms for additional weapons. All Joroans know to take the riverbanks to the woods and where to hide until they hear from me or Sisay. We even removed the Royal Galaxy Way from the palace, so no one can get inside our walls without us knowing. A lot has changed since Baraka was warrior captain here. Because of what he thinks of women, I'm sure he's underestimated us.

"Women of Joro, hear me." I wait for them to be quiet. "Practice is over. No longer are you training to become a warrior. You are warriors now! The time has come for us to defend this glorious land. We defend our children, our neighbors, our new freedom and way of life. No longer will we be subjected to the wills of those who think we are weaker because we are women. No more will we be put in a place of lesser than. A man who views us as nothing more than bedmates and baby raisers stands outside our gates with an army behind him. A man who thinks we have no army. He thinks we will run away scared. This man thinks overtaking us will not only be easy, but possible. Let's show him, let's show them all, just how wrong they are."

The women cheer in response.

Snapping the reins, I have my chariot race forward, with Sisay right behind me. We ride across the bridge over the Tehenu with warriors jogging behind us. I note a few straggling citizens who haven't made it to the woods yet. I hope most have made it to the woods already. We slow down as we approach the gates, and I put my hand up to let the gate guards know not to open the gates just yet.

Now it is time for me to address the few male soldiers we have. "Like your sister warriors, for most of you, this is your first battle. Today we make history. Today, we put on the most united front Joro's ever seen. Do not let what's on the other side of this gate intimidate you. We will defeat our enemies, and we will do so together!"

Looking up, I see our archers ready for my command at the top of the gate walls. I order the gates open, and the male soldiers fall in line behind the women as they line up outside the gates.

My and Sisay's chariots line up side-by-side with our warriors behind us. Baraka positions himself across the field in a chariot of his own. I watch disgust fill his face as he notes the double snake emblems on our shields that form the first letter of our god's name.

"You must have a death wish, Baraka," I yell.

"You've corrupted this land and that of Ginawa with your worship of the priestess," he responds. "Your blasphemy against the gods and the unnatural order has brought death to everyone who stands with you, unless they give up now." Moments pass, and no one on my side moves.

"She's not a priestess anymore. You call my order, my rule, unnatural when you stand there with soldiers from San, the only other land with a queen and no king?"

"I take it you haven't heard. San's queen and ruling class stepped down after my Himban soldiers and I talked some sense into them. Women get heightened clarity when the lives of their children are at stake."

"Steady," Sisay says to our warriors.

Like her, we know Baraka will say anything to get what he wants. His statement about Himba was not only to share information, but a threat to our women.

"All I have to do is go through those gates and snatch up a few of the children, and the women here will give up. The men will side with other men, as men do. I'll do the same in Ginawa after establishing my rule here."

I smile. Baraka has no clue what his words just confirmed for me and my warriors. He's not been there yet because he see's Joro as the weaker of the two. Ginawa has a king. Baraka won't go up against him without the strongest of forces.

"You'll have to get through us first," I say. "Joro!"

"Ha!" they respond and beat their swords against their shields twice.

Addis takes over the chant, yelling, "Joro!" Our warriors respond the same way they did with me. We fall into a rhythm, doing the simple chant repeatedly.

Baraka raises his hand and swings it down to signal for his army to attack. I stand in my chariot with my fist in the air for my warriors to hold their position while Addis keeps the chant going.

Sisay stretches her arm into the sky with her hand open. She does a silent countdown, putting down a finger at a time. When her hand forms a fist, the archers release their arrows. They take out most of the third and fourth rows of Baraka's army. The archers quickly reload, and Sisay signals for them to fire again.

"Now!" I yell when the first two rows of enemy soldiers get within reach. My first line goes down on one knee while the second line throws their spears, impaling several opponents.

"Forward," Addis commands.

Our first three lines of warriors charge forward, clashing swords with those too close for the archers. I watch from my chariot as Joroan women hold their own against Baraka's men. They are fierce and awe-inspiring to watch.

Blood sprays into the air before falling to the ground and mixing with trampled crops. The metallic stench reminds me of the early morning I killed Gainde. I did that for my freedom. Defeating his father will be for the freedom of Joro and the other lands in the galaxy.

The women make their way across the field, leaving dead bodies in their wake. Baraka deploys the rest of his army, and I do the same. Baraka, however, has hundreds more soldiers than I.

"Sisay," I say.

"Yes, Mother."

"Pray to your mother. Tell her what is happening and if she can't come herself, then to send reinforcements."

"You want her to send the snakes?"

"Our soldiers have prepared for a lot of things, but fighting alongside snakes is not one of them. Plus, they are hibernating during this time of the year. Let's save them as a last resort. Have her send Ginawa's warriors."

"Do you think she can get them here fast enough?" our Ginawan trainer asks.

"For Joro and Ginawa, she will find a way." Sisay answers.

Chapter 30
Medusa

A prayer feather appears in front of me as I make my way through the crystal mountain. Listening to it, I hear the clashes of war in the background of Sisay's prayer. Fighting the gods, I didn't realize how long I'd been away from her. Then again, time passes differently for gods. It feels good to hear her voice, but her message concerns me. If I wasn't already worked up, her message would make me feel that way. I focus on doing something I did only once in my cave. Even then, I couldn't hold it for long.

Breathing deep into my lungs as my body shakes, I create a projection of myself. The walking and talking projection transports to Ginawa while I continue walking up the interior of the mountain. My projection lands before the throne of Ginawa's king and queen, Khartoum and Juba. I grew up with them both as children.

"Goddess Medusa, it is an honor that you're before us," Queen Juba states.

The king and queen rise from their thrones and bow to me before returning to their seats, as do those standing nearby. "This is a projection of myself, but thank you for the welcome."

"What do you need from us?" King Khartoum asks.

"An army has risen out of Himba, led by Joro's former warrior captain, and they've conquered San and are in Joro now. Gather your warriors quickly. The survival of Joro and Ginawa depends on it."

The king stands and signals for the alarms to be raised.

"Thank you," I say. "I'd go myself, but I'm still tied up in Muhabura."

"Your will be done," King Khartoum replies.

"Only so many can use our galaxy way at a time. How are we going to get everyone there while keeping the element of surprise?" Queen Juba asks.

"I'll take care of that part. Gather in the field. Move quickly. We have little time."

The people of Ginawa move with efficiency. As I wait for them in the field, an earthy, familiar voice calls my name. It never ceases to amaze me how she becomes more beautiful with age. Her thick white locks are so long that she drapes them over her arm to keep them off the ground. I have my father's height, so she's been shorter than me for more than half of my life.

"Mama." I smile. This is the first time I've seen her since before my change. Looking at her, I wish I would've come home more often to visit.

Her wise eyes scan up and down my body, noting all the changes she sees like only a mother can. Her thoughts tell me she's worried about me.

"I'm fine, Mama. Better than, actually."

"I didn't want to believe what I heard, but it's true."

"It's true."

She studies me some more. "I guess I should bow."

"Never. You never have to bow to me. You're my mother."

"Are you sure you're okay?"

"Yes, Mama."

"And my girl? Where is she?"

"Sisay is healthy and safe. I wouldn't have made it through these changes without her."

"Goddess," King Khartoum says to get my attention. He stands before me with Ginawa's warriors at the ready. The queen walks up in her armor. "Oh, no you don't," he tells her.

"You're not going to stop me, Khartoum," Queen Juba says.

"I'll be back to see you as soon as I can," I tell my mother. She nods and blows me a kiss.

Waving my arms in a circle, I open a portal to Joro. We can see the battle taking place from behind Baraka's troops. I bring a finger up to my lips to instruct them to keep quiet, then direct them to go through the portal. I look on for as long as I can. Just before my projection fades, I spot Sisay across the field in a chariot. The ache I have to be with her and keep her far away from the fight ignites something in me. I need to finish what I came here to do.

Climbing to the top of the steps, I enter the throne room I've seen multiple times, but have never been in before, at least not in real time. Kemet and Songhai stand behind the six remaining serving gods. "You've known for so long that I would come," I say.

"Had we known you would cause all this death and destruction," Ife states, "I wouldn't have answered your mother's prayers for a child."

There is something interesting about Ife's memory of finally answering my mother's prayers after years of asking for a child. It's not something for me to address with Ife, but I make a mental note to address it later. "I was talking to the two who received the prophecy about me… before the Great War."

"Abominations do not speak here," Songhai snaps.

I smirk. "If I'm such an abomination, why have you feared me from the moment Asmara told you of me?"

"Blasphemy!" Kemet shouts. "We do not fear the likes of you. We created all that is, all there was, and all there ever will be. You are nothing more than a lowly mortal who attracted a god who forgot his place."

"You and I both know Moeder Heelal sent me here, just as Asmara prophesied."

The silence is thick and loud. There's nothing Kemet and Songhai can say to refute me. The minds of the serving gods in the room run rampant with questions about my statement and the Elders they serve.

Kush calls my name to get my attention. "Explain."

"Asmara did not kill Kinshasa and Malabo," I say.

"Silence!" Songhai demands while using her powers to mute me. Being exposed are her and Kemet's greatest fears. "You know nothing!"

I smile. "Still lying, Songhai?" The other gods in the room gasp. "That didn't work on me, by the way. Moeder Heelal showed me everything." I look each god in their eyes before continuing. "Asmara killed no one. Neither did she lead demigods here. Kinshasa and Malabo brought her here in confidence and out of duty and respect. Asmara prophesied about the end of the Elders and everything they built. She referred to me as a demigod. I believe because she had no other terms for what I would become, for what I am. Asmara told of a mortal forged into an immortal being by Moeder Heelal herself, who could create and destroy life, even the life of a god.

"Until then, the Elders used Asmara's gift whenever it was convenient for them. The moment Asmara foretold their demise, they unjustifiably destroyed her. To cover their tracks, they also killed Kinshasa and Malabo, and then blamed Asmara for leading a revolt, which of course got the gods ready to fight for the revenge of Kinshasa's and Malabo's deaths. The demigods never wanted a war with the gods and Elders, but the Elders created one with them out of fear of the demigod Asmara prophesied of. That is why the Elders started the war and why they forbid you all from creating demigods and interacting directly with mortals. Kemet and Songhai didn't know they were playing right into the prophecy. All the gods who died before you died believing their lies; they died in vain." I let my words sink into their minds. I can see the serving gods will need more than my words to convince them. The Elders aren't helping matters with their consistent denial.

"Lies!" Kemet and Songhai shout in unison.

I bring forth the viewing crystals, something only the Elders have ever done, and set them in place. "Show them what happened, Songhai."

The Elders' anger and the growing fire below shake the room. Songhai, proving to be quite stubborn, doesn't move. Reading her mind, she knows she won't be able to hide or lie about their actions.

"They will know the truth, whether you do so willingly, or I force you."

"I'm an Elder! The first creation in this galaxy. How dare you think you can force me to do anything!" she yells.

I sigh before moving her body across the room with my mind, then force her to wave her hand in front of the crystals. The events of that fateful day and the great war play out for everyone to see. No one can deny the truth.

"I don't understand," Kush says, still battling with the new information he has and what he's always known.

"There are other galaxies out there, Kush, beyond what any being could ever count. All of them have gods and mortals.

There is nothing special about the Elders. They are two of many. Eshu was the only other being to know the truth about what happened that day, which is why they kept him close to them and had every god not serving lands searching for him high and low after Jata exposed him. But Eshu figured out there was more beyond our galaxy's borders. That's why they couldn't find him. He was hiding just beyond their reach with Nthanda."

The six serving gods turn their attention to the Elders. Their anger is like what I felt the night of my change. Lies and betrayal by those who are supposed to protect you will make you question your own existence.

"You lied to us," Ife says.

Songhai directs her anger at me. "This is all your fault."

"To prevent this from happening," Kemet responds to Ife.

Songhai continues to ignore the others and talk to me. "You were never meant to exist."

"That plan went well," Kush says to Kemet.

"Save me your smart tongue, Kush," Kemet snaps. "Remember your place."

"My place? My place! I thought my place was serving Ginawa until recently, and, from what I know now, that was all a waste. The lives lost today, the lives lost in that war, were all a waste."

"This ends now!" Songhai shouts. She creates two short swords of white light and charges towards me. I spin out of the way and manifest my kapingas.

"A slow, agonizing death to anyone who touches my flesh," I whisper, casting a spell over my body. I want Songhai to make the mistake of touching me. Our weapons clash as Kush and Ife turn on Kemet. The serving gods of Himba and San stand to the side and watch, unsure of what to do.

The battle rages on for minutes, which is hours for mortals. As much as I want to check in with Sisay's mind, I keep my focus and energy here. Any wrong thing that happens in Joro will make me lose my focus in the fight right in front of me.

Grunts and the sound of weapons clashing and slicing through the air fill Muhabura, along with smoke and flames. Songhai hasn't touched me yet, and she's trying hard not to think about her next move, to keep from giving me that advantage. She catches me off guard, and one sword sinks into my leg. I block the other with my kapingas as it comes down over my head. The goddess of the gods screams as she uses both hands on the one sword to make me bend. Letting out a scream of my own, I shift my weight to the leg with the sword in it and swiftly bring my knee up to Songhai's torso. The force makes her fold and stumble back, allowing me to punch her in the jaw before pulling her sword out of my leg.

"All you had to do was change your ways and tell the whole truth to the gods and mortals who worship you," I say, panting.

"I decide what the truth is," she says after standing straight up. I can hear and see her frustration grow as she watches my wound heal.

"That is where you are wrong!" I charge towards her and swing my kapingas crisscross. Songhai blocks some of my swings, but others tear through her body. White light peers through her wounds as I keep attacking, driving her back into a pillar after knocking her second sword out of her hand. I put my forearm into her neck, and she places her hands on my arms. "How does it feel, Songhai?"

"What?"

"Consequences. How does it feel to face consequences finally? I am your consequence. If you had done right by your creations, Moeder Heelal never would have shared her power with me, which was then activated by Nthanda and Jata. I know you think they created me, but no. You and Kemet did."

"One mistake and Moeder Heelal will turn her back on you, too."

"Silence." I mute her, like she tried to do with me earlier. "Your rants and screams aren't necessary for your slow death." I take a couple of steps back and watch her as she slides down the column onto the ground. Songhai scratches at her face and body as her godly flesh slowly burns from the inside out.

I make eye contact with the four gods who've been watching everything. They fall onto their knees and bow to me. "Do you think that will save you, Mutapa, Nok, Medjay, and Twa? Do you think me that stupid?"

"We did not know," Medjay, the god of San, says. "But we will serve you if you spare us."

I look at them with disgust. Playing both sides for their advantage is something I've watched Kunle do my entire time in

Joro. "Die," I say. I have no reason to fight them or make them see the error of their ways, like I've done with the others.

There is one more who still needs to face their consequences.

When I turn to Kemet, Kush, and Ife, both Kush and Ife are on their knees, dying. I almost feel sorry for them. They were lied to and killed by their creator. As I did with his partner earlier, I move Kemet over to stand before me.

"Did that last victory feel good?" I ask him.

He says nothing, so I ask a question that's been burning me since Moeder Heelal showed me what happened with Asmara.

"Why?" I ask.

Still, nothing.

"Asmara had never been wrong. You had no reason to believe you could prevent her prophecy by destroying her and continuing on the same path."

"When you've lived as long as I have, being able to do and create as you want, you become power hungry and set in your ways. Hearing from a lesser being about your end will not sit well with you. Keep that as a lesson for yourself."

"Fortunately for me, I learned accountability as a mortal. You and I will never share the same fate."

He gives me an understanding nod, and I touch his face before he slowly fades to dust.

Chapter 31
Medusa

Rising above the flames and smoke that now engulf Muhabura, I can hear the cries of the people of Joro, Ginawa, Himba, and San as their rivers harden as Muhabura's crystal mountain melts, cools, and hardens in the rivers. The statues of the gods in all the lands that still worship them have crumbled as well. In the lands that had not already accepted me as their god, the people are worried about what's happening.

"You've done well, my daughter," a familiar voice comes to me. She materializes beside me.

"I am your vessel, Moeder Heelal."

She looks around at the foundation of the mountain and now crystalized rivers. "How do you want it?"

"What do you mean?"

"This is now your galaxy. You can set it up however you like."

"My galaxy." I haven't thought about this. Never did I think about having a domain, even after accepting my new status as an immortal. Vengeance and protecting Sisay have been my only focus. I think about how I grew up with the king and queen living amongst the people and the people living amongst the trees. We didn't need a priesthood because we're taught to have our own relationship with our gods. "That's not how I want to rule."

"That is no surprise."

"Was this worth it?" I ask.

"Hmm." She pauses for a moment before continuing. "If you had asked me that on the day I first called you to me, I would have told you nothing in this galaxy was worth the moments I took to create Kemet and Songhai outside of you. There was so much corruption, lust, and greed, I couldn't see the good for the bad. You've shown me there is still good in this galaxy. Good in the mortals and that they can accept change. Most of them want to do good, to be better if given the opportunity. It takes only a few rotten fruits to make the who bunch appear spoiled."

I don't have a response for her. I'm just glad I could get her to see things differently. There is still a matter we need to discuss, but she speaks again before I can bring it up.

"You may want to open up the rivers to the lands and get back to Joro now."

"What's happening?"

In an instant, Moeder Heelal is gone. Panic rises in me. Rising higher in the sky, I manifest my kapingas before flying like a shooting star into the hardened mix of crystals. My kapingas crack the thick shell that's formed, and the cracks travel over the lake and down the four rivers. Water springs forth through the cracks, shooting up high into the sky in some areas, and fills the rivers. Satisfied the lands have water again, I transport to Joro.

Chaos is the only word to describe what I see in Joro's fields as I float above them. What were once lush fields for growing food and raising cattle is now scorched barren land. "What has happened here?"

As I move above the land, I see that many of the homes in the Commons are black from fire. Some even still have smoke rising from them. The cobblestone bridge I walked over many times is now gone. Pieces of it stick up from the Tehenu River. Locating Zendaya's home, I transport to it and find it empty, as if she's never been here. "Where are you?"

I search the land with my mind to locate her and Sisay. Not only do I not find them in the Commons or the Proper, I do not come across anyone outside of the palace other than Baraka's army. Baraka is in the palace talking to a woman he holds captive in his former chambers.

"Mother," I gasp. Baraka's already been to Ginawa, and he's holding my mother as a bargaining chip. *How long has it been?*

Just when I decide to transport to the palace, something catches the corner of my eye. A thin canvas lies on the floor near a large vase. It looks just like the ones I manifested for Sisay when we lived in the cave.

Without searching it first, I transport to the only place that was safe for Sisay and me for a while. I hear multiple gasps and murmurs as people acknowledge my presence. Looking around, I see discarded armor, limbs, and heads with blood-stained bandages in every direction throughout the cave. The physical and mental pain of these people is great, but they are all thankful to be alive.

"You're here!" Sisay collides into me and wraps her arms around me.

I hold her tight and thank Moeder Heelal for my daughter still being alive. I don't want to let her go, but I need to set my eyes on her again. Looking her over, it seems she's grown so much in the time I've been away. I rub her head, face, and arms, taking her in. "How?"

"Sometime ago, I went to the woods and asked Moeder Heelal to show me how to get up the mountain so I can save the people. She sent the ejo nla. It took some time and convincing, but the people got comfortable enough with it to let it take them up the mountain."

"Clever girl. You are going to make a great queen someday."

Queen Nia, King Khartoum and Queen Joba of Ginawa approach. The king assists his wife, who is missing a foot.

"You could have warned us about that monster of a snake," King Khartoum jokes.

"It's a sort of pet of Moeder Heelal's and mine."

"Is your business on Muhabura done?" Queen Nia asks.

"It is. Tell me what happened out there?"

"Baraka lived up to the tales of his glory days as a great warrior," Queen Nia states.

I nod and listen as the two queens, the king, and Sisay tell me how they ended up here. Baraka is indeed everything people have said he was. He came to Joro with only half of his battalion. The other half used the Galaxy Way to get to Ginawa after we left. We assume they had a spy there. The battle in the field had gone on for nearly a week when the rest of the battalion arrived in Joro with Ginawan hostages, including my mother and Princess Imani and Prince Ismail, King Khartoum and Queen Joba's twins.

"Baraka gave us a choice of surrender or death," King Khartoum states. "Surrendering meant my children would live.

Your daughter convinced us to run to the mountains with them because you'd return and get my kids back. You've returned, so now what?"

Those who can, gather closer and circle around me. The rally of their hearts with me here makes a boisterous sound in my head. All of them need something, including healing of a broken spirit. Without saying a word, I send a blessing of healing to them all. Wounds close, limbs that were gone or barely hanging on reappear and are made whole again, and infections clear. One by one, the people and warriors of Joro and the warriors of Ginawa are themselves again. Soon, everyone is standing and rallying behind me.

"Thank you, Goddess," many say.

Others say, "How much more than the old gods is she, for they would not give such a blessing!"

"Iṣẹ́gun àwọn oríṣà." That is *the highest praise to you, goddess.*

The room fills with praises to and for me. There is a certain level of praise one receives as a member of the priesthood for doing the work of the gods, but this…this is unlike anything

I've ever heard. I can feel my spirit lifting just as theirs did upon my arrival in the cave.

I raise my hands to quiet them. "The enemy known as greed plagues the lands of this galaxy. This is not a new enemy; no, it was passed down from the Elders. Greed for attention, greed for praise, greed for taking life, greed for stealing dreams, greed for more of self. I stand before you now, after having wiped this greed from the heavens, declaring we will wipe it from the lands as well. The gods of old are no more. No longer do you have gods who sit up high and just watch you go through life. As your goddess, I will live among you. Today with you, we will make history. For the first time in this galaxy's history, your god will fight alongside you. We will take back our lands and correct the ways of San and Himba. Because you all believed in me first, I will bless you above others."

One by one, each warrior has weapons made of yellow and green light appear in their hands. Everything from spears, swords, double-headed axes, spiked clubs, long clubs, and war hammers, based on each warrior's specialty. As they admire their weapons, hundreds of small snakes come into the cave.

"Don't be alarmed. They are part of the blessing."

"I've heard tales of your fight with the former king here with the snakes. I can't imagine these tiny things are the snakes from that fight."

"They are not, but these snakes will provide you with protection, nonetheless," I respond. The snakes get into whatever space they have room in. Stretching my hands over them, each snake duplicates. They then climb to and up the body of every warrior and citizen three and ten years or older, wrapping around an arm and resting comfortably there. "Each snake has paired with a warrior and a non-warrior. The warriors have the original snake, and the citizens have the clones. This is your protection. Citizens, you will remain here where it is safe for you, but you must stay in constant prayer for the warrior with the original snake to your clone. Warriors, as long as your snake stays wrapped around you, no blade or arrow will penetrate your skin."

"This is an improvement from the one you gave me when you first sent me to Zendaya's," Sisay says.

"I've learned much since then. It appears we both have. Speaking of Zendaya, where…"

Zendaya approaches slowly, just as I'm asking about her. The wounds she had when I last saw her have now healed. However, she walks with the undeniable hurt of an invisible wound. "My friend." I greet her.

"Show them no mercy." Her mind replays a heartbreaking scene. Flashes of her running with her young son in her arms. Being the kind-hearted person she is, Zendaya didn't flee up the mountains with the rest of the royal household and villagers. Her love for my daughter wouldn't allow her to ride on the ejo nla's back without Sisay. So, she waited by the waterfall. Fed herself and Wambua berries and leaves until Sisay and the others who were fighting appeared. Baraka's men weren't far behind, so they all had to move fast. Just as the giant snake dashed up the face of the mountain, she lost her grip on her boy. He fell down the mountainside, landing on the ground a short distance away from the enemy. Zendaya watched as one of Baraka's men thrust his sword into her son.

When my eyes refocus on her, we both have the same tear-stained face. That young boy was innocent. Weeks before the death of King Ahmose, I healed him of the fever with a tincture and prayers. Wambua was a child who was happy just because. Now, he is no more. The pain she feels is heavy. "Let me provide you with some comfort," I tell her.

"Destroy them. That is what I will seek comfort in."

I didn't plan on killing all of Baraka's men. Looking into the grief-riddled eyes of my friend, I recall when Moeder Heelal first called me to her and made known her desire to destroy all life in this galaxy. Moeder Heelal was coming from a place of utter disappointment in her creations; Zendaya's request comes from a place of heartbreak and revenge. I can't help but wonder if that was what I looked like in the moments after the gods and crown betrayed me, or even to the gods as I destroyed them. I got my revenge. How can I deny Zendaya hers? What precedent does this set for me as a god? This is something I should have thought about prior to sending various vipers to end the lives of abusive men while I was practicing my powers in this very cave. The wives, sisters, and daughters who prayed to me would have said those men had it coming. I would agree. These men following Baraka, however, are merely following orders.

"Baraka will pay for what he's done."

"And the one who put his sword through Wambua like he was a rabid dog."

I nod and am grateful she seems to have accepted my compromise. While I go over the plan with the warriors and citizens inside the cave, Moeder Heelal talks to me in my head.

"You can always change your mind," she says.

"I won't."

"Look at your friend. There is so much corruption. I know I just thanked you for showing me the good, but now I'm asking you. Is the good worth all this death and revenge?"

"She's hurting, not corrupt," I explain.

"Your friend just asked you to kill hundreds of men for her one son."

"Her only son. You may be the mother of us all, but have you ever felt the pain of losing something as dear as a child?"

"Have you?"

"Don't you—"

Moeder Heelal interrupts. "I was merely asking a question."

"I have not, but I have something you do not. Something I gained as a mortal."

"And what is that?"

"Empathy. It's what you, the Elders, and the gods created in your name all lack. It is why you've destroyed countless galaxies in your time without a single word of correction to the gods or mortals. You let them go on in their treachery for millennia and then destroy them without a word, and you wonder what you are doing wrong."

"If I didn't know any better, I would think you're challenging me."

"You made me. For that, I'm grateful. In my time with you and in Muhabura, I've learned something about you."

"And what is that?" she asks.

"All of this is your fault." I let my words sink in before continuing. "Your hands-off approach has already cost a multitude of lives within this galaxy. How many lives has it cost throughout the course of your existence?"

She is silent, but I continue. "You had infinite instances where you could have corrected the Elders. In the same way they did nothing to stop Jata from pressing his actions towards me, you did nothing to stop them from taking the lives of Asmara, Kinshasa, Malabo, and so many other gods and demigods. Had you, I would still have my life with my daughter. You've forced me into a position to be hands-off with her as you were with me."

Silence again.

"That's right. I read Ife's mind in Muhabura, just before I fought with Songhai. It confirmed something I saw in my mother's mind when I projected myself into Ginawa. Ife said had she known I would've destroyed everything, she would have never answered my mother's prayer for a child. Only my mother prayed many, many times for a child. She was no longer of childbearing age when I was born. I was my mother's miracle baby. A miracle that happened because you touched my mother's womb and put it into Ife's mind to answer the prayer after years of ignoring it. The man I knew as my father is not my father at all. In fact, my mother was merely the vessel that carried me. I am the fleck of stardust you put into her womb."

Moments pass before Moeder Heelal says anything. "Yes, you are my child that I created. I could not give birth to you in the sense that mortals do."

"You can't create like you once did. You lost that ability not long after you created Kemet and Songhai. Mortals are taught you don't need our prayers and praise like our gods did, but that wasn't true. The lack of prayers and worship from all those who are under you, immortals and mortals alike, has weakened you. So has the constant creating, destroying, and creating again. You created me through mortals to do what you no longer could. The power you claimed to have given me was already there. You merely unlocked it before Nthanda could harm me. You said you wanted me to be like a daughter to you, when I am actually your daughter!"

"Your mind-reading skills have developed much more than I realized, and you found a way to keep me from seeing it. I've never been surprised by anything before."

"That's what your concern is?"

"What more do you want me to say, Medusa? I can't deny what you now know."

I'm not sure what I expected from Moeder Heelal, but it wasn't this. She's so nonchalant about me knowing the truth, but is interested in how I found out the truth without her knowing. No explanation or plea for understanding and forgiveness.

"Everyone, from you and the gods, has deceived me my whole life. Unbeknownst to me, I've been a puppet for you, the gods I served, and even to the former crown. I refuse to continue being used. I won't be your vessel of death and destruction. No longer will I serve a being, mortal or immortal, who lacks the simple tenets of humanity and expects those under them to be better than they are. Stay out of my way."

If she responds, I don't know it. I lock her out of my mind. Returning my full attention to everyone in the cave, I say, "Gather on the cliffs and ridges on the mountainside wherever you can stand. Declare protection over the warrior you're assigned to, in my name. As long as you continue praying and the warriors keep their snakes on their person, they'll have protection."

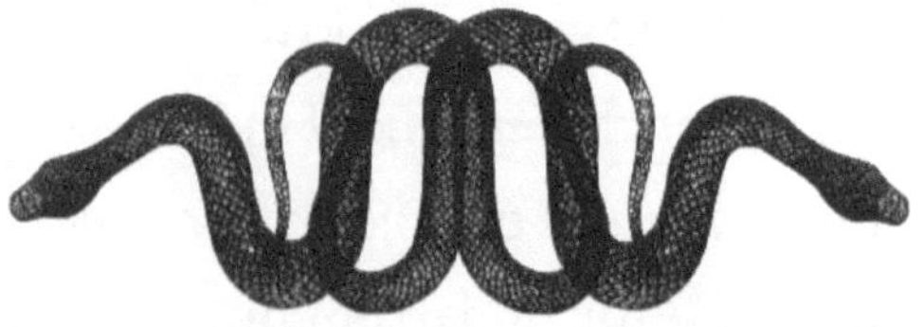

Chapter 32
Medusa

While everyone prepares, I search for the ejo nla. Either something has happened to it or its presence is hidden from me. I suspect Moeder Heelal has something to do with this as I can't imagine mortals taking it down. I need another plan to get my warriors down the mountain. Mentally, I scan the woods. As I thought, Baraka has warriors patrolling it. One by one, I transport one of my warriors to where Baraka's warriors are, and each time, his numbers dwindle. Once the woods are clear of Baraka's men, I transport my remaining warriors to just inside the walls of The Proper. They bang their weapons against their shields to get the attention of Baraka and his warriors while I transport inside the palace, first to get the prince and princess of Ginawa, and then my mother.

The kids are the easiest to get to, as there is a single guard outside of the chamber doors where they are and none inside with them. They are sitting side by side on the bench at the foot of the bed. The boy notices me first. Upon seeing me, the prince defensively puts himself in front of his twin sister. Though he tries to put on a brave face, his eyes and mind tell me he's scared and tired.

"I'm a friend of your parents."

The boy doesn't believe me. "I know all of my parents' friends," he retorts.

"I moved away to this land when I was of declaration age. Only for their wedding, your birth, the death of my father, and to visit my mother have I returned," I explain.

The princess stands and speaks. "Why did you move here?"

As I had hoped, my statement intrigues her and has stirred something inside of them. "To be a priestess. I had hoped to show the Joroans a better way to worship and have their own relationship with the gods, like we did in Ginawa."

"You didn't enter through the door," the prince states.

"No, I did not."

Both children, about four years younger than my Sisay, visibly relax and bow their heads. "Goddess Medusa. Our parents have told us about you," the young prince says.

"Good." I look them over and read their minds to see if they've experienced any type of mistreatment. It is a relief to discover the twins were fed, clothed, and bathed regularly. Baraka has kept them taken care of outside of regular threats to harm them if their parents try to oppose his rule here and in the other three lands.

"A guard will be here to serve us dinner soon," the princess states.

"Then let us get out of here, but first let me make it harder for them to realize you two are missing." I cause the guard outside the door to lie on the floor for a nap while looking at the ornate metalwork on the top of the double wood doors. Staring hard at the metal, I keep my focus on it until it bubbles and becomes a bright red, piping hot liquid. The melted metal moves to where the double doors meet each other and the surrounding frame. Walking closer to the doors, I inhale deeply before blowing in a wide arc, instantly cooling the metal and effectively welding the doors shut. Now there are the doors hidden in the room's wall paneling I need to deal with. Metal doesn't surround these doors like the chamber doors, so I make the wood doors expand so much that they jam into the surrounding frames. Satisfied that no one can easily gain access to the room to find the twin princess and prince gone, I instruct them to take my hands.

I transport them deep within the cave, and I ask Zendaya and those wise with age to keep watch over them.

"Our parents aren't here?" the young prince asks.

"No. They are getting ready to fight by my side, but you will be safe here."

"What can we do?" the princess asks.

"Everyone not fighting is praying, but you two, I want you to give thanks."

"Give thanks?" they ask in unison.

"Yes, give thanks and praise for our victory, like it has already happened."

"Your will, our honor, goddess," the princess responds.

The kids move to the center of the area, near the bubbling stream, and they clap and sing.

> *Victory is ours.*
>
> *Victory is ours.*
>
> *Praise be to our great goddess*
>
> *For making victory ours.*
>
> *She delivered us from those who desired our death.*
>
> *Praise be to our great goddess Medusa*
>
> *For making victory ours.*

Their praises vibrate through my body like small currents of lightning. Some of those within the cave catch on to the song and join the twins, adding to the increase in power I feel. It isn't long until the lightning I feel inside me manifests outside of me as well. Little bolts of lightning flash here and there across my body. I am in awe of the feeling because I've never felt the power of such strong praise before. When the women I avenged praised me, it was individual praise. They never came together to praise me as one. I almost… almost understand Jata a little more. Unlike them and my true mother, I don't need the praise of others to survive. For that, I am grateful.

Now that the future of Ginawa is safe in my cave, it is time for me to get my mother—the one who birthed and raised me. It will not be as easy as it was with the kids. There's a small battalion of guards covering the inside and outside of the chamber she's being kept in. Baraka even has guards stationed in the secret passageways leading to the room and on the balcony. Getting inside the heads of the guards, I count two dozen of them. Just when I think about dispatching some old slithering friends of mine, I notice the concoction of scents filling their nostrils as if I were standing in the room myself.

I hop from mind to mind, trying to find the source of the smell that I find outright repulsive. Despite how long they've been smelling it, the guards hate the aroma and are moving about the room in an ever-failing effort to get away from it. I look into my mother's mind as she watches the maids who just entered with large buckets, dipping towels into the buckets before wiping the walls and floors of the room with them.

"That is a nasty combination," my mother says. "How do you all get used to it?"

"Used to it?" one maid retorts. "We don't."

"We just do what we are told," another says. "Like everyone else, we have to stay alive somehow, so we have to obey Supreme Ruler Baraka."

Supreme Ruler? That's the title Baraka has given himself?

"What all is in that?" a guard asks.

"Lemongrass, garlic, wormwood, snakeroots, basil, clove, and yellow alder."

Snake repellant.

"It must work," a guard responds. "I haven't seen a snake since we got here."

"Or the stories are just stories," another says.

"They are not just stories, I assure you," one maid states. "I was working here at the palace the night she used the snakes to kill almost all our warriors. I stood on that balcony and watched the whole thing. She was brutal." The woman looks at my mother. "No offense."

"My daughter had her reasons."

The woman nods. "I will tell you this," the same maid says to no one in particular. "Your guy says Me—"

The guards all stop and unsheathe their swords.

"I caught myself! I caught myself!" The woman waits until they return their swords to their resting place. I quickly gather that my name has become forbidden to say. "She did not kill the king that night. My sister was one of the queen's ladies. She told me she saw King Gainde enter the queen's chambers hours after the priestess left him in the courtyard, and there were some servants who said they passed him as he went to the dungeons before that."

"Why would the king go to the dungeons if what you say is true?" a guard asks.

"Rumors are that's where his father was being kept."

I tune out the rest of their discussion as I formulate another plan. My snakes aren't able to go inside the palace with the walls and floors soaked with the essence of every snake-repelling plant that grows in Joro.

I don't want to be anywhere near it myself. But I have an idea.

Transporting down to the woods where the combined forces of Ginawa and Joro are a few feet behind the temple, I inform Ginawa's king and queen that their kids are safe in the cave.

"What about your mother?" Queen Nia asks me.

"I'm going to get her next. Stay low to the ground and move to the temple ruins. Wait there for my signal, then rush in and attack."

Queen Nia, Sisay, King Khartoum and Queen Joba, all nod and I fly into the air.

Medusa Untold

"Wait, what is the signal?" King Khartoum asks.

Chapter 33
Medusa

Using the water from the Tehenu, I form one large water snake to rival the size of the ejo nla and have it slither through the air. That it's made from the pristine river makes my creation almost invisible to the human eye…almost. The guards patrolling the courtyard outside the palace don't spot the water snake, but a guard on the balcony is questioning his sanity. He isn't sure if his eyes are playing tricks on him. I hold the snake in place as he tries to make sense of what he sees, if he is seeing anything at all. The man calls another guard to see if he too sees something in the sky. His comrade immediately notices that something doesn't look quite right.

Getting into my mother's mind, I instruct her to move to the center of the bed and to stay quiet.

Just as the second guard yells for the attention of the others, I send my water snake charging into the room, through the doors separating the balcony and the chambers. The water forces one guard back into the chamber, and the other falls off the balcony, breaking a leg on his landing. Inside the chamber, the water snake turns into a flood that sloshes over the floor and into the walls. Screams can be heard outside the room as the water sweeps the guards and maids off their feet.

I swing my arms behind me to rush the water, buckets, palace staff, and any remaining snake repellent out of the room. The mortals, I drop into the river. Hopefully, all of them can swim. Anyone who can't get out of the rushing river will undoubtedly drown and/or go over the edge. I send the water mixed with the snake repellent up above Muhabura for the sun to evaporate. I don't need or want large amounts of repellent in the ground or water. Placing my feet down on the now wet balcony, I walk into the chamber and find my mother exactly where I told her to go.

"Am I looking at you or is this more of your magic?" she asks me with wild eyes.

"It's me, Mother. I am here."

Her eyes and mind tell me she's not sure, so I go to her and take her hand in mine. Placing her hand against my cheek, I sink into it. "Mother, it's me."

She quickly snatches me to her and wraps her arms around me. In her mind, I can see when Baraka's men took her captive and brought her to Joro as a prisoner, as a bargaining chip for my inevitable return.

"Why didn't you pray to me when they took you? I could have done something."

"And be a distraction from what you were called to do? Absolutely not. Besides, I've been so worried about you since I heard about your change, I couldn't pray."

"I'm fine, Mother."

"You're burdened and will be for all eternity, beyond anything any mortal can comprehend. Everyone else sees what's happened to you as a blessing, but all I can see is the incredible burden you must feel."

I want to tell her about how I once felt the same as she does and how now I've come to see it differently. I also want to tell her that no one in existence is better equipped for this blessing and burden more than I. But I can't tell her any of that without also telling her I'm not her child, well, at least not in the traditional sense. It would break her heart, especially since I know she prayed for a child for so long and how she and Father struggled to start their family. We also don't have time for any of this conversation.

"I need to get you away from here. There is a safe place."

"I take it we aren't walking?"

"No, Mother, we are not," I chuckle. Embracing her again, I transport her to the cave, where the twins and others are having a full-on revival. "I have to go, but I'll be back. We'll talk then." She nods. "Feel free to join them."

I give my mother a small smile and transport to float above the courtyard. A full battle ensues, but Baraka's soldiers cannot keep up with my energized army. Swords clash and blood sheds, but not the blood of my warriors. With snakes wrapped around an arm and others on the mountainside praying, the skin of my warriors is impenetrable. Even Sisay fights more boldly than I've ever seen her before with this added protection.

I search for Baraka in the crowd and find him standing just inside the veranda with several guards surrounding him, much like his son Gainde did when I finally confronted him in this same courtyard. I can hear his frustration growing as his numbers dwindle and mine stay the same. A servant woman appears from within the palace and is allowed to get close enough to whisper into Baraka's ear.

"The children and the mother are gone," she tells him. "No one saw them leave. It is like they vanished."

Baraka expresses his dissatisfaction with the news by shoving her into one of his guards, whom she nearly trips over. The guard rights her until she has her footing again, and she hurries away into the safety of the palace.

I watch him as he rushes toward the battle while unsheathing his sword. Baraka skips the last two of the palace steps and charges in, yelling and swinging his sword like a man with everything to lose. His target is Queen Nia, but there are a few soldiers between them. Like a madman, he knocks them out of the way as he makes his way to the queen. Baraka thrusts his sword forward, but Sisay puts herself between Baraka and her second adoptive mother, raising her sword to cut off his blow.

Sisay raises her foot to kick Baraka, but he jumps back to dodge it. "You're the brat child of the priestess everyone's made up stories about. I've been looking for you."

"I am also the daughter of Queen Nia and heir to the throne of Joro."

"You'll never take the throne. It is mine, or haven't you noticed? I will make sure my legacy lasts throughout all the lands forever."

"Your legacy is having a failed king for a son and idiotically thinking you could best my mothers."

"I will end your life and that of your so-called mother."

They stand off for a few moments before Baraka charges towards her. I watch as their swords clash and they block or dodge each other's offensives. Sisay is a formidable fighter, but Baraka is more experienced and stronger. The daughter I've raised doesn't give up, and it frustrates Baraka. Using his momentum against him, she sidesteps one of his wild swings before kicking him in the knee of his back leg.

The older man falls to his knees and overextends his groin in the process. For only a moment, he lets his pain show on his face before replacing it with anger and determination. Baraka spits at Sisay's feet, something people tend to do to parentless children to get them to go away. The disrespectful gesture sets a fire in Sisay, one that I've not seen since my early days of taking care of her. Mourning her parents, adults and other children didn't fail to remind her of her place as an orphan: the least worthy of anything good. There were days when she would return to me in the temple in tears and others when she didn't leave my quarters at all. Even from high in the sky, I can see my daughter's tears from here. She charges at him, and he punches her with the hand holding his sword. Baraka tries to grab her as she staggers back, but all he grasps is the snake coiled around her arm. The small snake comes loose. Baraka turns it over in his hands as the snake hisses at him. I wish it were a lethal viper so it could hurt him, but being such a tiny constrictor, it can't do much damage to him. I watch as Baraka easily crushes the snake's head between his fingers as he rises to his feet.

As Sisay tries to gather herself, Baraka pushes the tip of his sword against the front of her leg and cuts.

Blood. Blood and her scream.

Baraka lifts the tip of the sword to his lips and licks it, relishing the metallic taste. I've never witnessed such a disgusting act.

With a loud voice he shouts, "Remove the snakes, then remove your enemy."

His soldiers, who hear his order over the commotion, repeat the words until it spreads to all of them. In small numbers, their tactics change. Baraka repositions the sword in his hand so that his thumb is near the end of the handle, before moving to stand over Sisay. She's still not aware of what's happening in front of her as Baraka places his free hand over his other and raises the sword above his head.

Before he can thrust the sword down, I transport him and his sword into the air, a few feet away from me. It happens so fast, Baraka is still thrusting his sword down until he realizes his surroundings have completely changed. When he does, his mind races with confusion about how and why he's floating in the air until he notices me. This is his first time seeing me since before his son tried to force himself onto me. As the golden hue of my eyes and other subtle changes to my appearance register in his mind, he loses his words.

"You thought it was all a myth," I say.

The slight quiver on his lips confirms the fear that has now replaced the confusion in his mind.

"My son—"

"Is dead, which you know, but not by my hand. I would have preferred he suffered quite longer for what he tried to do to me; for the position he put me in." I let my words sink in. "Gainde didn't act alone, though. The others involved are no more, just as he is. I'm curious, Baraka. What do you think should be your punishment for attempting to kill my daughter, the princess of Joro?"

"Death is a companion of war." The man has the nerve to say it with a puffed chest.

I find his fake bravado insulting.

I release my hold that's been keeping him in the air, letting him drop quickly towards the ground. His screaming gives me an odd sense of pleasure and draws the attention of the people fighting below.

Just when he drops into the tree line, I raise him back up to me. Baraka pants as he tries to catch his breath. His fear leaks through his skin as a heavy sweat. He's also wet from…

I turn my nose up at him when I catch the pungent odor of urine. "Not so bold now."

"Priestess—"

"Goddess," I correct.

He shuts his lips, and they form a hard line.

"You're still not willing to submit. Hmmm. We'll see how long that lasts, but what about your men?"

I look to the ground, where every eye is looking up at us. Projecting my voice, I speak to them. "The rest of you don't have to die today. For those of you who do not wear my symbol, all you have to do is throw down your weapons, remove Baraka's symbols, kneel, and proclaim me as your goddess. Do this, and you will live."

A handful of his men act without hesitation, doing exactly as they've been told. Some men react after seeing them and follow suit. But there is a small group of five men who stand not far away from Queen Nia. The only move they initially make is with their eyes, going back and forth between each other and the queen. I catch the small nod one of them gives the others, and they move to strike her down, raising their swords either above their heads or to their sides to thrust forward. In a flash, I turn all five men into stone, cutting off their plan to kill the queen for Baraka's favor and their lives.

After quickly gathering herself after what just happened, Queen Nia addresses the crowd now. "Let these men be a testimony of the goddess' power and the grace she has shown all those here today." She turns slowly to look at everyone to let her words fall heavy on them. "Place them on the temple ruins to be a constant reminder to the people of Joro and all those that come here. The days of gods who do not live among us are gone. There is only one god now. We are all under her eyes," she says, pointing her sword in my direction in the air. "And she will deal with each of us justly."

When she finishes, she stares at Baraka, wishing she had killed him instead of giving him a chance to have a life with his daughters. He wouldn't have been able to drive her out of her home or come close to killing Sisay if she had.

I get into her head, reassuring her that everything happened just as it should've and that I will take care of Baraka.

I know the answer before asking it, but still I do. "Seeing that what you've heard about me and my transformation are true, and witnessing a small part of what I can do, are you now willing to put down your arms and submit, Baraka?"

Vile disgust fills his eyes. "I didn't pray often, but when I did, it was always only to Jata. When I gave the gods praise, it was only to Jata and Kemet. I would rather die before submitting to or admitting that a woman has power over me."

"Very well. You have committed treason against the crown of Joro, unjustly started wars in the lands of Joro, Himba, San, and Ginawa. You committed war crimes by taking the prince and princess of Ginawa, mere children, hostage, along with my mother. As I stated earlier, you tried to kill my daughter." I think about turning him to stone, to be a familiar Joran face with the other statues on the temple ruins, but like his son, I want him to suffer. Mostly because Gainde didn't suffer as I would've liked, though I don't blame Queen Nia for what she did. Any woman would have done the same. Without touching him, I force his limbs to stretch out as far as they will go without dislocating, and I stiffen his body. One by one, I give his veins minor cuts, each one exploding in his body with a burst that no one but I can see. Baraka screams in pain.

"For each of those crimes, you will pay with your life."

Blood flows freely throughout his body with each burst of a vein, filling any cavity it can find. I intentionally save the major arteries for last. Just when I get ready to cut the ones in his legs, Sisay calls to me.

"Mother," she says while stepping forward from the crowd.

"My daughter."

"Who is better to be a testimony about rising against you?"

"He must pay, Sisay."

"I know, and he will, but find another way."

Turning my attention back to Baraka, I note the blood trailing out of his nose and mouth. I move him closer so only he can hear me. "Even with multiple changes in parents, my daughter still shows more grace and is wiser than you in all of your years. Your son never had a chance at being anything other than a waste with you as a father and role model. You are going to join your five men at the temple ruins. Unlike them, your soul will remain trapped in your statue figure."

Baraka's eyes grow large enough to rival the size of Joro's four moons combined.

"That's right. You won't be alive in the mortal sense, but you will be aware of your surroundings, able to hear every whisper about you as people look at your statue and you look right back at them. No one will hear your screams but you. For all eternity, you will suffer this way, all while in the temple Joro will rebuild for me. You're going to serve me, anyway. I'll make sure that wherever you're placed in the new temple, bird droppings can land on you."

Though I don't think this is exactly what Sisay had in mind, I'm grateful for her suggestion. In this way, his punishment will serve two purposes: one, he will suffer for his actions, and two, his failed coup will be a cautionary tale for all others throughout the galaxy. I reposition his arms and legs so his statue will be in a standing position. Unlike his men, I don't turn him into stone instantly. It starts at his feet and creeps up his body slowly. Baraka screams more now than when I was destroying his veins. Those screams turn silent when his chest hardens, but the pain is all over his face.

With a tortured expression is how his face remains when it turns.

I move Baraka's statue to the temple ruins, adjusting the position of the five men that were already moved there, so that Baraka is front and center, where he's always wanted to be all his life.

All of that to be the ruler of nothing.

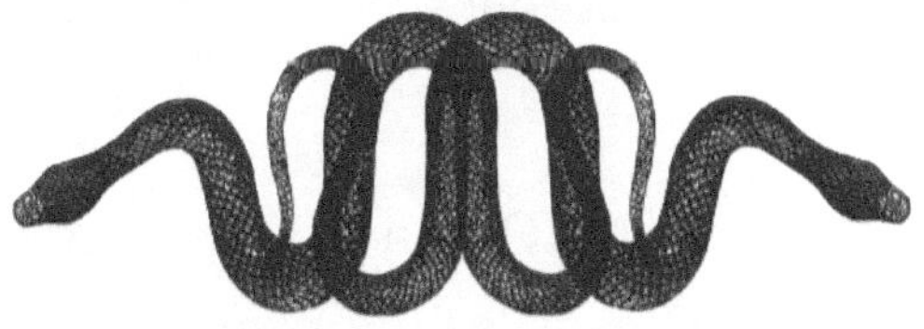

Chapter 34
Medusa

Slowly, I descend to the ground. Sisay bolts to me and jumps into my arms before my feet hit the ground. I'm so glad that at her age of ten and four years, she still feels free to express herself so openly with me, despite two years of separation.

"Thank you," she says. "He was going to kill me."

"You never have to thank me for saving your life. That's what mothers do." In saying this, I realize Sisay and I have something in common. We both have multiple mothers, birth and one who came later. Only she has one more than I do.

Queen Nia approaches. "What would you like us to do with Baraka's men?"

"That is up to you, Queen Nia. The throne of Joro is yours again." Turning to Ginawa's King Khartoum and Queen Juba, I tell them the same. "You have your thrones back as well."

"Who would have known the girl we grew up making mud pies and weaving banana leaves with would one day become the most powerful being in the galaxy?" King Khartoum states jokingly.

"And our goddess, no less," Queen Juba adds.

Queen Nia lifts her sword high over her head. "All praise to the goddess Medusa!" she shouts before bowing to me. Everyone repeats her words and drops to one knee.

As the praises come in for me, a prayer feather appears before me, carrying the panicked voice of my mother.

There's a strange woman with a human head and a body like the night sky here.

Without answering or dismissing the prayer, I immediately transport to the cave without a word to anyone. In the cave, my eyes go right to those of my mother and then to my other mother, Moeder Heelal. The mother who created me is standing directly behind my birth mother. Moeder Heel's arm is around my mother's neck.

"You have grown in your power in ways I hadn't expected. Never have I not known what was going to happen. I could always see the end based on the person's decisions until you figured out how to block me out of your mind."

No response comes from me. I knew what I was doing when I practiced making my mind go incognito and then calling her name to see if she could hear me. As I told her, I would no longer be anyone's puppet, and that includes the mother of the gods whose star I'm formed from. From the beginning, I sensed there was more to her story of needing a daughter as a companion, and the only way I could get to the truth of it was to read the minds of the gods without her knowing.

"Given who you are now, which of us would you choose?" she asks.

"This is between the two of us. Leave my mother out of it."

"I am your mother."

"So is she."

"Which of us means more to you, hmmm, Medusa? The mother who created you, planted you as a seed in this mortal's womb, and gave you your powers, or the one who merely birthed and raised you?"

My eyes go to my mother, the one I've always known as my mother. This is the first time since accepting who and what I am now that I've not known what to do. Before I can think of anything, there is a muted pop and my mother's limp body falls from Moeder Heelal's arms.

At the sight of my mother's lifeless body, I blast beams of power out of both of my hands at Moeder Heelal without thinking about it. She counters with blasts of her own. My white beam and her blue beam clash, pushing back and forth against each other for dominance. Though I hold my own against her for some time, she is, after all, a much older being than I am and more well-versed in using her power. As I struggle against her power, her beams shorten the length of mine and get closer to me, and I scream. Just as the mortals I've fought and killed were nothing compared to the gods I've had the same interaction with, facing the gods is nothing like facing Moeder Heelal, the mother of the universe. My intent is only to banish Moeder Heelal from this galaxy so that I and those under me could live in peace. With everyone else I faced, I went into those fights intending to end their existence. Baraka is the only one who had a different fate.

The power of her beams takes me over, and I am overcome with burning pain. As the excruciating pain courses through my body, a prayer feather catches my eye as it floats near me. *The others in the cave. They're praying to me, for me.* I try to focus my thoughts away from the pain I feel and on opening a portal for them to escape through. After Moeder Heelal's total disregard for my mother's life, I know she doesn't care about theirs. I struggle, but open a portal to the courtyard for a moment. Only two people make it through the portal before it closes.

I scream louder as the pain increases. It feels as though the magic, the power that was forced upon me that fateful day, only instead of being fused to me, Moeder Heelal is trying to rip it from me. For the sake of my people, I can't let that happen. I must get out of her grasp and lead her away from the mountain if the people here are to have any chance of safety.

It is such an odd feeling to, on one hand, feel your power being overtaken and destroyed, and on the other, feel it restored by prayers. The people in the cave are still praying. The increase in feathers lets me know that the two who got out have told the others in the courtyard, and they are now praying. Again, focusing my mind, I receive the prayers. Using the power from them, I bolt to the top of the cave. Moeder Heelal shoots another blast my way, but I transport myself high into the sky above Joro.

To give myself time to recover, I go incognito as fast as I can. I try again to connect with the ejo nla, and this time I find my pet. Its mind is groggy, like it was in a deep sleep that it's still trying to shake off. It hisses loudly.

I'm sorry I had to leave you. Come on, my pet. I need you to get the people in the cave down the mountain.

Trying something I've practiced less than a handful of times and something else I've never done before, I lie in wait for my other mother. The urge to pray that this plan works is strong, but I have no one to pray to. I have only myself to call upon, with an untold number of lives counting on me.

Chapter 35
Medusa

It isn't long before Moeder Heelal appears not far from me. Her entire body now looks as it did the first time we met face to face, blending in with the stars of the sky that seem in perpetual darkness this far away from Joro and Muhabura. I watch as her star-filled body moves slowly across the sky. It dawns on me that in this state, her most natural state, is her incognito mode. She's never had a reason to be completely invisible, like the gods she created. If it weren't for my powers and knowing this form of hers, I wouldn't be able to make her out against the sky.

"Medusa, I know you're here. I can feel you."

I stay silent, and I watch her as she continues to look for me. She stops and focuses on one spot. It takes everything in me to keep my heart at the same pace. Moeder Heelal stretches her hand forward and snatches me by my neck, releasing my body from the incognito mode I've been in.

"Did you really think you could hide from me? I created every star here, so I know when they don't look right."

I don't respond.

"None of this was supposed to go this way," she explains. "When I realized my ability to create new galaxies, new gods, new life, was diminishing, I put the last of that power into creating you. Though you didn't turn out deformed and unstable like the galaxies I created before you, you have now become my biggest disappointment. Maybe I should have been more honest with you when I first called you up to me."

"You should have."

The flicker of light in her eyes let me know those three words anger her. I've struck a chord.

"I can kill you just as easily as I killed the dirt suit that birthed you."

Repeatedly, I tell myself not to respond to her insults. "But you don't want me dead, at least not yet. Why is that?"

This time, she doesn't respond.

"You still need me, Moeder Heelal."

Still, she's silent.

"Without me, you cannot create. Without the ability to create, you have no real purpose. Your creations have no purpose for you after you've made them, but you want them to desire you. That was your biggest problem with Kemet and Songhai, and why it was so easy for them to spin the story that they were the beginning and end of everything. Tell me, *mother,* how many of your *creations* have you destroyed because they refused to turn back to you?"

Her grip on my throat tightens, and I vanish from her grip like smoke, only to appear a few meters to the side of her.

"Am I truly the only child you've created through a mortal, or are there others like me out there?" I say as I wave my hand in the general direction of the distant galaxies surrounding us. "Or did you destroy them, too?"

She looks at me and back at her hand that was just gripping my neck. The confusion on her face brings me a little satisfaction, but she quickly replaces it with anger. She flies towards me like a comet, but another me appears in the distance.

"Is that your plan with me?" I ask. "To destroy me, since I want nothing to do with you?"

Moeder Heelal stops in her tracks, looking back and forth between the two versions of me before her. A third version reveals itself.

"Have you ever wondered why your creations abandon you?"

A fourth appears.

"Did you ever think that the problem was indeed… you?"

"I am in no mood for games, child," she screams.

All of my clones, ten and five in total, reveal themselves, and I stand with them. "That is where all of you have made a mistake. My life is no game," we all say together. For my plan to work, she can't find the real me early on.

We float in the sky surrounding her, and I can feel the waves of anger coming from her. The stars can feel it, too. Everything trembles from the energy she's projecting.

"You've never been challenged in such a way," we say. It's not so much a question as it is an educated guess. To be ignored like you don't exist by your creation is one thing, but to be challenged by them, by me, her one creation most like her, is an insult beyond reason.

Most like her.

Most like her.

Saying these three words repeatedly in my head unlocks something I hadn't realized before. Something even Moeder Heelal may not have realized yet, but it is why she couldn't inflict as much damage on me as she wanted inside the cave.

Still, this won't be easy. This plan has to work.

"You asked if there are others like you. No, you are truly my only child. You also asked if I plan to destroy you. At first, no. But now that you know everything…" She raises an eyebrow to finish the sentence. "But before I destroy you, I'm going to rip every magical cell from your body and take your power from you. With it, I'll restore my power to create and be rid of you and your insolence altogether."

She puts two of her hands out, blasting at two of my clones that were on opposite sides of her. I and the other clones continue flying around her, intermittently blasting Moeder Heelal and dodging blasts from her. The first of my clones goes down, and I fly into the smoke-like essence it leaves behind.

"Neem stewig vas," I whisper while going through the smoke. It gathers into a near-translucent point fixed in the sky just like the stars.

I repeat this after Moeder Heelal takes out six other clones, blasting at her in between each to match appearance with my clones, goading her into attacking them. As I come around the side of her, I notice her looking at me out of the corner of her eye as she blasts at two of the remaining clones. Something about the way she watches me puts the image of my mother's lifeless body back into my mind, and I'm overcome with anger. I throw a quick series of light balls at her and mentally instruct the clone out of her line of sight to do the same.

Moder Heelal fires back at me as she destroys another one of my clones. She's observing me. *Is she watching to see if I will fly into the essence of the now-destroyed clone? Has she figured out my pattern?*

Instinctively, I have the clones fly into the essence of their fallen twins, leaving the fixed anchor points just as I have.

"Just as I thought," Moeder Heelal states.

Only one clone gets to leave an anchor point before Moeder Heelal spins and flips, shooting beams to take down the remaining clones all at once, leaving only her and me in the sky.

"Clones…smart," Moeder Heelal compliments. "I wouldn't have been able to grab a projection as I did."

"No, you wouldn't have. But you are forgetting a couple of things, *Mother*."

"What could the creator of all things, the creator of you, forget?"

"Even projections carry some powers of the original; clones even more so," I project myself into the various spots where the essence of my clones still lingers. "*Neem stewig vas,*" we say together. The anchors form and I do a single loud clap. White power beams shoot out to Moeder Heelal, trapping her in it.

"What is this?" she screams.

I ignore her question and continue with my next point. "The second thing you forgot is that I am your daughter. You've reminded me of this repeatedly, but it wasn't until a few moments ago that I understood what that truly means."

"Having second thoughts about shutting me out?" she asks.

"No."

We stare at each other for a few moments before I continue. "You made me from a speck of stardust from your body. Your makeup, everything that makes you powerful, is in me. It has been since I was born. But because I didn't have the knowledge of being your daughter, I didn't know those powers existed in me. It makes sense, though. It explains the attraction and love for the gods I had at even a very young age, and the favor of the gods I had in Ginawa and Joro. I embodied the best parts of you, of the gods. Add that to the mortals' ability to create life, I have the best attributes of both worlds. You merely brought the existence of my powers to the surface, where I could easily access them. In protecting me from Nthanda, Jata unintentionally gave me the blessing of the gods to rule over them. Had he not done that, the powers I was born with would have protected me, anyway. Asmara's prophecy was as much for you as it was for the Elders."

The anchor points and the beams coming from them tremble as Moeder Heelal screams and tries to break free. I clap again, and an electric shock goes through the beams and hits her. She screams some more and emits a large blast of power of her own, destroying my anchor points.

Crap. I didn't use the anchor points for what I really wanted to use them for, which was to drain her of her power. Now I have to improvise.

"You will not replace me," Moeder Heelal growls.

"If replacing you means better for those I love, watch me." I fly towards her at high speed, and she charges towards me. My hands light up with magic, enveloping them like fireballs. I throw one at her, and follow quickly with the second. Only the one that hit her do I recall back to me.

I dodge her blasts as best as I can as she rants about me and her creations being ungrateful. My magic balls keep coming at her two or more at a time, with me recalling only the ones that hit her. With each one I recall, I absorb more and more of the power it takes from her. Moeder Heelal's frustration grows and the entire front of her body lights up and hits me with a powerful blast that sends me tumbling uncontrollably through the sky.

It takes a lot of effort to right myself, but I'm disoriented. I don't know where I am in relation to where we were. While I try to get my bearing, I also try to spot Moeder Heelal coming my way, but I don't see her. My skin burns from both the blast and healing itself.

I watch the stars around me for movement, but what I see isn't a cluster of stars moving. There is a single star hurrying towards me, growing the closer it gets. I dodge it and am immediately hit again. This time it is Moeder Heelal that collides into me. I grab her arms and swing her around and off of me, but I make sure to absorb some of her power through my touch.

My wounds finish healing, and I'm feeling as I was just before she blasted me. With a grunt, I light my body up. Fire surrounds my entire body. I shoot a series of blasts in her direction and chase her with them as she moves around the sky. When a couple hit her, I follow them up immediately with another blast that I hold on her.

"You said my power was second only to yours, but if you need me to create, that isn't true. Your ambivalence towards your creations led to their indifference towards you, which then led to your jealousy of their lack of need for you. Though you showed me much, you left me to figure just as much out on my own. Had you been more involved, I may never have learned the truth about myself or you. I would have thought I needed you. Thank you for failing at your own lesson."

The direction of my beam changes, sucking the power from Moeder Heelal. I absorb it as her form changes to the one she used most when I was living in the cave, human head and star-filled body.

"You can't do this. It will be too much for you."

"Asmara's prophecy mentioned a forged demigod. Like the perfected sword, to be the goddess worthy of my people, worthy of all creation, I've been forged multiple times. As with the sword, I get better, more balanced, and stronger. The perfected sword is only perfect for the person it was made for. With each forge, every trial I've had, those who no longer had use for me went away. Their unworthiness to me was their death penalty. The same goes for you, *Mother.* I told you I would no longer be your puppet, and I meant that. Too bad you didn't take heed."

With my last words to her, I absorb the last of her power. The sky trembles with her screams until she is no more than dust. Moving my hands around, I gather the dust into a swirling ball between my hands, and I light a fire to it.

Looking around me, there are countless galaxies. How many of them have gods as selfish and corrupt as the ones Joro used to have? Do I let them continue as they have been, or do I give them the same fate as the gods of my galaxy? I have several unknowns right now, but the one thing I know is I want to see my daughter.

Chapter 36
Medusa

I look over the burial cloth my mother lies under. Queen Nia was gracious enough to lay her to rest in the tomb of the kings while I was battling Moeder Heelal. My hand hovers over her chest as I play out the consequences of what I'm considering.

As if she can read my mind, the queen speaks. "If you do that, those who serve you will ask you to do the same for them. I know I will be first in line."

"Hmmm." I bring my hand to my side. "When I was the age Sisay was when I took her in, my father died. Like yours, it was due to sickness. I wanted more than anything to bring him back to me then. The pain Sisay must carry at losing both of her parents just before her more formative years…I don't know how she copes with it."

"She had you," the queen states.

"And now she has you."

"She has us both." Queen Nia steps further into the cave. "The body is only a part of who they are, who we are. The kindness and love they shared lives on in those they were kind to and loved."

"So much of my life has changed, and I never got the opportunity to really talk to her about any of it. A couple of quick conversations between battles were not enough. She doesn't know," I correct myself, "didn't know I'm not her daughter in the way she thought."

"You are her daughter in every way that mattered," Queen Nia now corrects me. "Just as I am King Ahmose's daughter and heir. Just as Sisay is the daughter of us both, and the rightful heir to Joro's throne. She loved and raised you as her daughter. Nothing will ever change that."

We're quiet for a moment before she continues. "I want to talk to my father every day. To ask him how he would rule in this situation or that. Or show him the evidence of why forcing me into marriage with Gainde was a horrible idea with all the best intentions."

At this, we both laugh.

"Father could have saved us both a lot of strife had he left me to rule on my own like I asked."

"Mhmm. My fate was sealed regardless."

"Have you thought about what you are going to do with the other galaxies out there?"

We head out of the cave and into the woods as we talk.

"I sent clones to the equivalent of our former Elders to show them our battle. Many were easier to convince than others, stating they felt a shift in their energy or power at the exact moment I destroyed Moeder Heelal. There are some who are challenging me right now."

"As you're standing here with me?"

I nod. "Several clones are in battle at this very moment. I will have to leave to make appearances soon."

"How soon?"

"I will be here for Sisay's sixteenth birthday."

She releases a sigh. "Thank you."

"I wouldn't miss it."

"No, for everything. Thank you."

We stop amongst the trees, and I look at her. "Thank you for taking her in. For being the mother I could no longer be. And for being the guiding light to the people of these lands. Getting San, Himba, and even Ginawa under control with all the changes wouldn't have been possible without your leadership."

She nods, and we walk again.

"You know she's already picked out her heir?" Queen Nia states as we cross the bridge over the Tehenu.

"What?"

"According to our daughter, men are messy, untrustworthy, and not fit to rule, with my father being the exception, of course."

"Of course," I chuckle.

"As my father accepted me as his child knowing I wasn't, and as we accepted her as our daughter even though we did not birth her, she will take in her heir. It didn't help that she had witnessed a few births while you were in Muhabura. The sight traumatized her."

I shake my head.

"How is Zendaya?"

A somber look comes over the queen's face. "Some days she's good. Today is not one of those days. Apparently, one of the five men you turned into statues is the one that killed her son." Queen Nia tilts her head up, and my eyes follow hers. "On the bad days, she doesn't leave her room. She sits on the front balcony and stares at the collection of statues, with a constant flow of tears coming down her face. I've offered her new rooms that didn't face the temple ruins, but she refused."

"I'll go see her."

Queen Nia bows to me and heads up the palace stairs. Slowly, I float up to Zendaya's balcony and sit next to her. We sit in silence for a bit before I speak. "Tell me which one he is, and the statue goes over the edge."

She doesn't respond immediately, and I don't push. I will sit here next to her for all of eternity, if that is what it will take to make my friend whole again. As much as I still want to take the pain away from her, I understand her need to feel it and to work through those feelings. It was the same I had to do after the night the gods and old crown betrayed me.

"I'd rather smash him to dust and set the dust aflame, like you did with your other mother."

"Say less."

I transport us to the temple ruins, just feet from where the statues sit.

"The one to the right of Baraka."

I lift the statue into the air, and she stops me. "I'm sorry. To Baraka's right."

"That makes a difference." Putting the wrong statue down and lifting the correct one, I place it down in the middle of the ruins, behind the remaining statues. "Hold your hands out."

Zendaya does, and I manifest a long-handled, block-head hammer into her hands. While she tests the weight of it in her hands, I turn Baraka's statue around so he can witness the destruction. When I turn back to Zendaya, I can see the question all over her face.

"His soul's trapped inside," I answer.

Zendaya's eyes grow large. "Can he still hear and see everything?"

I nod.

"That is…" she laughs. "That is diabolical. I love it. You should let the queen know so she can come out here every day and tell him how his son bled out all over her when she sliced his throat."

"I didn't think she told anyone the truth about what happened to Gainde."

"She told only those she trusts." She eyes Baraka's statue. "What is he doing in there?"

I hold my hand out to give him some volume. Those near the temple freeze at hearing him scream about what evil dogs we are before I silence him again. "He's done nothing but scream and rant since he's been in that form."

After a few moments, everyone continues going about their business, but I can hear their thoughts. Soon, word will spread that Baraka is still alive inside the statue.

"Not much different from what he was before," Zendaya states.

I nod towards the statue I moved for her. "His soul is not inside of him. Baraka is the only one cursed that way."

"I don't care. I just want to destroy the last of him."

"Do you want me to stay?"

"No, I need to do this on my own. I'll let you know when I'm done."

While walking down the steps of the temple ruins, I cast a spell over it so it appears as usual to everyone, but with one less statue. No one will see Zendaya exercising her grief in this way.

The people in the courtyard stop and bow to me as I pass on my way back to the palace. Some whisper praises and thanks to me.

This is how it should've always been. Yes, gods are more powerful than mortals. But we need direct access to mortals so we can show up for them when they need us most. Mortals need direct access to their gods for their own relationship and to remember who is in control. Without that closeness, it is easy for one to think the other doesn't truly exist.

Epilogue
Queen Sisay

"Does it have to be so soon?" I ask.

"You're still grieving, I know, but the people will grow anxious without you officially crowned as queen, Sisay," Zendaya responds as she continues to fuss over my dress.

"I thought I had more time."

"So did your mother. You remember the stories she told you of when her father died?"

I nod. The way people gave their "all hails" and "long lives" before her father's last breath left the room bothered her.

The first ones came from the two who had the most to benefit from the crown, Baraka and Kunle.

It's only been a week since my mother's funeral, and here I am preparing to be crowned queen. I am grateful I'm taking the crown at plus thirty years instead of my early twenties, like my mom. And that she didn't force me to take a husband.

"Speaking of my mothers," I say before I'm interrupted.

"You look gorgeous, as always," Praia, the oldest of my adopted daughters, states as she enters my dressing room.

"As do you, my love. Are your sisters ready?"

I have four beautiful daughters, one from each land in our galaxy. We named three of them after my mothers—Praia, Medusa, and Nia, with the youngest named after Medusa's mother, Moroni.

"Yes, we are," my daughter Medusa leads the younger two in.

Behind them enters Mother Medusa, as I came to call her after settling into my role as both the daughter of the goddess and the former queen.

"You made it," I say.

"I wouldn't miss today for the world. Your mom and I talked about this day often. She is proud of you."

"How is the coronation going to work?" Praia asks. "Wasn't Íyá Àgbà crowned by a high priest?"

"Actually," Mother Medusa answers, "I crowned your Íyá Àgbà, Queen Nia, and I was just a priestess then. A high priest was there, but we don't need those anymore. Now, I get to crown your mother, too."

I remember that day vividly as their grandmother, though she prefers them to call her Mother Medusa as I do, tells the story of the coronation of their Íyá Àgbà.

A servant steps in, interrupting the story. "Your Highness, it is time."

"To the Great Hall, everyone," Zendaya says. Everyone except myself and Mother Medusa leave to take their places.

"How are you feeling?" she asks me.

"Fine. Not ready, but fine."

"No one is ever truly ready to wear the crown and take on all the responsibilities with it. But you had an outstanding teacher and role model. As great as Queen Nia was, your goal is not to be her. You are your own queen, your own person. Rule as you see fit—"

"But always be just," we say together.

"Thank you," I tell her.

"You don't have to—"

"I do. None of this would be possible without you. You made great sacrifices for me, broke rules for me. Joro wouldn't be as prosperous as it has been for the last two decades if it didn't have you as its goddess."

"Joro is prosperous because of its leadership," Mother Medusa corrects. "You've been a part of that from the moment Queen Nia took you in as her daughter. She trusted your judgement and the ideas you brought forth for community between the lands, agriculture and war advancements, which all led to the prosperity you speak of. There wouldn't be a people of Joro if it weren't for your thinking that got them away to safety when Baraka invaded all those years ago. You think you are not ready, but you are. You've been ready."

She pinches my cheek. "Let's go. Everyone is waiting for us."

"Please, let's take the mortal route and walk. I don't think my stomach can handle transporting right now."

"As you wish, Queen Sisay."

THE END

Acknowledgements

I need to that the following writer friends who encouraged me during the long road that has been this story and/or beta read for me (some more than once):

Chelsea

Audra

Ashley D.

Daja

Vix

Dom

This story is very different from the original Medusa story that came to me in 2019 (if you were following me on the former bird app, you know what I mean). This story stressed and stretched me so much. The original inspiration came while I was driving home from work on northbound I-75. A motorcycle came up beside me and passed me, scaring the crap out of me because he wasn't there the last time I checked the mirror. He had on a Predator helmet. As he continued on about his business, the "hair" of the helmet was blowing in the wind and reminded me of the snakes often depicted with the Greek Medusa.

I got off at the very next exit and sat in a fast-food restaurant writing the premise of the story that came to mind, which was very much an erotic fantasy.

The one thing from the original idea to the finished product you've read that remained the same is this: Medusa was going to be Black and thicc!

We all know the Greek Medusa story, and the Medusa of this book bears some similarities to her: both are exquisite, were betrayed by the gods they served, and were cursed because of that betrayal. Because this Medusa was going to be Black, I know that much of the Greek pantheon has some origins to various African mythologies; I did some research. Low and behold, the Greek version is rooted in African mythology. She wasn't a monster. She represented feminine power, wisdom, and transformation, which is the essence of this story. Her hair wasn't made of snakes, but were locs, possibly clay covered, similar to the Himba tribe of Namibia.

Medusa Untold

There is one more thing I knew from the original conception of this story: this Medusa was not going to be a victim. She is vengeance and justice; power and grace.

Of all my books, this story took the longest from idea to publication. I'm so grateful for the journey.

A Note from the Author:

Thank you for reading my book! I feel honored, truly.

Did you enjoy **Medusa Untold**? Be sure to leave a review wherever you can!

You can purchase the rest of my books on my website, as well as with your favorite online book retailer!

<u>Love Lost Series</u>
Love Lost
Love Lost Forever
Love Lost Revenge

<u>Addict Series</u>
Addict—A Fatal Attraction Story
Addict 2.0—Andre's Story
Addict 3.0—DeAngelo's Story
Addict 4.0—DeMario's Story

<u>The Hot Holiday Series</u>
Santa's Pleasure
Cupid's Lust
Jack's Thrills

<u>Standalones</u>
Intoxic
In Over Her Head
<u>Children's Book</u>
Princesses Can Do Anything!

<u>Devotionals</u>
Childlike Faith

<u>Fantasy</u>

Medusa Untold

www.ingramcontent.com/pod-product-compliance
Lightning Source LLC
Chambersburg PA
CBHW020332010826
48970CB00010B/88